METHODOFCHOICE

RDSTONES

I. PUT UP YOUR DUKES

WHEN I GOT home from school, I stretched, smoked a few cigarettes, went out into my front yard, took off my shirt and glasses, and put them on top of my mom's car. I knew Silent would be rolling up to my house at any moment with my sister in his car. When he stepped out, I told him, "Those are some nice shades. Let me see them?" He gave me his sunglasses and I put them on top of the car next to my glasses. "Put your hands up. We 'bout to get down,"

"I'm not gonna put my hands up. What do you wanna fight me for?"

"You know what it's about. Put your fucking hands up." The night before, Silent had shown me what appeared to be a picture of my butt naked sister. He had been hanging out with her a lot lately and the picture on his phone was of a girl lying on her belly, same hair color and skin as my sister. You could see her pussy but not her face. I should have fought him then but I was drunk and my reaction was delayed. It took me all day to get angry enough.

"I'm not gonna fight you," he said. My sister yelled at me to go in the house. I already had my hands up but I wasn't going to swing on him until he agreed to fight back. My legs were shaking. Silent put his shades back on, got in his car and left. Many neighbors came out of their houses and asked me what it was about, suggested different ways that I should fuck him up when he comes back and generally instigated and egged me on because they all wanted to see a fight.

When he returned, he had brought Beto with him and appeared to be a little drunk and wired, his preferred state of mind. Fucking crackhead. He had a Bud Light bottle in his hand.

"Come on, why you got a bottle?" I actually said, "Put up your dukes!" I was stepping towards him with my hands up. He was holding the bottle as a weapon now and backing away from me. If he was going to use a bottle on me, I might as well back him into a corner, so I pressured him into the space between Dogoberto's house and his grandma's van. I was looking Silent dead in the eyes, ready for them to point at whatever target on my body he might swing the bottle at. Simultaneously, the focus of my peripheral vision was on the bottle, ready to snatch it out of the air if it made any sudden movement.

All the neighbors started heckling Silent, calling him a pussy and telling him to put down the bottle and fight like a man. What the fuck was he so scared of anyway? He responded to the peer pressure and put the bottle down. I backed up and let him out of the corner. We squared up in the middle of the street.

We were walking around, feeling each other out, learning the range. I sensed that he thought he was at a safe distance, took a step forward with my right foot, and used all the rotation in my body to throw my longest reaching straight right, aiming to try to break his eye socket but hitting him on the forehead. I was southpaw now.

He loaded up and threw a big, telegraphed right hook at me. I blocked it with my left, but this guy was a much harder hitter than I expected and the force of his blocked punch caused my right ankle to roll. I jumped back and got a better footing. He came at me with his head down swinging wildly with both hands. He was wearing a wife beater and I snatched up the part of it that was on his right shoulder with my left hand while quickly sidestepping to my right. I twisted the sleeve around his neck and jerked him around by his shirt while hitting him clumsily on the head with my right hand until he disentangled himself. We paused for a moment and he looked at me with disgust as I held his shirt in my hand. I thought about throwing it in his face but dropped it on the ground instead.

Again he came at me with the big loaded right hook, and this time I leaned into it when I blocked it so that it wouldn't roll my ankle. I backed up and he rushed at me again with his head down. I leaned into his shoulder with my left forearm. In the clinch I hit him on the jaw with my right hand, but it wasn't really loaded up and I doubt it did much damage. At the same time his right hand hit me hard on the jaw.

"¡Ándale puto!" he said. I got dizzy and felt my arms and legs get weak. That was the decisive hit of the fight. From that moment on he had the advantage.

It's a blur to me how it went after I got my bell rung. I remember getting knocked down twice and being allowed to get back up. I remember chasing him as he backed away with his knowledge that he had a better stamina than me. He knew that if he could evade me long enough I'd get tired first because I smoked a lot of cigarettes and he didn't, and then I'd be at a greater disadvantage. It was too late by the time I figured out his strategy to wear me down. As soon as I noticed that I was out of breath and he wasn't, I stopped chasing him, stood my ground, and waited to be attacked, ready to do something desperate.

Again he rushed with his head down; I braced my forearm against his shoulder, and this time, with a last crazy reserve of adrenaline, I swung my overhand right down onto his spine with all my might. Later on people would tell me that it had made a hollow thud that was heard way down the street.

He backed up, had a crazy look in his eyes. I had given him the fear of paralysis or something with my dirty spine punch. He rushed me again with his head down. This time I tried to put him in a headlock but he got out of it, wrapped his arms around my torso, lifted me up off my feet, slammed me on the ground, mounted my chest, and started dropping furious hammers and downward punches all over my face. I made a feeble reach up at him with my right hand and jammed my fingers uselessly into his neck. My hand slipped off without damaging him. He was on autopilot now, mechanically trying to beat me to death. He gripped my shoulders and started banging my head against the ground. A cloudy little baby blue spot appeared at the center of my vision. It expanded instantly every time the back of my head hit the ground, getting bigger and bigger until Beto jumped in and pulled Silent off me. I didn't get knocked out, but I think he must have knocked a couple of screws loose in my head because after that I was never the same.

Beto, the neutral referee, told me to get up. I did. He asked me if I had had enough. I said yeah, I'm done. Then he told us to shake hands and we did. The fight was over and I had lost badly. It was my first fight as an adult.

I went into my house. My sister had no respect for me. She played that song from Ludacris – Move Bitch really loud from her room. Maybe she even left with Silent; I don't remember. I don't remember my mom's reaction either. I looked in the mirror.

Silent did a number on me. I didn't expect to see the blood on my face. My right eye was damaged far more than my left; both would soon turn black and swollen. The best wound he had inflicted was from a punch that must have been done by his left hand landing on my right eye at such an angle that it had also fractured the bridge of my nose. I also had a cut under my right eye that corresponded to the sharp bottom edge of its socket. I washed my face. I got in my car in a daze and drove to a convenience store. I don't even remember which one. I bought a bunch of King Cobras. The girl at the counter asked me, "What happened to you?"

"I just got fucked up, and now I'm about to get fucked up."

"Does the other guy look as bad as you?"

"I got some shots in but I don't think he looks bad at all."

"Why did you fight?"

"I can't say." She looked disappointed at hearing that and seemed unsure of whether or not to have respect for me. Was I the good guy or the bad guy? She didn't know and I didn't give a fuck what she thought.

I went home and got drunk. Then I went to the bar, SLUGS and joined the poker tournament. The bartender, Eightball, who had always hated me, was now happy to see me for the first time in his life. Had I been beaten twice as badly, he would have been twice as happy. He laughed at my wounds and bought me a shot of something or other to go with my bucket of beers.

The next day, all of the muscles of my abdomen and my back were sore from swinging as hard as I could. I went to school with a mangled face. All the girls who might have thought I looked tough before now had their doubts. Some seemed sympathetically concerned, others scared, and others just totally turned off. I didn't feel like talking to anyone. I had a mean, numb look in my eyes, and any guy who looked at me shrank back when I turned my ugly face on him.

The fracture to the bridge of my nose had caused a post nasal drip of blood that I was constantly swallowing. It was starting to make me gag. I had to leave in the middle of one of my classes to go to the bathroom and vomit up some stale blood.

I was a sore loser and I took it out on my family. When I wasn't at school, I was at home, getting drunk and verbally abusing my mom and sister. One day my mom told me she had good news. She had found an apartment for me. To me this was the worst possible news. I had just fought to defend the territory of my home from a shady guy who had wormed his way in through its weakest point, my dumbass little sister who didn't have any loyalty to her family and would still hang out with him after he had whooped my ass, even like him better for it. For me to leave would appear cowardly, like I had made the decision myself and was running scared. Also my adversary would have the satisfaction of seeing how easily he could turn my family against me. And he would probably be allowed into my mom's house as he pleased, along with any other dickhead who could weasel his way in, since my sister would bully her into it. There was nothing I could do about it. They kicked me out.

II. HILLVIEW TERRACE

I MOVED INTO Hillview Terrace Apartments on September 11th 2010. I didn't have a job yet, so I tried selling coke. I had a quarter ounce of the best coke ever from a connect of Dogoberto's. I managed to sell one dub at a bar before I dipped into it for a few days. One night I randomly woke up in the bathtub. It was a little Mexican girl with green eyes just like mine who woke me up and ran off. My daughter? I don't have a daughter. A ghost? The water was cold and I didn't remember getting into the bath. I wondered how the fuck a little girl could have gotten into my house. I washed myself, dried off and looked around my tiny apartment for her. The doors were locked. The blinds were closed. There was nobody.

There were a mattress, a lamp with a glass surface, a cheap Taurus 9mm pistol, some pieces of bloody toilet paper, a digital scale, the coke and the razor blades I had bought to cut it up. A bunch of shit a little kid should never see. That was all I had except what was in the fridge and some dishes. The morning after I finished all the coke, I felt so shitty, I held the gun to my head. But I had a couple hundred bucks to my name so I figured I was too rich to die. I went out and got something to eat. I ended up selling the gun when my money ran out before I got my job at Jakarta Kitchen.

My only friends were a guy named Starvin Martín who had wandered over to my sliding glass door one night following the smell of weed and this chick named Xiomara, the most constantly battered woman I had ever seen. Her boyfriend, who paid her bills but lived somewhere else, would give her a fresh beating as soon as the old one would start to wear off. All I wanted to do was whoop his ass but I knew I'd lose and that wouldn't accomplish anything; I would be beat up just like her.

I loved and pitied Xiomara. I wasn't sure if she was a prostitute or not. It constantly depressed me that I couldn't figure out a way to help her. One morning I saw her boyfriend walk by my apartment with scratches on his face. I knew who he was but he didn't know who I was. He was probably going to the office to pay her rent. I put a little league bat up my sleeve, walked outside and stood against the wall around the corner where he'd be coming back. I waited for a long time but he wouldn't pass by. I guessed he must have gone another way so I went back inside for a cigarette. Right then he passed by and I missed my perfect shot at him.

I worked nine to five every day except Sunday, dropped out of school, smoked a lot of weed and drank constantly. I bought some weights and started working out a lot. Every once in a while I hung out with Xiomara.

I used to go to the bars and try to pick up chicks but even when one was into me I didn't know what to do with it. I was always too drunk and I'd ruin it somehow. I had very little confidence.

I was full of hatred and anger. I was desperate. I had cut off ties with all my friends. I felt betrayed by my family. I hated my life. My neighbors were threatened by me because I appeared to be a drunk, musclebound creep who wanted to fuck their wives. I felt used. Everybody had some hidden agenda for me. It really seemed to me that there wasn't anybody who really gave a shit about me, and I barely gave a shit about myself.

III. GOING INTO PEOPLE'S HOUSES

I USED TO go into a trance sometimes and leave my body. It would happen often when I'd get home from work and sit on the couch and be half asleep for a while. I would go into my neighbors' houses and shake hands with them, pet their dogs, and later find out that those were the people who really lived there.

One time it seemed as if I left my body and fucked a beautiful girl in her room on the other side of the apartments and later I started seeing her walk past my house. She was one of those really proud top of the line chicks, classy and smokin' hot. I hit on her a couple times, not at all disrespectfully, standing on my porch all drunk with a forty in my hand and no shirt, and she snubbed me both times. I am a handsome guy and was in great physical shape, but it wasn't hard for people to tell that I was fucked up in the head.

I had been doing this out of body shit for a long time and I was pretty fearless about it. It was so easy to do that it would happen by accident. It had never occurred to me how dangerous it could be if I was to run into the wrong person. I thought I was safe because as much anger and hatred I had in my heart, I had no ill will towards anyone in my new neighborhood, except Xiomara's boyfriend, who didn't even live there, and I wasn't about to try to figure out how to use some type of psycho voodoo shit on him.

It seemed that I was in a community of psychic people and my mind was open and unafraid of what I might find out there. At the same time, my mind was also in a dangerous state and I didn't really know it. By the time I would get home from work my hands would already be shaky, in need of alcohol, and I would feel violent and confused.

One day something strange happened that changed my life forever. I had just gotten home from work and was sitting in a chair smoking weed and looking out the glass door. (By this time, I had acquired a chair, a desk, a sofa, and a coffee table.)

This part of the story requires a geographic layout. Looking out my glass door there is a sidewalk that leads to a flight of stairs. Down the stairs is the front parking lot of Hillview Terrace Apartments, then across the street called Blue Agave is the parking lot of another apartment complex. Along this same straight line, in that parking lot there is a small wall and a chain link fence that has a hole torn through it. That hole leads to the parking lot of the old bar, Los Reyes. Then across Mesa Street is Jakarta Kitchen. From my glass door I could see and walk a straight line all the way to my work. I would jump over that little wall and through the hole in the fence every morning as a shortcut.

As I was smoking a blunt and looking out the glass door after work, I noticed someone standing at the bottom of the stairs. From my viewpoint, all I could see was the top of the person's head. This person had a blue hood and sunglasses and that's the only part of the body I could see. I could not determine the person's gender or age. He or she stared at me for about five minutes and I thought it was kind of strange but didn't see it as a threat. I decided to go see what this person wanted. As soon as I stood up, the person ran away without exposing anymore of his/her identity to me and when I got to the stairs there was nobody around.

I didn't give it too much thought and pretty much forgot about it. I spent the rest of the night drinking and getting high until I got sleepy. I turned out the lights and got in bed. Half asleep, in my mind's eye, I had an overhead view of the sidewalk outside my apartment. Someone was slowly walking by my house. I couldn't see the person clearly, as if the body was made of crude geometric shapes, but I knew it was the same person who had been watching me from the foot of the stairs. I got the impression that it was a short person with a frail body, but who was powerful, the most powerful person I had ever encountered. A heavy, oppressive mental force from this person paralyzed and suffocated me. It was unlike any other sleep paralysis I had ever felt and I struggled as hard as I could to break free. All the while I could see this person slowly walking past my house. Then, it felt like some foreign electricity took complete control of the nerves in my left arm, like it was someone else's arm, and I punched myself right in the mouth.

I jumped out of bed, opened the door and looked outside. Nobody was there. I turned the lights back on. I smoked and drank some more and went back to sleep without any problems, but I had a strange new fear of a vicious person with mysterious and highly developed powers who had decided to show me how easily my mind could be dominated.

After that, it gets hard to explain exactly what happened to me and the things I did.

IV. THE PRESENCE OF EVIL

I TRIED TO forget about the mystery person, but something started happening. It didn't bother me when I was at work, but when I was at home, especially when I would sit in the chair by the glass door, I would feel the same suffocation of sleep paralysis while I was awake. Like something was choking me. At first it wasn't so bad and I was easily distracted from it, but it slowly got worse until was bothering me all the time. I tried to drink it away but nothing worked. It got so bad that I couldn't sleep at night and eventually I stopped sleeping altogether. I started to believe that that person with the blue hood was doing some kind of brujería on me.

I started to believe that person was evil and search for him/her.

I stopped going to work.

One day I turned off all the lights and closed the blinds, tried to make it look like I wasn't home. I stayed peeping through the blinds and watched everyone who passed by my house all day. I knew that if that person passed, I would recognize them even without the disguise of a blue hood and sunglasses, but everyone who passed was normal and didn't appear to be evil.

I started seeing a blue demon, like a little horned beast floating in the air. The demon wanted to show me something but I would never allow myself to know what that was or let him dominate me. He wanted me to follow him somewhere but I never would. I would bark like a dog and growl whenever the demon came around.

I started walking around the apartments, trying to feel out where the evil person was who had their hex on me. It was getting harder to breathe every day, and I imagined these disembodied flying hands with long skinny fingers digging their nails into my throat, not my physical throat, but the throat of my soul, the electrical body that goes out when you leave your physical body. I would stop and carefully study the people I would pass. Then I would say, "Ok. It's not you," and warn them that I sensed the presence of someone very evil in the area, all the while sort of wheezing and gasping for air. This scared the shit out of everyone I met.

At night I would walk around with the bat so quietly and cover every inch of my apartments. When I would come across someone who was not evil I would turn the bat around and hold it by the end with my fingertips to show that I wasn't going to use it on them, and continue sneaking around quietly.

I called the cops to come to my house one night. I was extremely drunk and I don't remember exactly what I told the 911 operator to get them to come. I told the two cops that there was someone very evil in the area and I wasn't sure what they were up to. I gave them the description of the person I had seen watching me, the blue hood with sunglasses, but I didn't tell them anything about the invisible hands strangling me most of the time. They asked to come inside and if I had any weapons. I said my house was full of improvised weapons but I had no intention of using them on the cops and they could come in if they wanted.

My house was a mess. I had rocks of different sizes, pieces of that rusty brown metal bar used for construction, various metal pipes that I had found around the apartments, a random prison style shank I had found in the street, like a sharpened piece of rusty metal with electrical tape on one side, the little league bat and the razor blades. I had them arranged so that no matter where I was in my house I could always reach a weapon. And I was always moving around to different spots because if I stayed in one place for too long the hands would find me. My house was the most uncomfortable place for me to be. I remember the cops telling me that it was ok for me to be that drunk, but I was not allowed to leave my house like that or it would be considered public intoxication, and that there was nothing they could do about a person who I merely suspected of being evil. I guess they figured I was just drunk wasting their time and they left.

I tried meditating and using my soul's hands to pry the ones off my throat and break their fingers, but they didn't want to let go and play mercy with me. I wanted my own hands to fly off and choke the evil person back, but I could not locate a body to strangle.

I hadn't slept in two weeks and was in so much pain that I went outside my door and started yelling as loud as I could. It sounded similar to the way the guys in *Dragon Ball Z* power up, but it wasn't exactly like that. It was an expression of my rage at the pain I felt in my strangled throat. It was a homicidal roar to let my enemy know he/she was hurting me and that I wanted to find them. It was a sound like nothing I have ever heard and somehow, like the singers of death metal bands, I was able to do it all night without it hurting my voice. Sometimes I would yell, "Show yourself! Where are you?!"

My roar was so loud that it reached the people at the Tequila Mirage; I heard some guy over there try a roar back one time, but his roar sounded so weak and lame that he must have gotten embarrassed by it and he didn't do it again. I knew he wasn't the person I was looking for. I also knew that when I saw the person I would know without a doubt. No neighbor dared to come outside and tell me to shut up and there couldn't have been one person in the whole apartment complex or even a few blocks away from it who didn't hear it. When I wasn't yelling I was completely silent, listening for the quietest indication of where my enemy might be hiding.

I stayed in front of my door all night alternating between my roar and complete silence. In the morning I saw Xiomara pass by. She had a bag with two 211 Steel Reserve beers in it. I was so relieved. She came in and gave me a beer. As we drank, I explained my whole story to her. She said that whatever was bothering me, it was like the police; they can't come into my house unless I let them in. The beer relaxed me and brought some sanity back to me. She said she thought she was pregnant, and I told her I thought she was pregnant too. She said, "I know I'm fat," but I explained that she didn't look pregnant, she just felt different, like there was something missing, like the egg got fertilized. She looked at me like I was crazy as hell for saying something like that. I asked her if she knew who the father was; she said it could be anyone but it was probably some black guy. Then she started panicking and saying that she lost her wallet. We went around the apartments searching for it. She kept saying it over and over, "I lost my wallet."

V. DO YOU HAVE A GUM?

XIOMARA WAS SO hot. I first met her one night when I was smoking a cigarette sitting on the same stairs where I would later see the blue hood. She came out of nowhere, walked up to me so fast that it reminded me of those zombies in the movie *28 Days Later*. She scared the shit out of me and my first impulse was of violent self defense, and then I realized it was a beautiful woman. She was average height for a woman, pale, Mexican, long wet black hair like she had just gotten out of the shower, thick soft body, huge ass, beer belly, nice small tits, beautiful face, especially the lips, everything perfect about it except for her very crooked teeth, which didn't matter. She smelled strongly of some cheap strawberry body spray.

She spoke rapidly. Her head would sometimes snap sideways suddenly and then look back at me. I had never seen someone that wired before. She said her boyfriend had just beaten the shit out of her, torn up her house and broken the door. "He turned my house upside down!" she kept saying over and over. She had a black eye and bruises on her jaw and arms.

She was wearing some flip flops and showed me a long, deep gash on her foot that was stitched up from where she had stepped in broken glass during a previous situation like that with him. I didn't know what to say. She asked me for a cigarette and told her I had some in my house.

Talking to her in the kitchen, I felt like I wanted to give her a hug or something. She picked up a steak knife like she thought I was going to rape her. I was surprised. I asked her if she wanted some water. She put the knife down and relaxed a little. I washed out my only cup and filled it with water from the sink. I told her I had nine dollars, I could go to the store and get some beer. I figured anybody that wired needed a beer. She looked around my house at nothing but a mattress and realized how broke I was. She declined on the beer.

We sat together on the bed and I told her about how I had ended up there. She told me about her boyfriend. He was nineteen years old and in the army and did this to her all the time. As soon as she would heal, he would beat her again. I asked if he was only good at beating up girls or if he could actually fight. She said she'd seen him fight many times, that he was really good and I didn't stand a chance against him.

I ended up awkwardly putting my arm around her. She was sitting at my right side and her head kept snapping to the right and her wet hair would whip my face, smelling like shampoo. I noticed the outline at the bottom of her shirt of a crackpipe and a torch clinging to her body. I thought about kissing her. She asked me, "Do you have a gum?"

"Yeah I got a gun right here," I pulled the Taurus out from behind the mattress, "Do you want me to shoot your boyfriend? You could call him over here right now and I'll kill him." I didn't give a fuck. I had just held the gun to my own head a few days ago. I didn't really have much to live for and I wanted to make the world a better place.

"I asked you for a gum, not a gun!"

She freaked out, got up, begged me not to ever shoot him and I said ok; then she said she had to go. I asked her if she wanted me to go with her to her apartment and stay with her tonight but she said no.

The next day I sold the gun because I was flat broke and I needed the money. Ironically, I got my job at Jakarta Kitchen that same day.

VI. XIOMARA AND STARVIN MARTÍN

SHE CAME TO my house all wired again one night. She walked right in through the glass door all fast and scared me again. I don't remember what we talked about so much. We sat against the wall smoking weed. She was definitely mad at me for selling my gun, I remember that. When she decided to go, we both got up at the same time, our heads banged together and she knocked me out. Only person who has ever knocked me out to this day. I'm hard headed and I have a great chin but she must have got me just right. What a beautiful face to come together from my double vision, like an angel looking down on me. She helped me up off the floor and kissed my head where she had hit it. I always regretted not kissing her head back.

I didn't see her for a long time after that. I walked by her apartment a few times and could see that the glass door was off its track and anybody could walk in and rape her if they wanted to.

At the convenience store I was buying a 30 pack of Budweiser and she got in line behind me. She had no visible marks of being beaten and her hair was straightened. We smiled at each other and I waited for her to make her purchase so I could walk back to the apartments with her. When I saw her buy a pack of grape Phillies I said, "Hey grape Phillies are my favorite. Do you got weed for those blunts?"

She said no, afraid to admit to being a pothead in public.

"Well, that's cool, I got weed. Let's go smoke and drink these beers." The cashier, a really huge bald headed guy who always appeared to be happy, and had once told me that he had never had a drink or smoke in his entire life, smiled at us. He had met both of us before, but didn't know we knew each other, and it must have appeared to him that she and I were just meeting each other for the first time that way.

As we walked to the apartments Xiomara looked me up and down and said, "You have a nice body."

"Thanks. You look good. I like your hair that way." It was nice to see her not all beat up and wired. She was sort of timid and shy like that, moving slowly now.

Xiomara's house was now spotlessly clean and well furnished, although the sliding door was still busted. She didn't know how to roll blunts, so I rolled them. I always rolled perfect blunts and joints. She told me about her life. She used to be a stripper, met this nineteen year old army guy who whooped her ass until she wasn't allowed to dance anymore and paid for all her material needs after that.

"How come you never just call the cops on this

guy?" I asked.

"Because I'm afraid it will come back to me and if I call the cops my son will end up in prison someday," she said.

Before she was a stripper she had a good husband and two kids but somehow that didn't work out. She was really nice, but I could see how it must be difficult to try to keep a woman like her as anything more than a fuck buddy without eventually getting your feelings hurt. She was bored easily, anxious, and didn't like being idle or alone.

She told me to keep lifting weights, made me some spaghetti and toast. It turned me on to see her in the kitchen cooking for me. I wanted to bend her over and fuck her from the back against the stove. The food was gross but I ate it all because how often does a woman cook for me?

Her boyfriend called her on the phone and I got up from the table and held her from behind, got a boner and poked her with it. She had to talk to her boyfriend and act like I wasn't there and nothing was going on. When she got off the phone with him she pushed me off but she was smiling. I think I asked her if she wanted to fuck and she got offended and told me to leave.

Another day I was on my patio drinking and she passed by looking hot as hell. She was wearing some tight pink and black Nike gym clothes. Her hair was straightened and it had what looked like some dried sperm on the side of it. She told me she had been out all night with her friends rolling on ecstasy. Ridiculous. My dick popped up and she stared at it for a second. I wanted to give her a hug like how guys and girls casually greet each other but the jizz in her hair repelled me. I wonder if she knew it was there. We walked to the store together. Inside, there were a lot of old men in line in front of us staring at her. One guy said to me, "That's a nice girl!"

"She is really nice," I said.

On the way back she asked me to carry her beer for her. I said no problem. Then she profusely explained that she wasn't trying to be a bitch or tell me what to do but that her hands get cold very easily. I thought it kind of surprising that she would be so apologetic about it and I said it doesn't matter to me I'll carry your beer for you anytime. I tried to get her to hang out with me but she said she had to meet her boyfriend right now. Then she surprised me by giving me $60 to hold for her because otherwise her boyfriend would take it from her. I put her money under the mattress separate from mine and wondered if I was becoming a pimp for this woman. She could have easily hidden it from her boyfriend but for some reason this woman was giving me her money that she had made somehow without a having a legitimate job.

Maybe an hour later she passed by my house with her boyfriend. He was a huge, muscular guy. No way I could take him back then. He appeared to be a calm and normal guy but from something subtle in their body language as they walked together it was easy to discern a sadistic pleasure he had in his hatred for Xiomara, like she was his favorite toy. She had told me that he cheated on her with many women but she was the only one he beat. She was freshly showered and dressed much more conservatively than before. They didn't look at me. He didn't know I existed, but she wanted to show me who he was.

I used her money to buy two ounces of weed, separated it into eight dimes, and sold them to Starvin Martín one or two at a time, making a $20 profit. The guy had started weirding me out so much that I didn't smoke with him anymore or let him into my house. He never admitted that he was gay, claimed to have a girlfriend although it sounded like bullshit, and one night he called me a fag. I told him that I was not gay and that if he ever said I was again, I was gonna knock him the fuck out. That was the last time I ever allowed him into my home.

I had had many gay friends before and none of them had ever given me any problems. I had never had to make a violent threat to a gay guy before. Starvin Martín struck me as a guy who had been to jail and gotten fucked a lot in there, and now had a certain kind of predatory sexuality. He would often try to act tough and attempt to intimidate me, but it was obvious from the way that he moved that he was a complete pussy who didn't know how to fight for shit, and I couldn't imagine how anybody could be scared of him.

Doing business with him was annoying because

he didn't have a phone, so he would often knock on my door to try to buy weed when I didn't have any. He had been doing that a little too much lately and was really starting to get on my nerves. Sometimes, when I would go to the store, I would find him waiting outside for me. How long had he been standing there? It was starting to look like I had myself a gay stalker.

I was extremely drunk and feeling particularly violent, thinking about Xiomara's boyfriend when he knocked on my door. He had a big bruise on his left cheek. He begged me to let him in so we could smoke and chill because he was running from someone who had just hit him with a bar. That was a lie, because the bruise looked too developed to be a fresh wound. It might have been two days old. I imagined that the mark on his face was probably from a guy he had been stalking and sexually harassing. I told him that he had to leave; I wasn't gonna let him in. Then he tried to take a step in and I shoved him out with my left hand. He stared at me wildly, started panting like it turned him on to get pushed around like that, "Come on, just let me in." He tried to open my door more and squeeze past me. I grabbed him by the shoulders and threw him out.

"No. You need to get the fuck off my property and never come back or I'm gonna whoop your ass right now."

"Oh no, I'll be back. I'm gonna keep coming back," he said, smiling.

Can't say I didn't warn him. I glared into his eyes, he looked down and smiled, maybe even blushed a little; at that moment I gave him an overhand right to the same spot where he was bruised. He threw his hands up, and with my same right hand that hit him, instead of pulling it back empty, I grabbed his right wrist, pulled him into a hard left elbow that hit him on the neck, right under the jaw, and he went down. I stood over him. He took about five seconds to wake up.

"Had enough?" He got up and started caressing my arms, groveling.

"Look, I know, I'm sorry I fucked up and you had to check me but we're brothers, we have something special—"

I blacked out with rage. I have no visual memory of this, just pitch black. My feet were planted firmly on the ground, my whole body swinging my arms as hard and fast as they could hit, digging hooks into his face and body. My vision returned and he was lying on the ground again. There was blood on his face and on my hands.

"The next time I see you," I growled at him, "I'm gonna break your fucking bones."

He got up and stumbled away, said in really effeminate voice that I had never heard him use before, "I'm gonna tell my mom on you!" Some neighbors were standing outside their doors watching. Starvin Martín left and I figured he wouldn't be back, but the neighbors were freaking me out. I had weed and pipes in the house and I thought they might call the cops. So I washed my hands, put my paraphernalia in a little box, pocketed all my money, locked my doors and left. I went to another apartment complex and stashed my box in a bush. Then I started walking to my mom's house, a long journey across most of the Westside.

I heard a loud noise in my head and everything went black for a second. I almost fell down but I got control of my legs before I could hit the ground. I stood up and looked back. It was the revenge of Starvin Martín, the rock thrower. This motherfucker. I ran into the shadows of some apartments, picked up my own rock and decided to kill him. One rock to the head can kill you so this guy had made an attempt on my life and now it was mortal combat. I was quiet like a ninja, creeping from shadow to shadow, always feeling like another rock might come out of nowhere. I was trying to sneak up on the guy but I couldn't find him anywhere, and I figured he was gone. I dropped my rock, hopped a fence, and started walking down Mesa Street.

Then I saw him walking parallel with me on the other side. We started walking sideways, staring at each other. There was heavy traffic moving fast between us. As soon as I saw a little gap in the cars, I sprinted across the street, got on the sidewalk, grabbed Starvin Martín by the collar and threw him in front of some little white car that slammed the brakes. It was a woman driving with children in the passenger and back seat. I looked at her terrified face for a second and disregarded it. I started stomping all over him right in front of her and her kids.

As I was doing this the lady changed lanes and drove on; then the next car saw what I was doing, changed lanes, and kept moving, and a third car did the same. Starvin Martín was screaming. I kept stomping him faster and harder, but nothing seemed to be breaking and it was making me angrier. I felt my foot bounce off his collar bone inaccurately and saw it as a weak point. He tried to block it so I stomped him in the nuts and smashed them twistingly like I was putting out a cigarette, and as he was clutching at my leg with both hands, I jumped up in the air and gave the collar bone a final stomp, landing with all my weight on the heel of my right foot and felt it break, heard it break. My foot dropped into his collapsed shoulder. It was disgusting. Now he was really shrieking.

I ran as fast as I could; I ran through back roads and motel parking lots, jumped every fence in my path, put my hands on a rock wall and almost jumped over it before seeing the three story drop on the other side. I had so much adrenaline I thought I might have a heart attack. I sat down behind a dumpster and caught some air. I could hear Starvin Martín screaming in the distance. It sounded like a woman's voice.

I took every shortcut I knew and didn't really feel like I got away with it until I got to the closest convenience store to my mom's house. I opened the door and everyone stepped back like a murderer had just walked in. I got three King Cobras. The cashier's hand was shaking when he gave me my change.

I told my mom I had just gotten in a fight and I didn't want to be at my house if the cops came for me. I didn't mention that it was a gay guy or that I had tried to kill him. I told her it was a guy I had noticed casing my house for a burglary. She could tell I wasn't really telling the whole story but didn't seem to really want to know. I was ashamed of myself that night for beating up a homosexual, although I no longer am. He was a fucking creep and he deserved it. A gay man is still a man; he has a dick and balls and the right to get his ass whooped for being out of line just like any other man, regardless of his sexual orientation. Starvin Martín ruined gay people for me and I would never trust them again. I never wanted to have to beat one up again either. It was very unpleasant. For the rest of my life I would generally avoid homosexuals.

I tried to convince my mom to let me stay the night but she wouldn't. She smoked me out and let me finish my three 40oz beers, which I chugged very quickly and thirstily, faster than I could have possibly drunk water. I regretted that I had not bought six of them. I noticed the little league bat, a Louisville Slugger, thought it might come in handy, and took it with me, the same bat that I would later put up my sleeve to try to ambush Xiomara's boyfriend with, also prowl around my apartment complex with at night sometimes, and got a ride home from my mom.

We passed by the scene of my crime and there was no evidence that anything had happened there at all. For the next few weeks I would be afraid of some cops knocking on my door, but I guess Starvin Martín kept his mouth shut about me and I never got in trouble for that.

I was sitting on the couch a few days after I beat him up thinking about Xiomara. Was I some kind of pimp now who never fucks his hoe? I didn't like thinking about it that way, because I thought of her as a friend and didn't want to take advantage of her in any way, especially because she was in such a bad spot, but she was a certain kind of woman. I knew she fucked around a lot, probably for money sometimes. I liked the idea of being a money manager for her and I wanted to encourage her to give me more money. I often fantasized about her moving in with me, letting her wounds heal, putting her to work at Prince Machiavelli's, the nearby crappiest strip club in town, and using her money to be a stay at home drug dealer (true, I had beaten the dogshit out of my best customer, but I could easily find more). Through her I could meet more strippers and pimp them out too, also drug dealers and customers. She already seemed to be hoeing the streets though, so maybe my strip club idea was regressive. Under my management, nobody would ever be able to beat her again, I thought, but I also wondered if maybe she liked being hit and would be unable to get over that addiction.

The little weed sessions I would have with her were the only moments of happiness in my bleak life. Maybe I was in love with her, which was a mistake in itself, and that's why I made the wrong decisions.

I got a knock on my door and there she was. She had on these jeans that were all cut up, showing a lot of skin. She had told me that her boyfriend liked to cut her jeans while she was wearing them, sometimes cut off all her clothing, and fuck her with a knife to her throat. I hadn't been laid in almost two years. Every time this chick came around I knew she had probably experienced every possible type of kinky hardcore porno shit and even been raped, hands down the freakiest chick I've ever met to this day. She made me feel like an amateur. I was twenty two and she said she was twenty eight.

She looked so good that when I saw her, I started panting like a dog and so did she. She took off her jacket, had a pink shirt like a tube top, exposing her shoulders, which I had never seen before, and sat next to me. She had a tattoo that said Angel on her shoulder. When I asked her about it she said it was her son's name. I said I thought it meant she was an angel. I could see she had some stretch marks on her belly from pregnancies and that was alright. She had a nasty bruise on her jaw, and her arms had grip marks all over them. I couldn't stand it.

I explained to her how I had used her money to make a little money and I had some chronic I had been saving just to smoke with her. And if she ever wanted her money back I would give it to her of course. I always had this feeling like I was talking too much when I was with her, never knew what I was doing, was even scared to really look her in the eyes, and she had beautiful eyes. She was very happy with my little two-bit hustle and said she hadn't smoked chronic in years.

We started smoking and next thing I knew I was feeling her up, she was moaning, I undid her jeans, no panties, and started fingering her. Just then her boyfriend called her. She started talking to him in some sexy babytalk voice that I had never heard before. They were arguing in Spanish. She was saying, "¡Tu me engañastes, tu me golpes!" You cheat on me, you beat me! I kept fingering her but it was awkward. Then she lost her argument, lost whatever we had, whatever she had gained from being with me, got up and left to go with him. My fingers smelled like some nice fresh pussy, nothing wrong with it at all. I felt like such a loser.

I didn't see her again until that morning when we went looking for her wallet.

VII. IT'S YOU!

WE NEVER FOUND her wallet that morning. She went home. I went home and finished the can of beer she had left me. It had a sobering effect. Everything became clear to me all of a sudden. I had been acting completely insane all night and for... I didn't really know how long. I needed to go get my job back and register for the spring semester at UTEP.

So I walked down that fateful straight line to my work. Just as I was about to jump through the hole in the fence behind Los Reyes, I heard a voice behind me.

"You're going through the hole again." A chill went down my spine. I knew that it was the person I had been looking for, yelling at the top of my lungs for. I turned around and there she was, a little old Mexican lady with sunglasses and a blue hooded windbreaker.

I pointed my finger and started walking slowly towards her, yelling as loud as I could, "IT'S YOU! IT'S YOU! IT'S YOU!..." She ran away from me. For some reason I popped a boner. Weirdest boner of all time.

Neighbors started poking their heads out the windows. They had heard me yelling all night and now they wanted to see who it was I had been looking for. Just some frail old lady. A woman came out and helped her up the stairs, said she was calling the cops. I said, "You don't understand! This is a bad person; she's been doing something bad to me! This woman is a bruja!" The old lady in the blue hood made a face like she was scared to the lady who was helping her, but looked back at me and smiled, an evil smile confirming that we both knew exactly what was going on, and went into her apartment. I realized that this old lady had a perfect view out her window of me going to work every morning and coming home every afternoon.

The fact that she was a bruja and not a brujo made things worse. Had she been a man, I could have just beaten him up to solve our problem, but I couldn't hit an old woman.

I went to my old job. All the doors were locked like nobody was there. It wasn't a Sunday and it was past ten o'clock. There was no reason the place should be closed. Were they hiding from me? It didn't make any sense.

So I walked to UTEP. I struggled to breathe. Worse than ever I could feel those sharp fingernails digging into my throat. It was because I had come into such close contact with her; the connection had become stronger. I stopped at Whataburger, got a nice double cheeseburger with mayonnaise and no mustard. I sat down at a table outside, relaxed, and watched the beautiful college girls pass with my dick hard. So many beautiful girls passing by I couldn't believe it. Me, with my juicy fat burger and such a view; I felt like I was in heaven. All my troubles left my mind. It was a moment of pure bliss.

The last girl passed by. I watched her walk all the way up the hill until she disappeared, and then I was alone again. I got the feeling that someone was watching me. I looked around, and sitting at the table behind me to my left was a big fat dirty gay bum with fucked up black teeth smiling at me.

"What the fuck are you looking at," I said. He turned and looked away from me and put his hand down his pants and started masturbating! I couldn't believe it. I stood up, picked up my half finished burger and said, "Hey, puto!" He looked at me, still masturbating. I threw my burger as hard as I could, hit him right in the face with it. He picked up some lettuce and sort of tossed it in my direction but not close enough to reach me. Blackness started closing in around my field of vision as I looked at him. I would have liked to beat him to death, but not with my bare hands. I turned around and walked away.

When I got to UTEP to register, I couldn't talk right to the lady. I couldn't breathe. The words I was saying didn't make sense. I was telling her about how a witch put a curse on me and I needed a limpia. No registration happened and I left.

The reason that the word "limpia" came to my

mind was that there was a psychic shop right next to Los Reyes. In El Paso there are many psychic shops like this. They have a big sign with a hand on it. This one had a sign that said, "PALM READINGS, TAROT CARDS, FREE LIMPIAS WITH EVERY SESSION". The one by Los Reyes I had passed by before and looked through the glass door one time. There was a pretty old lady with long hair sitting on the couch with her legs crossed, her eyes closed in meditation. She seemed like some kind of a good witch to me. And I wasn't quite sure what a limpia was but it sounds like it means cleansing. Maybe this lady could help me with the bruja who had put her hex on me.

VIII. YOU WON'T SEE ME

I WALKED ALL the way back to the palm reading shop. The neon sign said OPEN. I tried the door but it was locked and dark in there. A woman in a white robe was standing with her back to me, doing something with her left hand, waving it back and forth over a table. I knocked on the door and begged her, as if she could hear my voice, "Please, you gotta help me. A witch put a curse on me. I need a limpia!" It seemed like she could hear me, but was ignoring me, then she suddenly whipped her head around and looked at me with a wicked left eye over her shoulder. A wave of disgusting energy came from her whole body and hit me hard, almost physically knocked me down. All my hairs stood on end. I jumped out of my skin and took off running.

It was gross, like my entire body was filled with a sickening nausea but I didn't want to throw up. It felt like every base and disgusting emotion, every fear and weakness I had within me had been recognized and pulled to my surface all at once, and also like some kind of mark had been placed on me. It's impossible for me to describe the feeling I got from that one quick look. She had given me the real evil eye, and not only that, it was the same lady with the shades and the blue hood. I wondered if she wore shades all the time like Cyclops from the X Men because her eyes were so evil. On second thought though, they might not have been the same woman. The one with the evil eye seemed different, more powerful. I couldn't be sure. If they are two different women, they must be in league against me. Who knows how many of them there might be?

I saw a girl I knew from college walking down the street. I explained to her, all out of breath, about how a witch put a curse on me and gave me the evil eye just now; she's right over there in that shop. She put her hands over her ears, said she couldn't hear me and kept walking.

I went into the convenience store and got some King Cobras. I saw a friendly old woman in there and when I looked into her eyes, they terrified me. She saw my expression of terror and became scared herself. I looked away. I told the cashier that a witch put a spell on me. She was a tall, good looking lady for her age and her gorgeous daughter sometimes worked there.

"You mean like she put a spell on you so you'd fuck her?" the lady asked.

"No, she put a curse on me so I can't breathe, the witch from the tarot card shop over there..." I started explaining my whole story to her from the beginning, hyperventilating, starting with the part where I first saw the witch and how she made me punch myself in the face. She cut me off.

"I can't hear you right now." She put her hands over her ears. I suspected that she must have been a witch too in cahoots with the other one, that I was in a whole community of witches and friends of witches who didn't like people talking bad about witches.

When I got to my apartment there was a note on the door saying that I needed to go to the office. I put my beers in the fridge and went down there.

The lady in the office said that there were many complaints against me from my neighbors and that if I wanted to keep living there (I never did in the first place) I had to just stay in my house and not bother or talk to anyone or make any noise.

"You don't understand, there's someone evil, a witch put a curse on me—"

"There's no such thing as witches, you're the only person around here who's been acting evil and weird. I don't want to see you anymore. Just stay in your house except when you're going to work."

"Ok. Don't worry, you won't see me anymore," I laughed and went home with my mind made up.

I drew the blinds. I was so full of adrenaline that I felt no pain when I took a razor blade to my wrist. Blood started gushing out, slowly clotted and stopped. So I made more cuts on my arm, all the way up to my elbow. When I cut my right wrist, I went too deep and cut the tendons that controlled my thumb, index, and middle finger, making them completely useless. I had also cut a nerve so most of my hand was numb and I could cut my fingers up without any sensation. A surprising amount of blood came out of my fingers. I guess they have a lot of veins in there. As I slashed myself up, I sometimes paused to smoke from a pipe of chronic, holding it with my mouth and lighting the weed with my left hand. It got me ridiculously high, mixed with the unexpected euphoria that came from losing a lot of blood. I put my finger in an empty forty and watched it fill with blood, then I drank the blood because fuck it. I made cuts all the way up my right arm to the inside of the elbow; I could no longer cut my left arm because my right hand was dead.

I had to keep changing blades as they would get dull. I was pulling out the veins and re-cutting them so they'd bleed again. I was getting light headed and thirsty. I had to run to the sink and drink water a few times. I was walking around squirting blood at the carpet. Fuck that carpet. Fuck Hillview Terrace. It was wrong how good it felt to bleed out like that. What reason could human evolution have to make it feel good to let blood?

I could see the dark angel of death following me around like a black shadow of smoke, and I started chasing him, but he wouldn't let me touch him and I slipped on a puddle of blood and fell down in the bathroom. I climbed into the bathtub and leaned on myself, applying pressure so that the blood would shoot out of me in spurts with the rhythm of my heartbeat. It was not as easy as they make it look on

TV to kill yourself by this method. Just some dead lady in a bathtub full of blood with two little cuts on her wrists. "If only we'd gotten here five minutes earlier we could have stopped her!"

I had barely any strength left in my body when I crawled out of the tub, pulled myself up and sat on the bathroom counter in front of the mirror. I figured I could finish it like this. I made a vertical cut down the right side of my neck. The skin burst open. I could see all kinds of guts in there. I was about to attempt to dig around in there for the jugular or the carotid, when my body suddenly collapsed and I fell off the counter, hitting my head on the ground.

I was lying on the floor in a pool of blood, blind, in a beautiful dream. I could feel my soul trying to leave my body but hitting this infinitely thick wall of steel that I believed was God. I couldn't pass through the authority of it.

IX. 1/11/11

I WOKE UP at three in the morning. I had passed out around noon. I peeled myself off the giant scab on the floor and crawled around looking for my phone. I didn't have the strength to stand. Real blood doesn't look like the movies at all. It's thick in some places and thin in others as it tries to clot. It's not the same shade of red all over; some places are dark, almost black. Blood seems to be alive, still trying to do things even when it's not in your body.

I crawled around for about an hour. Standing was impossible. I could barely even crawl without taking breaks to catch my breath. I didn't have enough oxygen in my brain to remember where my phone was. Now the pain was there, the most pain I had ever felt. I thought about cutting my legs but I didn't have the strength and this time it would hurt. It would be easier to call 911 and see what they would do with me. It seemed like I had searched those pants a million times and didn't find anything but then there was the phone.

The same two cops who had visited me before came to my house. "What the fuck?" I remember one of them saying slowly, horrified and disgusted. I asked if I was going to jail, since it's illegal to attempt suicide, and they told me yes. I said that's fucked up, I can't defend myself at all like this, I can't do shit! They put me on a stretcher and loaded me into an ambulance. I remember saying over and over "I need blood! I need blood!..." They took me to the hospital.

I'll never forget that date, January 11th, 2011. 1/11/11. Whenever I see five ones in a row it still looks ominous. I had lived in Hillview Terrace Apartments for exactly four months.

I woke up on a hospital bed surrounded by surgical instruments and said, "What the hell am I on? What did you give me to make me feel so good when I'm all fucked up like this?" It was a high that I didn't recognize, a different kind of downer, not an opiate. They told me it was Fioricet, a barbiturate. Hands down the best high I've ever had. I felt fucking amazing. The doctor said he was going to do surgery on me and he seemed like a cool guy. I immediately trusted him.

I woke up with a cast on my right arm. They had done some serious work on me. I could move my fingers again and they even had partial sensitivity, although they would never be the same. My left arm was covered in sutures. I had an obscenely gay male nurse. I kept laughing at him when he would talk and he would get offended. I said, "I'm sorry, I'm all high on these drugs, I have nothing against you, it's just so funny to me how you talk, dude. Please, just give me more morphine. As much morphine as you are legally allowed to give me." And he was cool about it. He would keep coming back and putting little cartridges of liquid morphine on my IV.

There was a tall, skinny, old, black guy from somewhere in the South they made keep watch over me. I told him my whole story of the witch and everything that happened, asked him if he believed in supernatural shit like that. He said he absolutely did. He had heard stories in his childhood of people going up to an open casket at a funeral and the dead body coming back to life for a moment to sit up and slap the person looking down at him.

I remember a red haired woman coming into my room and saying an intense prayer for me. She said that she had heard about me, that everything that had happened to me was real and that Jesus could save me from any evil person or demon. She told me a story of a ghost that haunts the hospital in bloody rags and that she has to pray to Jesus all the time to keep him away.

Two creepy psychiatrists in white lab coats came in and offered me antipsychotic medication. I turned it down. I wasn't crazy. Everything that happened to me was real and I wasn't going to let them take that away from me. They came back again the next night. They said that I had been found cowering in the corner with all my tubes pulled out, pointing at the window saying that there were witches on brooms flying around out there. They had to shoot me up with tranquilizers and put me back to bed. I had no memory of this and I wasn't sure if they had made it up; I had never thought of them as riders of brooms, but it scared me enough that I accepted their antipsychotic meds. They started giving me Haldol twice a day. It made me feel upbeat and happy and refreshingly dulled my senses.

X. MY MISTAKE

THE HALDOL MADE me unable to feel vibes from anyone, even witches. It made me passive, lethargic, hungry and sleepy all the time. When I would sleep I would have the most violent, murderous dreams, killing all these people just to escape to the convenience store to steal a King Cobra, cop cars and helicopters all over the place coming for me as I tried to chug as much beer as I could before being captured.

They had given me a blood transfusion, and explained to me that I was anemic. I needed more blood and I had two options. I could get another transfusion, which is not completely safe, or I could eat and rest and my body would make its own blood over time. I chose to make my own blood.

They took me to El Paso Psychiatric Center and I talked to the lady who ran the place. You rarely get to talk to her. I told her my story. She told me that she believed in brujería and asked me why I believed this witch had put a hex on me. I had been asking myself that question a lot lately and gave her the best answer I had come up with.

On my way to work every morning, in clear view of the witch's apartment windows, I would see a girl washing a truck. She was tall like me, and I'm 6'1", had long black hair down to her waist, and I could never tell how old she was. I would stare at her and try to determine her age. I did not lust for her, because I didn't know if she was old enough, but I wanted to know, so yeah, I would stare. She always had her back to me so I never could see her face or if she had tits. It's not like I ever spoke to her or flirted with her. I doubt she even knew I existed.

"So maybe it was the witch's granddaughter or something?" the lady asked me. Maybe. Might have just been some young girl who lived around there. I had made a mistake. Regardless of physical maturity, no girl of age would wash her father's truck every morning. Who knows how young she might have been.

That was the only possible reason I could come up with for why the witch had put a hex on me. What else had I done wrong? How come the witch hadn't chosen a more evil target, like Xiomara's boyfriend?

I tried to spend the night in one of the waiting beds of the El Paso Psychiatric Center but I got too cold, started shivering, didn't have enough blood, and had to go back to the hospital for another week before I was ready.

When I returned they asked me a lot of questions. When I told them how much I used to drink, five King Cobras a day, they were shocked and gave me

Librium for alcohol withdrawal. I didn't understand how that was shocking or think that alcohol withdrawal was anything serious enough to need pills for. They kept me on Haldol and I would get two Vicodins a day for the pain. A mind numbing mix of drugs that made me not really give a shit about anything while I killed time in the looney bin. Except for the constant hunger and cravings for alcohol. I was a chainsmoker and I would have killed for a cigarette too.

EPPC is divided into three levels. The first floor is where they put you when you first get in. Most people in there are pretty crazy and have just recently attempted suicide. When you stabilize they send you to the third floor. Everyone is calm and boring up there and you miss the stupidity and entertainment of the first floor, but it's good because it means you're about to get out. The second floor is an all male unit reserved for the criminally insane. The guys in there look a lot like how guys in prison look, but kind of retarded or something. You don't want to end up on the second floor.

They pretty much baby you in EPPC, although there is a creepy air of power tripping authority. You have no privacy, but that was ok because I didn't want to be left alone. Although the food is delicious and healthy, they keep you on a 2000 calorie diet, so you're always hungry and when you get your food you wolf it down. For a big twenty two year old man with a fast metabolism and barely any blood in my veins it was never enough. No matter how hungry I was I would never stare at the food on someone else's plate. Still, I was the second most violently wounded person in there and very obviously anemic so people would give me all kinds of extra food every day out of pity.

My first roommate on the first floor was an old Mexican man who liked to sing in Spanish all the time. Religious songs and the most sorrowful love songs you ever heard that made you want to slit your wrists all over again. When he saw me with my shirt off and all those stitches all over me with the cast he did the sign of the cross. I really liked his songs and I told him in Spanish. I wondered what he had done to get in there because he had no visible injuries.

My second roommate was cool. It has been my good fortune in life to always be assigned cool roommates. He was a young guy named Cervantes, but he didn't like his name and I forgot what nickname he liked to go by. He had a good sense of humor and he was always joking around. They had him on a heavy dose of Zoloft, a drug I associated with the Columbine shooters. Never knew his method of attempted suicide either.

My roommate on the third floor was one of those effeminate guys who have gay mannerisms, but somehow seem to be completely straight regardless. He had a wife and kid who would come visit him sometimes. He was in there for being high on PCP and stabbing a cop in the head. He showed me the scar where he had gotten shot in the stomach. He falsely believed that he was in there for life.

Only one person in there was more mutilated than me, and by far. An ugly, sad, fat, lonely, one legged lesbian in a wheelchair who had put her leg on the train track to get cut off.

There was a little chola girl I would always kick it with named Rosie. One time we were walking around in circles, as we often did, since we didn't have shit to do on the third floor; she flashed me in the hall and I sucked her titties in the laundry room when nobody was looking. She was one of the worst whores I've ever met in my life. We would later meet again on the outside. Looking back, she strikes me as a girl who must have been molested as a child.

I would dream and fantasize about Xiomara and all the girls I liked on the outside, girls from the apartments and bars. I wondered how I could ever face them again. I felt so much shame for what I had done. Would they have any sympathy for what I had become, or treat me with disgust? I had gone from a proud, strong young man, to a deranged and partially crippled guy who no woman could ever love. I used to see people like that, people who looked like fucking creeps to me. The stigmatized mentally ill. I never knew I would have to walk in their shoes.

Eventually my medication made me impotent and unable to masturbate. Also I could barely even get out of bed, I was so lazy. I explained this to my psychiatrist. Ms. Lara was a hot middle aged lady with a personality that was notoriously cold as ice. She switched me to Risperdal and got me off the Haldol. This was a painful psychotic transition and I had to act like I was doing ok in order to get out of there even though I felt like shit.

One violent suicide attempt equals one month in the looney bin, at least, if you make an effort to get out. If no damage is done to your body, you might only have to stay for three days.

My mom would come visit me often. She always had dark circles around her eyes and looked totally freaked out. We had to convince them that she would take me back and not throw me out again no matter what. She didn't know how much I resented and blamed her. I had never wanted to get kicked out of her house. I only wanted to defend it. I may have been acting like a complete fuckup in many ways, but to kick me out right after I fought for righteous reasons and lost showed me a certain dark side of human nature that I didn't think I would ever forgive her for.

The trick to getting out of the mental institution is to tell them lies. Say you feel good. You like the medication. Say you're happy. If you feel like being honest and telling them every day how fucked up in the head you really are, you can stay for as long as they will have you until they need to make room for someone who's crazier than you, who's not just being a pussy hiding in there. I was hungry. I would have told them anything to get out of there and be able to eat as much as I want.

They took me to the hospital, cut off my cast, cut

out all the sutures. I had one normal arm and one skinny, pale, Frankenstein looking arm that was far more mutilated than the other. I would have to treat my right arm carefully until the tendons healed back together or they would tear apart again if stretched too far. I wasn't supposed to move my wrist very much.

I went back into the psych ward and everyone gathered round to see what had been hidden under the cast for so long. That was my last day in there before I went home.

XI. NEVER LEAVE ME ALONE

I WAS STOKED to be out of there, even if I was completely fucked up in the head. I whistled at girls out the window of the car, even ugly girls. I got a fat triple Whataburger with just bacon, mustard, pickles and onions, a large fries and a strawberry milkshake, and I wolfed it all down. As I rode back into my old neighborhood, I barked out the window like a dog.

That night I had to see Valdo, Silent's evil older brother who had gotten ahold of my sister. One of the worst people we've ever had to deal with. He started crying when he saw me and what I had become. I looked like hell. I had a long beard and long hair, that zombie look in my eye from being on too much of the wrong medicine. I had become skinny and I was always cold so my jacket looked too big for me.

My mom cooked a big pot of chili and I ate too much. A weird feeling came over me and I threw up all over the place. That night many people in the neighborhood and many dogs threw up around the same time. It was a phenomenon.

Every voice I would hear in a song or on TV sounded like it was talking to me, like the TV was watching me and having a conversation me as it read my mind. I could never tell who anybody was talking to. Everything seemed to have a double meaning and a superstitious significance.

Someone in the mental institution had told me that you can do a limpia on yourself by passing an egg over your head a few times, putting it under your bed, under your head where you sleep. When you wake up, you crack the egg in your garbage can and if it has a black spot in its yolk, someone has had their hex on you, which is then lifted when you take out your trash. They also told me about another one you can do on your house that involves leaving a little cup of laundry detergent on your windowsill, but I couldn't remember exactly how to do that one.

I passed an egg over my head and put it under the couch. That night I dreamed that I cracked the egg in the garbage can; it had an ugly greenish black spot on the yolk and I took out the trash. When I woke up in the morning I cracked the egg in the garbage; it was normal and I took out the trash.

I told my mom that I didn't want to be ever left alone. I had become used to the constant observation of mental institution workers. When I was left alone I would often make half assed suicide attempts, which is common, I have heard, for people who have just gotten out of there. I dropped the toaster in the bathtub. All it did was give me a crumby bath. Sometimes I'd go wait for the train, but I never had the balls to stick my head on the track to be cut off. I would stand on top of tall buildings and look down, get that tingling on the soles of my feet and chicken out. I tried suffocating myself with a plastic bag and wondered how good it's supposed to feel to jerk off while doing that, since so many people die from it, but decided I was weird enough without being one of those guys.

XII. I FOUND A REASON

THEY KEPT ME on the highest legal dose of the antipsychotic Risperdal and added the highest legal dose of the antidepressant Lexapro. At first it was cool, like being on a very low dose of ecstasy all the time, but an ironic side effect of antidepressants is constant suicidal thoughts. It felt good to fantasize about killing myself and it was hard to think about anything else. Also, I found it difficult not to fidget all the time when I was on that combination of drugs. My hands would just do it all by themselves if I didn't make a conscious effort to keep them still.

I was still terrified of witches, although it seemed I had gotten under the radar of the one who had hexed me. I was afraid of old women, especially ones with sunglasses, and sometimes I would see one and think she was a witch. I suspected that they all knew about me and were popping up here and there to check on me every now and then. I would have nightmares where I'd be talking to someone, my mom, my sister, a friend, who seemed to be acting weird, like an imitation of themselves, and then I'd realize it was the shapeshifting witch with her evil eye and she'd morph into her true self, paralyzing me with her gaze, walking towards me with her bony hands open to strangle me.

I was eager to explain my story and it would scare the shit out of most people who knew me well, seeing what I had become. In those times it was very real. Most people believed me and would get goosebumps and a chill down their spine, but some were defiant and told me that the only way brujería can hurt you is if you believe in it.

One time I got so scared, I walked to the steps of a church in the middle of the night, got on my knees and prayed for hours for God to send me a beautiful woman. I couldn't stop crying. I couldn't believe how fucked up my life had become. When I ran out of matches and needed to light my cigarettes, I went to the nearest convenience store to buy a lighter and the girl working there was the most beautiful I had ever seen. Just the sight of me, all deranged and bleary eyed, made her flinch.

I fell in love hard the moment I laid eyes on her. You don't know what it's like to be so low, so close to the bottom, and then suddenly see such a beautiful girl, the rush of euphoria, all kinds of chemical reactions in my brain. I needed her. She was something good to think about, something to lean on, a beautiful distraction from my pain and an inspiration to become normal, or even better than normal. She was stuck up, proud, and gorgeous. I needed to change for the better if I was ever going to get this girl who was the immediate answer to my prayers and a coincidental suggestion of God's existence.

Her name tag said Paloma. I had never met a girl named Paloma, the Spanish word for dove, or popcorn. I estimate 5'4", pale Mexican with kind of a Spanish looking face with very fine features, black almond shaped eyes with long lashes, a perfect little nose, great teeth untouched by braces, hard to make her smile though, a serious girl. She was thick with wide hips and a tiny waist, nice small breasts, tasteful tattoos of flowers on her wrists, a little silver piercing of two silver studs under her right eye, long shiny straight black hair down to her big ass. A flawless, slightly gangster looking chick, but not a chola. Perfect El Paso beauty. Young, but something very mature about her that I couldn't put my finger on. So perfectly healthy and ripe you just wanna stick a baby in her.

My tendons healed and the doctor told me that it was safe for me to lift weights again. I got back into shape. I returned to UTEP. UTEP has so many beautiful girls, it's unbelievable. I became impotent as a side effect of being overly medicated. Once again I couldn't even jerk off. Nothing could make my dick hard. I couldn't stand to be there like that. It was the beginning of my mistaken belief that I had actually died after I slit my neck and was in hell, everything I want right in front of me but just out of my reach.

I dropped out of college again and went off the meds. Every day I would cut a little more off the pills with a razor blade than I had the day before, and I was scared of sharp objects, although I didn't believe it was even possible to kill yourself with a razor blade. I was scared of the sight of blood and guts, surgery on TV or anything, like razor blades, that would remind me of the sight of my own gore in that moment when it had been completely painless to vivisect myself, a shocking, unbelievable image that would suddenly flash brightly in my mind every now and then.

Antidepressants/antipsychotics are the hardest drugs I have ever quit, but it felt good. I became extremely depressed, seemingly more depressed than when I tried to kill myself, but I felt less suicidal every day and my sex drive began to return. I masturbated constantly. I began to talk the way I used to, walk the way I used to, or at least similarly. I would never be the same.

I had a collection of about 60 porno clips on my Ipod, mostly Latina, a lot of Rebecca Linares, Yurizan Beltran, Abella Anderson, Melanie Rios, Jenaveve Jolie. I once jerked off 28 times in a day. On number 27, blood came out of my dick; number 28 was just a test to see if blood would come out again and it didn't. It took about a month of that for me to get off everything. I think I went too fast.

Normally I like to buy a gun every time I get a student loan but I didn't trust myself to have one at that time, and once you go to a mental institution you can't buy one from the gun store anymore without lying on the form you fill out before the background check. The form asks if you have ever been in a mental institution. To lie on the form gets you ten years in a federal penitentiary. But supposedly, if you lie on the form, your medical records will not show up when they do the actual background check and you can still get your gun. So it's sketchy. It's a violation of your constitutional right to bear arms. Who's to say that former mental patients should be deprived of the right to arm themselves and protect their homes like everybody else?

Coming off antidepressants left me with that burnt out feeling, like a rough morning after a long night of rolling on ecstasy, all the time. My brain felt like a dried out sponge and I started drinking again. I had been afraid to drink while on my meds. I had tried a little sip of beer one time and it was scary as hell. But off the meds I had an appetite for alcohol like nobody's business.

I couldn't smoke weed anymore. It would put me on a bad trip and make me paranoid and confused. I had been a constant pothead since the age of fifteen and it blew my mind that I couldn't hack it anymore. I compensated for that by embracing alcoholism more completely than ever before, except that I had decided that forties, especially King Cobras, were evil and I would drink nothing less than Budweiser. First thing I did when I got off my meds was get a bottle of Stolichnaya. I remember feeling a hot, black, animalistic rage project out of my body in all directions when I took my first drink in six months. It was good to have my normal human emotions back.

XIII. I'D RATHER BE WITH YOU

BEFORE I WENT off my meds there was a time when I was hanging out with Lost and Alizé. After I got off my meds too. It's hard to remember, because I know there was a time when I was going to school on my meds and I also remember being there off the meds but high on morphine. The phase of cocaine Lost and Alizé had been fun back in the good old days, but that was over and now it was pain pills and black tar heroin. Unlike alcohol, opiates complemented the medications I was taking very nicely.

We knew this weird white trash girl who was sixteen. She lived in a big house in Canutillo that had dogshit everywhere and smelled so bad that just to be in there would make you feel sick and pretty soon like you would throw up if you stayed any longer. For some reason she liked us young adults and would sell us all these crazy Oxycontin and Morphine pills, like 120mg Morphines, for ridiculously low prices. She didn't even care about the price; a lot of times she'd just give them to us for free. We knew a guy in an RV who had the black tar. I guess Lost and Alizé needed a car and I needed some friends I wasn't too ashamed of my new self to hang out with.

I didn't know how good I had it before, now that it was gone. I wished I could have been my former self again, but obviously there was something wrong with him too. I had to either become a better person than I had ever been before or die, and dying sounded a whole lot easier.

I remember this one beautiful summer day when we hung out at Lost's aunt's house and there was this boysenberry tree in the yard full of ripe juicy berries, and we were out there picking and eating them all day. I had never eaten fruit off a tree like that. They were so ripe, you could just barely touch them and they'd fall off. I've always had a weird thing about eating fruit. I never liked it that much and I rarely eat it, except I love all types of berries. And when you get a plastic box full of berries from the store half of them are blighted usually and they taste like chemicals. These were the best berries I had ever had.

A badass blue pitbull puppy escaped from the yard next door. He had his ears docked still with the stitches in them and his nails were clipped. He was friendly and appeared to be well taken care of. Lost took him home to his owners, said that the dog was always escaping and he was always taking him back to them. I told him I wanted to jack that dog. I had always wanted a pit but my mom would never let me have one. I asked her this time and she said it was ok. Next day the dog escaped again and ran up to us. But this one was a female and with a cuter face than her brother's and her ears not clipped. I immediately liked this one better. We put her in a wicker basket with a lid and took her to my house.

I named her Biscuits and she's the best dog I've ever had. The dream dog I always wanted. I used to sleep on the couch and she would come up and put her head on my chest and sleep with me like that when she was a puppy. Now she's huge. One of the most beautiful dogs I've ever seen. Tall, long-bodied, and stocky. Blue with a subtle brindle pattern and white socks. In the summer when the sun shines on her a lot you can see a little bit of red in her fur and the brindle stripes become more pronounced. You'd be surprised how much just having a badass dog who loves you unconditionally can make you feel better about almost anything.

My sister must have been gone to visit relatives in Florida after the whole Valdo thing was over. I'll tell you about Valdo and her later.

There was a day when I decided to try suicide again with heroin as my method of choice. I know I was off my meds at this time. I bought four dimes of that black tar and some needles from Walgreens. I had watched Lost and Alizé do it enough times to know how. Nobody was around. I cooked up the tar in a spoon, used the fuzz from a cigarette butt to filter out the solid debris, and had four syringes full of heroin. I planned to shoot all four of them, one right after the other, and figured that would be enough to kill me. And maybe it wouldn't be such an unpleasant way to die. I would just have to go wander off somewhere nobody could find me when I turn blue so they don't call the ambulance.

It wasn't easy for me to shoot up because the veins of my arms were all maimed and stitched back together and hard to hit. The scars on the insides of my elbows looked similar to track marks and sometimes they still give people the impression that I'm some kind of junky, although that day was the only time I've ever shot up. It took a few tries before I got it in the vein correctly. I took the shot, released the belt around my arm and within a few seconds, I suddenly felt so great that I completely reconsidered any thoughts of suicide. If it was possible to feel so much pleasure in life, I didn't want to die anymore at all. It was pure artificial bliss. I didn't care about sex. I didn't care about my lack of love, my loneliness, self hate. Nothing mattered at all. I went outside, sat on a bucket in the little alley between my house and my neighbor's, smoked a cigarette and didn't give a fuck.

I didn't give a fuck so much that I wanted to die happy. I figured that this was the best that heroin would ever feel before I'd build up a tolerance and quickly deteriorate into a hopeless fiend like Lost and Alizé, shooting up all the time just to feel normal and running out of veins, and mine were already in terrible shape.

I wanted to drive my car. I had three needles left and I wanted to go shoot up in some cool places. I wished that everyone in the world could know how it felt to be so artificially happy like me; at the same time I wished that I could know how it felt to be naturally happy like them. What better place to shoot up than the bathroom of the UTEP library? I could see some beautiful girls all high and shit. But I missed the vein in the bathroom there, a painful injection under my skin that yielded no high. Then I failed again the same way in the bathroom of Carl's Jr. I got home and it was night time. In my room, without all the pressure of being in a public restroom I had success with the last needle. It got me so fucked up that I stumbled out of my room with double vision and couldn't hide how high I was from my mom. I told her I wanted to go back to the mental institution, that I had attempted suicide so many times since I got out. I just wanted to go back in there and be high with all those mental patients.

She drove me to the place, had to stop the truck once so I could throw up. When we got there they said they wouldn't let me in like that. I had to go to the hospital first and get rid of my high. In the hospital they gave me two options. I could either take an injection of a drug that would make my high immediately disappear, or I could lie down on a bed and wait for it to subside naturally, and then they'd take me to the mental institution. I chose the second option. I would never get to be that high again so I wanted to ride it out. They left me alone in the room. When nobody was looking, I just walked out and made a break for it down the street. If I couldn't go in there high I didn't want to anymore. I got to a place called Juarez Burrito on Alameda, closed at night. I called my mom. She picked me up, angered by my fickle selfishness and took me home.

After that I got clean. It had been a long time since I had taken a shit. Opiates make you constipated and full of shit all the time. It wasn't the first time I had gone off opiates and it's never been something hard for me to do. I never understood how other people can't quit. It's painful and depressing for about two weeks and then it's over. Of course, I never got too deep into shooting up so I don't know how bad it can really feel, but I'm pretty sure I could quit. I can quit anything, or at least take a break.

XIV. FUCKING AND FIGHTING LESSONS

I WASN'T IN school or working. I was drinking a reasonable amount. I decided I wanted to learn some martial arts. The one that appealed to me the most was Aikido. I wanted to be like Steven Seagal in *Hard to Kill.* There's only one place in El Paso that teaches it. I called them up. The guy said it was $70 a month, Mondays, Wednesdays, and Thursdays from 6:20 PM to 8:30 PM, and on Saturdays in the morning from 8:00 to 11:00. That sounded perfectly reasonable.

The dojo turned out to be a great place for me. I really enjoyed it and I liked all the people there. I rarely missed a class, except I didn't usually go to the ones on Saturday morning. I'd come home and spar with my neighbor Dogoberto and teach him the moves I had learned. Dogoberto was my best friend and we exchanged a lot of fighting knowledge.

Aikido is the Japanese defensive art of redirecting your opponent's motion and using his own strength against him. So a smaller, weaker person can defeat a stronger, larger attacker. The moves are designed as responses to being attacked, so you don't really learn how to attack people so much. The moves require very little strength as well, just good timing, form, and flexibility; you use the strength of your attacker. There is the uke, the one who attacks and is thrown, and the nage, the one who is attacked and does the joint lock or throw. The uke learns the underrated lesson of how to be thrown without getting hurt and how to be comfortable in off balance positions. The uke and nage can switch roles as there are counters to the nage moves. It's a lot of grappling, neck and arm manipulation. The ideal is to defeat your opponent without injuring him, but almost any of the moves, if done a certain way, can break a bone or kill someone, so it is a dangerous martial art. Also you can figure out ways to assault people with the nage moves if you think about it. Any movement your opponent makes, even a non-violent one, can be directed into a nage move.

Aikido gave me a lot of confidence and discipline, just as many martial arts dojos typically advertise. It was good for me psychologically. I had a lot of rage and violence in me and it was good to have a controlled environment in which to practice. Nobody ever said anything about the scars on my arms and neck, and my maimed fingers were never a problem. There were old and young students. There was only one girl in the class, a cute little sixteen year old Chinese girl. I never hit on her at all because I'm not into young chicks. Occasionally we would have women, usually older ones with their husbands in the class. Not really a place to pick up chicks at all but that was ok. That's not what it was for.

There was still a problem that I had to do something about. It's not right for a man to go so long without getting laid, and although I looked good and was starting to develop some confidence, I didn't know how to get a girl and I needed professional help. My mom gave me $500 for my birthday specifically for that purpose. I went to The Mesa Inn and got a room. I went out and bought a bottle of Don Julio Añejo and a shot glass. I had a piece of paper with phone numbers of various escort services I had found on the internet.

The first two numbers I tried didn't work. When I tried the third one, a woman answered the phone, "Hello?"

"Hi, I'm looking for a girl."

"What kind of a girl? White, black, Mexican?"

"Mexican."

"Thick, thin, fat?"

"Thick with big tits."

"Long hair or short hair? What color hair?"

"Long black hair."

The fee was $150 for the escort service and $150 for the girl. If I didn't like her I'd still have to give her $50 just for showing up. That was alright with me. The girl who showed up was a little more than thick, I'd say chunky. And she didn't have long hair, more like shoulder length. Her face was alright. I was disappointed but I wasn't going to pay fifty bucks for her to leave. She said her name was Angelica. She didn't even look like a hooker. She had a dress with flowers on it, like something a woman might wear to church. Smart. Any girl might be a hooker if that's what they look like.

She took off her dress and her body beneath it was almost completely covered with tattoos of pink roses with thorny green stems. She had on some hot pink lingerie with a G string. Big huge tits. She told me to get comfortable so I laid back. She sucked my limp dick until it got hard. I put on a condom and fucked her missionary for a while, then when I thought I was about to cum, I pulled out, turned her around and fucked her doggystyle until I was about to cum, then I let her get on top and that's where she beat me. I knew I wasn't really pleasing her, but she gave a lot of fake moans to try to make me cum faster. I wonder if she even enjoys sex at all. She started riding me back and forth in the way that I would teach more innocent girls to do later. Then she was bouncing up and down on me and with the springy mattress and we were slapping against each other pretty hard. Fifteen minutes with her was all it took for me to bust a $300 nut. I didn't think to discuss the terms with her and try to get her to charge me by the hour so I could fuck her again.

I gave her a shot of tequila, we smoked some cigarettes and she left. Of course, I never kissed her on the mouth. I got her number so if I ever needed her again I wouldn't have to pay the escort service and it would be half price.

I still had some money in my pocket and a hotel room. I felt like a badass. A wickeder, dirtier feeling than just getting laid. I had fucked a prostitute who taught me a thing or two.

The Mesa Inn is right next to Hillview Terrace Apartments. Enough time had passed that Xiomara must have had her baby a few months ago. I figured I'd pay her a visit. A big black guy answered the door. He seemed like a nice guy and was probably the father of her child. I felt happy for her that she wasn't with that old boyfriend of hers, but who knows? Maybe she didn't even live there anymore. The guy asked me what I wanted and I said my bad I got the wrong apartment.

I went to the bar, Los Reyes (didn't take the shortcut though). Hung out and drank until the place closed, found no woman to take back to my room and didn't care. I finished the bottle and slept better than I had in years.

XV. NATURAL HIGH

THE NEXT DAY Dogoberto's grandpa saw me walking down the street and asked me, "Feeling better?"

"Yeah," I grinned. I felt way better. I went to the bar, Botellas, which used to be called SLUGS. This was the closest bar to my house and it was my favorite. Normally I would keep to myself in this place but that day I was socializing with everyone and flirting with the bartender chicks. I was still not quite right but definitely better. Banging a prostitute doesn't teach you everything you need to know. It doesn't teach you how to have a healthy relationship with a girl or all those other moves you need to get them into bed with you, but it's a start.

During this time I believe my sister was living in Canutillo with her new boyfriend Mike and my mom was living with a secret boyfriend she seemed to have and claimed to be house sitting for a friend, so I had the whole house to myself. My mom would stop by sometimes to check on me, cook for me, clean up a little bit, but mostly I was on my own and I was cool with that. I drank a lot, almost every night, but I also cooked and ate well, worked out and went to my

Aikido classes. Sometimes I would apply for jobs and not get them. At the beginning of my story when I fought Silent I weighed 160 pounds and was very skinny. At this point I had gained a little more than 20 pounds of muscle.

I now had the confidence to start making small-talk with Paloma from the convenience store. She had lost some weight, and although I preferred the way she looked when she was a little thicker, she was gorgeous. Every day it seemed like she had a different hairstyle, so much long black hair she could do all kinds of things with it. And she always smelled so good. She would wear a lot of different perfumes, but sometimes I'd smell her with no perfume and her natural smell was intoxicating. She would stare at me hard when I'd walk in and I'd look down. I knew she was a freak. Sometimes she'd have aggressive hickeys all over her. She was two years younger than me; she grew up in Arizona but moved to El Paso when she was sixteen, was not religious, didn't go to church, liked English and Spanish music, didn't drink or smoke or go out much, and lived with her parents. It was so hard to make her smile or laugh.

The first time I made her smile, I remember, I said something really corny. There's a show that comes on once a year called Nuestra Belleza Latina, a beauty pageant where they get the most beautiful Latina women from all over the world. I loved that show. Exotic dream girls, South American princesses, daughters of tequila barons, stuck up Mexican sluts from California, all kinds of gorgeous women. There's usually at least one girl from El Paso on there. I asked her one night, "Do you ever watch that show, Nuestra Belleza Latina?"

"Yes."

"You should be on that show. You could win." She laughed but kind of like she thought I was making fun of her. She didn't know I was completely serious. Looking back she obviously didn't think as highly of herself as I thought of her. Not to say that she seemed to have low self esteem, depression, or any type of mental illness whatsoever. Everything about her seemed so perfect and healthy, but I can't say I really knew her. I would sometimes get this feeling like she was attracted to me and mad because I didn't know how to get her. Also I think she disapproved of how much I drank and thought I could be doing something better with my life.

Sometimes there would be some sleazy looking guy or other who didn't look like he was good enough for her standing by the counter having a long conversation with her as the customers came and went. Ugly guys, fugly guys, cholos, stoners. I always wanted to have a conversation like that with her but I couldn't figure out how to talk about anything serious with her. I had too much to hide.

She had no idea how much I thought about her, how important she was to me, especially when I was feeling down. Whenever she would cross my obsessive mind, a very pure feeling that I would get from her, comparable to a serotonin reuptake inhibitor, would slowly increase in intensity until it became ecstasy. Sometimes I would fantasize about her all day, exploring the infinite variations of her natural high.

There were a lot of other girls I liked but none of them ever compared to the crazy attraction I felt to Paloma. Never have I met a girl who made me so nervous yet at the same time so comforted just by being near her, and sometimes, like a junky, I'd have to go buy some beer and get another small, powerful dose of her.

XVI. BLOOD SAMPLES

THE DAY OF my Uncle Mike's wedding turned out to be strange for me in many ways and it was the start of another change in my life. The first weird thing that happened was when, after a night of heavy drinking, I woke up and ran to the bathroom to vomit some blood into the toilet. I didn't even worry about it. I got dressed in my sharpest clothes and drove out to New Mexico.

Mike and I are not related by blood, but I consider him completely to be my uncle. He is the son of my maternal grandfather Richard's ex-wife Angie and a guy named Mike James. My Uncle David is the son of my grandfather and Angie so they are half-brothers. My Uncle Pete is another son of Angie and Mike James. The three of them were all raised together as brothers and have always been very close. They used to play with me and my sister when we were little kids and they're all wild party animals, although now they have all settled and calmed down a little bit.

The last time I had seen my Uncle Mike was in 2008 in Florida at my Uncle David's wedding. He had just broken up with his girlfriend who he had been with for many years, because Mike really wanted to have kids and she didn't. Mike was just starting to bald and he was going wild. He talked fast, moved fast, and was funny as hell. He banged the sloppy maid of honor at David's wedding.

By 2011 he had found an El Paso woman, had a son with her and was now about to marry her. David and Pete were there. David's wife was there and his two sons, my little cousins, Pete and Joseph, Joseph being the younger of the two who I was just meeting for the first time. Those were some masculine little sons any man would be proud to have, and handsome too, and it was interesting to see David as a dad. He seemed like an awesome dad. And Mike was so tight with his little son, who looked like a miniature version of him, it was like they were best friends. Angie was there too and although I rarely see this ex-step-grandma of mine, I always enjoy it when I do because she's so cool.

This wedding had an open bar to anyone who was family. I love weddings. There were some hot girls in the other family, one in particular that I wished I could bang. Technically there was no blood between us whatsoever, but I decided to consider her my cousin and felt protective of her when an old man kept hitting on her. She seemed to be going with it too, although looking back I think she was just being polite. It angered me and when I saw him go into the restroom I followed him thinking I might whoop his ass in there and get thrown out of the wedding. He seemed to sense it and offered to buy me a drink. I told him I was family so I drink for free. He tried to buy me a better drink and I declined. But I decided not to fight him, whoever the fuck he was.

When the wedding was over and I had already been cut off by both of the bars for being too drunk, I took the drive home. I was one of those drunks who fancy themselves masters of driving while intoxicated. I sped back to El Paso at 100 miles an hour because I wanted to get to Botellas and drink some more before it closed. Also I bought some beer at a convenience store for when I got home.

At Botellas, I was struggling not to fall asleep, and I couldn't help but notice these three beautiful girls sitting at the table next to me with a creepy cholo guy. Now here in El Paso we have all different kinds of cholos, but I had never seen one like this. He had real vampire fangs. The girls called me over to the table; we took a couple of turns buying rounds of shots. I asked the guy, "How did you get those fangs, man? Are you a real vampire?" I wasn't trying to make fun of him. I had seen the movie *From Dusk Till Dawn* and was drunk enough to entertain the possibility that vampires may actually exist in the El Paso/Juarez area. I already knew that witches were real. Either the guy was an actual vampire or he had had some kind of expensive dental work done on him for it to look so convincing.

He said, "I have not disrespected you, so don't disrespect me."

"Oh no, man. I meant no disrespect at all. I've just never seen anything like that is all. I just came back from my uncle's wedding and I'm drunk as fuck."

I noticed that the girls were scared of him and he was their pimp. He offered them to me but I politely declined because I didn't have enough money for prostitutes, surely not enough for ones as beautiful and nicely dressed as those. It's probably better that I didn't, since their fangs would have come out and they would have drank all my blood as soon as I got alone with them. I went back to drink at the bar and didn't look in their direction anymore.

Last call came. I left. I had a reserve of beer in my car for when I got home. But I didn't make it. Only a few blocks away from my house, I got pulled over by a traffic cop and could not pass the walking and saying your ABC's test for shit. I refused the breathalyzer, some bad advice I had gotten from some old people at a bar once. The guy took me to get a warrant for a blood sample. On the way there I asked the cop if I had been driving badly and he said that I was driving perfectly and had not made a single mistake, except that I threw a cigarette butt out the window and that gave him an excuse to pull me over for littering. He had started following me when he saw me drive out of the parking lot of the bar.

When we got to the hospital I decided that the only way they were going to get a blood sample would be against my will, as a matter of principle. I said, "This is my blood. You can't take my blood. Do you know how long it took me to make this fucking blood? All I can say is this. I'm not gonna swing on you, but I'm gonna defend myself."

Cops started surrounding me. I saw the traffic cop's hands rising up into a boxing stance. I quickly twisted his right arm using my favorite Aikido technique called Nikkyo and brought him to his knees.

Nikkyo is one of the most painful Aikido techniques, whereby you twist someone's arm and hand in such a way that it uses surprising pain to force them to comply while requiring minimal strength from you, if it is done in the perfect direction. It also has the potential to stretch the tendons in the forearm until they pop without breaking the skin if done with a lot of force. I went along with the upward motion of his rising hand and directed it quickly into a perfect Nikkyo that was just painful enough to put him on his knees, but not forceful enough to damage him, just like we practiced in class.

Then I was wrestling with five or six cops and I wouldn't give in but they eventually pinned me to the table. One cop told me, "Stay down, bitch!"

"You're lucky you've got your crew here to back you up, you fucking faggot," I said, "Try me one on one with no weapons and I'll fuck your world up."

When the female nurse came to draw my blood, I stopped resisting, not wanting to accidentally inflict violence on her or move around too much and get stuck wrong by the needle. Though the vampires in the bar had failed, she and my toilet had succeeded in extracting samples of my hard earned blood on a strange day that seemed to require it of me for some reason.

The traffic cop and I had become friends somehow on the way to the hospital, and I guess he respected me for putting up somewhat of a fight against the violation of having my blood being drawn against my will. He said that since I didn't throw any blows he wouldn't charge me for resisting. I don't know what it is about me, but I have a way with cops. They usually don't give me any trouble. Maybe it's because I'm usually polite and respectful of their authority. Probably it's just because my skin is white that I'm able to get away with so much shit. Had I been a black man and twisted the cop's arm, they would have beaten me to death. Had I been a Mexican, they would have beaten me halfway to death. I don't hate all cops or cops in general. There are good ones and bad ones; I have mostly come across ones who were good to me. I don't hate the traffic cop who arrested me and gave me a DWI because the DWI ended up changing my life for the better, although it was unpleasant and expensive.

My blood alcohol level was 0.21. 0.08 is the point where it becomes illegal in Texas. I got this DWI on Labor Day 2011. I went to jail. Everybody in the holding cell was respectful of each other. I can't say the same for the guard who came in and kicked a guy sleeping under a bench to wake him up and take him upstairs. I do hate prison guards in general. There is something sadistic about anybody who would ever choose that profession, to come to work every day and watch people caged like animals. Through the magic window of the holding cell, the fat ugly bitch who is a prison guard in the hall looks like the most beautiful woman you've ever seen and she knows it.

There was a man in there who got busted with 800 pounds of marijuana in a semi-truck. He realized that he would never see his family again outside of prison and started crying. Everybody in there was peaceful. We talked about women and what types of drugs we liked to do and what crimes we had done to get in there. It almost seemed like we were forming an alliance early on for if we were to go upstairs. I'm sure you can get in a bad situation in a holding cell but that's not what happened to me and I got bailed out in the morning along with some of the other guys.

One guy offered to buy us a round of drinks at a bar, and looking back, I don't know why the hell I didn't take him up on it. I think it was because I just wanted to go off on my own and look for some female company. I ended up drinking at that bar downtown, Viva Vida I think it's called, the one next to The Tap. I was the only customer and there was this gorgeous bartender and I was trying my best to speak Spanish to her, my dick so hard I could have jizzed in my pants if I would have allowed myself to. Then my sister's boyfriend Mike came to pick me up. I let him drop me off back at Botellas.

XVII. THE INSIDE OF A COFFIN ON A MOONLESS NIGHT

CHRISTINA USED TO be in love with me back in middle school. She was a goth chick, really skinny, wore way too much makeup and I thought it made her look like a clown. But she was cute. She had started making fun of me on facebook a lot, being mean to me. I took it as a sign that she was still was mad at me for not liking her back when we were in middle school. I knew I could fuck her. I got her number and one time I told her, "Christina, I'm actually goth. I dyed my hair black. I have a raven that perches on my shoulder at all times."

"You don't have a raven! You didn't dye your hair. You're not goth." She was giggling.

"My hair is blacker than the inside of a coffin on a moonless night." I always felt confident around her. I took her out for drinks one night. I would give her rides places sometimes. One night I took her to my house, made out with her, got her to suck my dick, put a condom on, stuck it in her and busted a nut in one stroke! I got embarrassed and took her home. Hey, but I still got laid and it wasn't a prostitute.

XVIII. THE WIDOW

I WORKED OUT all day, then drank myself to sleep, woke up and had eight dollars left in my pocket. It was past midnight so I couldn't buy beer at the store, but I wanted to drink just a little more, so I drove to the bar, Aceitunas. I sat down next to this tiny woman named Maricruz who had a pretty face, nice long hair, a gap in her teeth, big boobs, and a beer belly. She said she was thirty five. She wouldn't stop talking to me. First she asked me if I was a serial killer and I said no. She said, "You're so handsome but you look really creepy at the same time."

"Maybe the reason I look creepy because I tried to kill myself a while back and I still feel bad about it." She took pity on me. That's when she started buying me all those drinks. She said her husband just died. He was shot for no fucking reason. All she wanted to do was party and do drugs.

"Do you wanna party and do drugs with me?"

"What kind of drugs? I don't smoke weed."

"Me neither. Wanna do coke and pop pills, like Oxycontin and shit?"

"Well, it sounds nice but I don't have any money."

"That's ok, I got you. I need a ride so you just drive me around and I'll get you high all night."

"Alright, I'm down, and I'll get you back one of these days."

"Nah, don't worry about it."

This chick was cool, but she was a domineering chola type lady, real bossy, and it was annoying. We went to some black dude's house and got some coke. She gave me ten bucks because my gas tank was empty and we drove all the way to the Northeast side. It was me, her and her two big fat chola sisters, and each one of them had a seemingly infinite supply of a different brand of excellent coke. We sniffed coke all night until the sun came up without any alcohol to drink. I was so wired I couldn't even talk. And Maricruz was just crying and crying about her dead husband. I didn't know how to console her, almost like it wasn't my place to do so or something. It was really awkward for everyone. After a while she calmed down and we started listening to some good music. All of a sudden she said, "Take me home."

We got in the car and she asked me, "Do you wanna take me home or do you wanna take me to your house and fuck me and then take me home?"

"I wanna fuck."

We didn't talk much on the ride to my house. When we got to my bedroom she took off her clothes, I took off mine. She told me not to kiss her on the mouth or leave any hickeys. Prostitute style. Don't eat her out and she wasn't going to suck my dick. I prayed to God that my dick would get hard after doing so much coke. My heart was racing. I sucked her tits, started grinding against her belly and sucking on her neck without leaving hickeys. I stuck it in real slow, forgot about the condom, I was going as slow as I could trying not to cum, she said, "Fuck me hard!" so I did but I couldn't last like that, pulled out, skeeted on my boxers, wiped my dick off and stuck it right back in before it could get soft, then I really pounded her for a good fifteen minutes all out of breath. I had her long hair wrapped around my hand and a grip on the back of her head like that. I pulled out and nutted again.

We laid there for a while and I said, "I don't think I can get it up again. I'm too fucked up. I wish I could make you cum though." I went down on her. I love eating pussy, and it's normally something I never do after I have already stuck my dick in there, but hey fuck it. I did my best at eating her out while she rubbed her clit, but I couldn't make her cum. She said it's cool; it's really hard for her to cum when she's wired. Then we smoked a couple of cigarettes. She gave me some Oxycontin pills and said to take them when I start to come down. I drove her home, gave her a hug, went back to my house and found in my room a little leather Oakland Raiders cell phone case with a bunch of 40mg Oxymorphones in it and a bag of chronic.

I texted her and let her know I had the pills, said I would get them back to her later. But I just didn't wanna drive with them because I don't ride dirty. So long story short I gave the weed to my mom, never gave her back those pills or hooked up with her again.

When my mom woke up I really needed some beer and cigarettes. Especially the beer because my heart was pounding. I told her all bug eyed and excited the story of what had happened without any vivid details of sex. She was glad I got laid. She gave me some money and I waited for Dogoberto to wake up so he could give me a ride to the store. I told him the story. We got some forties, hung out in the street and got fucked up for a while. Then later that night I went to the bar, Texas T's and everybody was laughing at me because of how wired I looked. I told my story to a few guys on the patio. Then for the next few days I stayed ridiculously high on those Oxycontin and opanas. So it was like a four day high I got off that chick and some sex. I felt like some kind of dirty gigolo.

I've gone to the bar, with $200 in my pocket dressed to kill and not come close to how much fun I had off just $8 and being in the right place at the right time dressed all bummy. God bless that sad lady Maricruz. I hope she's doing ok. I ran into her at Albertson's one day and she looked hideous from not living right.

XIX. WHAT CAN I DO

I DECIDED TO give UTEP another shot while I was still doing Aikido. I got some student loan money. I took some basic classes and also a kickboxing class. I found it hard to concentrate in my classes because all I could think about was sex with so many hot chicks around. I don't know how guys can concentrate at all over there. I didn't last a minute before I dropped out. I failed all my classes and didn't manage my time well because I was partying too much.

This must have been the spring semester because I remember there was a Valentine's Day where I went all out trying to get a Valentine and get laid. It started at Texas T's one night. It was me, Dogoberto, and Slim X. I had gotten a new tattoo of the shape of Texas with a nautical star on my heart (right off the label on the Budweiser bottle). I had also been partying with Shameless James a lot. He had this house all to himself right on the golf course in Santa Teresa and he would party as much as he could.

There was this bartender at Texas T's who I couldn't take my eyes off. At first she looked kind of sad and like a stuck up fresa, but when I started talking to her she turned out to be a goofy pothead Native American chick and we really hit it off, so well that my friends bought me a pitcher of Guinness and left me alone just to talk to her. I don't even remember her name. She was so cool though and I was smooth that night. I asked her if she'd be my Valentine and she said yes. I even thought I could have fucked her that very night. After she got off work she stayed drinking with me at a table for a while. She gave me her number and I went home.

I called her but she didn't answer and texted me that she was driving. I texted back, out of concern for her safety, "You shouldn't text and drive, it's dangerous, just call me when you get home." Then the next message I get from her was "You ruined it!" After that I couldn't get any response from her. I still thought she was going be my Valentine and I wanted to spoil her. I really liked this chick. It was still a few days before Valentine's Day. In the morning I went to this place called Casablanca Flowers and got this crystal vase of a dozen perfect pink roses, and one extra white one that I added for some reason, for $80. Can you believe what I spent my student loan money on? You see my intentions for going to UTEP, the wrong intentions? You're supposed to go there to learn and I'll never trust myself to go to college again.

This chick went all bipolar on me. She said that when I told her not to text and drive it set off a red flag that reminded her of her ex-boyfriend or something and when I asked her to meet up with me at school she called me a stalker. I texted her, "I'm no stalker, and just to make it clear, I'm not even gonna go to the bar where you work anymore and I'm going to avoid you as best I can." I don't know what was up with her. She seemed so cool that night at the bar.

So I had these expensive roses and didn't know what to do with them. I went to Botellas in the afternoon. It was just me and an old man in there. I told him what happened, said I was thinking of just throwing them away because it wouldn't be right for me to give them to another girl instead, and he gave me some cool advice. He said, "Don't throw them away. That would be a waste. Go find a girl and give them to her as fast as you can. The roses will start to open up soon and they won't be as nice anymore. You never know, it might lead to something later on."

Just then it hit me. Why am I trying to give these perfect roses (and they really were perfect, flawless, not like the kind you buy at the supermarket) to some stupid chick I just met at the bar, when I don't even love her? There's only one girl I'm in love with and it's Paloma from the convenience store. I drank a couple more beers for courage and went next door to where she worked. First I walked in and got some money out of the ATM just to check if she was working that day and she was. Then I went back to the car and got the roses out of the passenger seat. There were a lot of old people in line in front and behind me so I had to stand there for a long time with the vase in my hands.

Paloma didn't know how to look at me. She kept making all these confused faces like trying to play it cool in case they weren't for her but how could they not have been? I gave them to her and said, "Here, Paloma. These are for you for Valentine's Day, even though it's not Valentine's Day yet. I won't ask you to be my Valentine because I know you probably have a boyfriend, but I just want you to know that I've always loved you since the first time I saw you. These are for you." It was totally worth it just to see the expression on her face, so sincerely touched and surprised. She just said thank you twice, in such a nice way. It made me feel so good. I almost felt like crying. I felt so bold to finally confess my love to her, and in front of so many people.

The next day I went into the store to buy some cigarettes. It was just me and her in there. I had something planned to say to her but when I got to the counter we couldn't look each other in the eyes and I completely forgot my words. She smelled so sweet. It seemed like there was humidity coming off her. I could feel her body heat. I just asked her for the cigarettes, paid for them, and when we exchanged money and her hand touched mine I jizzed in my pants. I just stood there for a few seconds dumb-founded, staring at her all bug eyed like an idiot with jizz running down my leg. She wouldn't look at me. The expression on her face was almost angry. I said goodbye and walked out.

I would wake up suddenly in the middle of the

night sometimes with my heart racing and a rush of adrenaline and ecstasy from the memory of her smell so fresh on my mind like she was right next to me. It was driving me crazy. I could think of nothing else but her, but at the same time I didn't know what the hell to say to her now that I had confessed my love.

XX. THE SANDPIPER

I HAD SOME student loan money to throw around, which is not what you're supposed to do with it. In fact, I don't really know what the hell you're supposed to do with it except go into debt. One day I decided to take my sister out for drinks. She was living with her boyfriend Mike in Canutillo. I wanted to show Paloma to her. We went into the convenience store and I showed them to each other. I told Paloma, "This is my sister," just to make sure she didn't think it was my girlfriend or something, and nothing more was said. I put some gas in the car. My sister didn't have much of an opinion about Paloma, except that she had very beautiful hair.

I took her to the bar, The Hoppy Monk. I chose this place because it was not a rowdy bar where I would end up fighting because of some guy hitting on my sister. It was a fancypants bar full of snobs, hipsters and pussies most of the time, the type of bar I can't stand but it has its purposes.

There we met Ceci, a beautiful girl we went to high school with. She was on a date with some dude and blowing him off just to talk to me. I got her number. Talked to her on the phone a few times, then one night I went to a show with her. Some God forsaken rock show of a terrible band I couldn't stand that she seemed to worship. I obviously wasn't her boyfriend and she was so gorgeous that guys kept coming up to us and hitting on her. What a stressful night. Still, I asked her to be my Valentine and she said yes. I had already bought her a heart shaped box of chocolates before our date and I gave it to her right there. What a sleazy guy I was.

On Valentine's Day she rolled up to my house in some guy's car, gave me some cupcakes, and I gave her a giant teddy bear. Then after the brief exchange of gifts in my front yard and a hug, she left with the other dude. I thought we were at least going to hang out or something. The nerve of her to roll up to my house in another man's car on Valentine's Day! Nothing is sacred to these girls. I cussed her out over text messages. The homemade cupcakes, chocolate with chocolate chips were delicious though.

And that's what I should have told her instead of cussing her out. I should have kept it cool. Of course she didn't know me well enough to trust me and come to my house alone on Valentine's Day. It was a test. I should have stayed cool with Ceci no matter what agonies she put me through. Any girl as beautiful and sweet as Ceci is bound to put you through agonies without even intending to be cruel to you because she has so many options. Damn, and she even knows how to bake. But this chick made my blood boil. She was so hot and nonchalant that she made me really jealous. Still, if I had kept it cool, I could have gotten somewhere with her I think. She might have eventually narrowed it down to me if I could have shown her some stability. But I had been going into a rage over a lot of things lately because I'd do coke every weekend. When I blew up on Ceci I knew I had been doing too much.

Now here's a fucked up story. I had been partying at Shameless James's house a lot. These parties were strange because he would invite a lot of high school kids. Just about anybody who wanted to go could get in. There were adults, even old people at these parties. A lot of coke. You never knew what kind of chaos you were getting into. One night I did a bunch of coke with Dogoberto and after he left I drove over to Shameless James's, thinking it was a cool place where I would be surrounded by friends. The thing I always liked about those parties was that I felt superior to everyone there. They were all a bunch of pussies; I was always the toughest guy in the place. I felt like the alpha male and I'd go around trying to steal their girls. So on this night Shameless James comes out of the closet to me and says he's bisexual and that every time after I leave they have orgies with guys and girls all over the house without me, like a great big clusterfuck.

All those guys who I just thought were just a bunch of pussies were actually gay and there they were, out of their shells, wrists bent, talking with lisps and being sexually aggressive with each other. Right in front of their girlfriends! What was the world coming to? Even these gay dudes have hot girlfriends and not me. But hey I'd rather be me than some gay dude with a girlfriend any day. I was so sleepy my eyes could barely stay open. An extremely effeminate guy came up and started touching my arm, "I know you. I remember you from high school…"

"Look, you don't know me and I don't remember you. When you touch me, it makes me wanna punch you in the face. So just get the fuck away from me." Everyone looked appalled, like there was something wrong with what I said. Someone came over and took the offended little guy away from me. "And that goes for the rest of you fucking fruitcakes too. I'm not gay. Don't touch me. Don't even look at me funny. And don't be watching me sleep." I fell asleep in the chair instantly. I was too tired to go back home. Who knows what kind of sexual deviancy might have gone down in front of my sleeping eyes.

I had a dream that Shameless James was crying, telling me he was a pedophile and that's why he doesn't spend any time with his daughter. He seemed like some type of guy who could be sexually attracted to any living creature. I wouldn't put it past him to fuck a dog or a chicken if he was left alone to be a farmer. Of course, those are some strong accusations, and who knows what the guy is really like, but that was just the exaggerated impression I got of him from my dream. The whole thing was weird as hell, because I'd known the guy since middle school and I always thought he was straight as an arrow.

When I woke up in the morning they offered me beer and ecstasy pills and tried to get me to stay. There were some more girls on the way over. But I broke the hell out of there as fast as I could. I wouldn't be caught dead hanging out with any of the people from those parties ever again.

I later heard Shameless James tried to kill himself, overdosed on bath salts or something, and lost his house.

This next story is horrible too. I still occasionally have nightmares about this girl. I had stopped going to Aikido class (after a little more than a year's worth of training, without ever trying to get any belts) and I would drink every day from morning to night. I made a lot of bad decisions and who knows how I treated people. I remember frequently waking up with my hands shaking. I was still enrolled in school but I didn't go anymore. And I was broke. I had chickened out of the kickboxing class when I saw the huge dudes in there ready to beat the shit out of me in the bodyboxing we were going to do every day. I wasn't about to go in there underweight, the lightest guy in the class, and be everybody's punching bag. I immediately went and got some more gym equipment. My student loan money was not completely squandered on booze, drugs, and Valentine's Day gifts because I bought a 100lb heavy bag with a stand, a bench press with some weights, and a machine that does a lot of different exercises.

So anyway, one morning Dogoberto and I went to the Circle K, not the Valero. Because I didn't want Paloma to see what a mess I had become, I had stopped going there. I had recently watched the movie *The Mack* and had been listening to Too $hort a lot and you could say I had my pimp hat on. This is a metaphorical hat you wear when you're thinking about pimping hoes. I figured I could do it, I just needed to find the right starter hoe. And there she was all nasty and gross, smiling at every man, Rosie from the mental institution. I got her number right in front of her boyfriend. What a sorry ass dude that had to be.

She would call me and say she was lonely. Her man was a trucker. She lived with him and he would be gone for two weeks and stay home with her for two days. She was fucking all his neighbors. When I went to pick her up way out on the East side, the mother of her boyfriend was glad I came, wanted this chick gone. We drove around cruising and drinking forties. I made out with her, which was gross, but when you're in that phase of alcoholism you just want everything to be gross and fucked up so you can laugh at yourself spitefully. Life is a joke and it always feels like you're swimming around, breathing underwater. I took her home and fucked her with a condom as hard as I could for about an hour until I got tired and gave up, unable to even cum because this chick grossed me out so much. She got pissed off and said she wanted me to call my homies and run a train. She wanted to get fucked all night. This was what I had been waiting for. I knew she was a real hoe and maybe I could make some money off her. I called up every guy I knew and all of them pussied out, except Dogoberto.

"How much money you got?"

"I got a dollar."

"Well I got this hoe over here, I just fucked her for like an hour and I couldn't cum. She says she wants to run a train. You could fuck her for a dollar."

"Is she hot?"

"Not really. Not at all."

"Let me come over and see her and if I like her we can take her to the RV in front of my house."

"Ok come over."

They hit it off on the couch just fine. We went to the RV, which was called The Sandpiper. Dogoberto was about to fuck her without a rubber but I tossed him one. "You better wrap it up with this one." He banged her for a while as I watched in the dark. He was a little more creative than me with the positions he used; he pulled her hair a lot. When he had her doggystyle he told me, "Put your dick in her mouth."

"Nah, I'm good."

Dogoberto couldn't finish either and he gave up. We went out in the street. He gave me four quarters.

"What's that?" Rosie asked.

"That's the money this guy paid me to fuck you. Guess what? I'm a pimp and you're a one dollar hoe."

XXI. TRICK

I TOOK HER back in the house, fucked her again and busted a nut in one stroke. That made her happy. She was glad just to get a nut. We spent the next couple of days fucking and being bored and drunk. I always used condoms without exception. Next thing I knew I had her moving in with me. Her boyfriend's mom was happy to be rid of her. I intended to make as much money off her as I could.

But I had gotten myself into a conundrum. This chick wanted me to be walking around with her and shit but I couldn't stand even to be seen with her, so she was just locked up in my house all day annoying my mom. Also I couldn't bring any other girls to the house with her in there. My scheme of pimping her out wasn't working because nobody wanted to fuck her, except this old man who offered a hundred bucks. She wouldn't do it. Her crappy little excuse was that she was scared of his wife. I told her nobody could come to my house and beat her ass. But there was no convincing her.

She wanted to be like me and go off her meds. She stopped taking them all at once, started getting this crazy look in her eyes like she was going to murder me in my sleep. To be a real pimp you've got to be ice cold and I guess I didn't have it in me. I had become a rest haven for a parasitic hoe. A real pimp might have slapped her around a little bit or talked real rough to her to make her fuck the old man and get his money, but I was too soft. I didn't even slap her when she bit my dick one time. She told me, "Your dick tastes funny. It tastes like you got trick. It's an STD. I sucked a guy's dick once that tasted like yours and later on we found out he had trick. I'm gonna call you trick."

"Bitch, you better not call me trick!" But it was true, she had made a trick of me. Still I made the right pimp decision to get rid of her as soon as she wouldn't fuck the old man for me. I took her to her dad's house but he wouldn't accept her. She had been deserted by her whole family. Finally I found some friend of hers from the mental institution who took her in. It was one of the best days of my life when I finally got rid of her. You have no idea how happy I was.

The next day Dogoberto asked me, "Where's Rosie?"

"Last night, I told her 'Get in the car, we're going for a cruise.' I took her downtown, drove into a dark little alley where nobody was there and said 'Get the fuck out the car and don't call me until you have $100.'"

"What the fuck?! You really left her there?! You

asshole!"

"Yeah, haven't heard from her since. I still got all her clothes and shit in my house."

"Dude, that's fucked up."

"Nah I'm just playin', man. I found a friend of hers she could stay with and I left her there."

"Oh, man! That was a good one." He gave me five and we laughed for a long time.

"Oh! If only to be young again!" said the old man she wouldn't fuck.

XXII. SLEEPING BEAUTY

AFTER ROSIE WAS gone I had a newfound appreciation for my freedom. I went to the bar, Liquor Dick's with Dogoberto and Slim X. It was when on Tuesday nights the drinks were one dollar you call it. There were so many bitches there that night, it was ridiculous, and I was horny as fuck. I got two girls' numbers. The first was this smokin' hot chick having her twenty second birthday. She was tall with a big ass and nice legs, long brown hair down to her ass pinned back, pretty face with fake green eyes, wearing a little white dress. She was acting all stuck up with all the other guys like she was some kind of good girl but I could tell she wanted to get fucked that night. She left a little early, made sure to come say bye to me and give me her number on her way out. Then I got this tall cute black chick's number. Nowhere near as hot as the first chick, but definitely cute and nice.

Slim X was our designated driver and we went home at two in the morning. When I got home the black chick, Tanya, was texting me that she wanted to hang out and spend the night at my house. I got all sprung and wired, jumped in my car all drunk and sped over to some Village Inn. She was there with some guys who were being very rude to her. I walked right up to her and made out with her right in front of them, took her by the hand, opened the car door for her, and took her home. We held hands all the way in the car and had some nice conversation. She was a sweetheart.

I was a little too eager. I practically ripped her clothes off when we got to my room, went way too fast with her and freaked her out, even tried to pry her legs open and then I felt like I was raping her so I stopped. She let me eat her out just a little bit and her pussy tasted like water. Freshest pussy I ever tasted or smelled. She said she just wanted to cuddle and sleep with me. I was ok with that. A hell of a lot better than sleeping with Rosie. This chick had a nice body and she smelled good. She arched her back and started moaning and grinding against me as we lay on our sides. I stuck my dick in her doggystyle with no condom. She was wet and tight as fuck. Really a nice pussy. It caught me by surprise. I pulled out and jizzed on the sheets. She rolled over and gave me a kiss. Then she started doing it again, grinding on me doggystyle. I stuck it in her, started off slow, got used to it and then really started pounding her.

"What the fuck?! I was asleep! You were fucking me in my sleep?" She pushed me off.

"I thought you were awake! You started grinding on me so I stuck it in. I swear to God I didn't know you were asleep. Were you asleep the first time too?" I wasn't lying. I really thought she was awake. To this day I still don't know for sure.

"You fucked me twice in my sleep without a condom? Oh my God. You didn't cum inside me did you?"

"Nah I pulled out, see the jizz right there?"

"Well, I'm on birth control anyway but I don't like having sex without a condom." Or while you're awake? She told me not to fuck her in her sleep again. But sure enough she started grinding on me again and I fucked her really softly so's not to wake her up. She even rolled over and gave me a kiss with her eyes open again. Then I had to go sleep on the couch because it looked like she was going to keep doing that all night and I really didn't know what to think of it.

In the morning my mom saw her sitting on my lap while we smoked cigarettes and she really liked Tanya. She told me I should stay with her. And I tried to but Tanya never came over again after that. We stayed friends and would talk on the phone sometimes but we both ended up crashing our cars and she lived all the way on the Northeast side. Then she got a boyfriend and stopped talking to me, eventually changed her number.

The morning after I had sex with Tanya, I questioned the morality of what I had done. Was I a fucking creep? A little bit. But not really a bad person. It was one of those things you had to laugh at with that dark alcoholic sense of humor. And the first thing I did after I dropped her off was buy some King Cobras. It made me wonder how many times she had fucked guys in her sleep without knowing it, woken up the next day and thought she had only had the platonic sharing of a bed. How many other chicks just want to cuddle and end up getting fucked without even knowing it? I never met another girl who fucks in her sleep again though, no matter how hard I would try.

I also noticed that that smokin' hot chick had been texting me trying to hang out the whole time I was with Tanya. I really wish I would have gone with her instead. In fact, I could have left Tanya sleeping in the bed, gone over to that other chick's house and come back and Tanya wouldn't have even known. I tried to get it to work with her but I guess her birthday was my only window of opportunity and she stopped responding to my text messages pretty soon.

I decided that raw pussy feels way too good to use protection, and I never wore a condom again.

XXIII. GOD DOES THINGS JUST TO TEASE YOU

AT THIS POINT I had gotten the DWI a long time ago and paid a lawyer half of what he wanted, so every time we would go to court, he would delay the trial, waiting for me to pay him the rest of the money. All we were going to do was plead guilty. So although I had the DWI, I still hadn't been convicted yet and was still driving around drunk everywhere, drunk all the time, morning to night almost every day, yet still eating and working out.

I went into the Valero to get some cigarettes and although Paloma was totally skinny and had a flat stomach, I sensed that she was pregnant. I don't know what it was about her but I could tell that she was pregnant without a shred of doubt in my mind. I don't know why this angered me so much. I thought she was my destiny but what had I really done to get her? I had improved a lot but I was a fucking mess, not good enough for her at all. It really freaked me out. I went to my house, gathered all my change, went to a Coinstar, got about ten bucks and drank the cheapest beer they had at The Brew.

An old friend of mine used to always say, "Sometimes God does things just to tease you." I had prayed for a beautiful woman and He sent me the most beautiful one I had ever seen, way out of my league.

After I noticed she was pregnant I didn't see her for a long time or even fantasize about her. Fantasizing about a pregnant chick was weird. I avoided her as best I could. I became a worse alcoholic, drinking more and cheaper shit. I was the worst alcoholic of anyone I knew. Part of it was because I knew I was going to be on probation soon and would be forbidden to drink, so I wanted to get in as much as I could before the deadline.

One morning I was kind of drunk; I went out to get some more beer and I crashed my car into the back of a truck. The truck only had minor damage to its bumper but my little Honda was totaled. I exchanged insurance information with the guy and then took off running because I had warrants and I didn't feel like going back to jail that day. I felt like drinking at my house. Plus it would have been another DWI. Imagine two DWI's when I hadn't even been convicted of the first one. It was advantageous to take off, jump some fences, run through some people's yards, get chased by a German Shepherd, and walk home through the gutters. It gave me a cool adrenaline rush.

I stopped at the Valero. I could almost always sense whether Paloma would be working or not before I got there, and on that day I knew she would be there. Before I went in, I got an unusual vibe from her, sort of an insecurity about her looks that had never been there before. Inside, she was now visibly pregnant, but only slightly. So I had been right. I was so happy to see her. I would always run into her at my shittiest moments. And she looked so cute pregnant. I didn't tell her about how I had just crashed my car or anything; I just smiled at her, bought some beer and left. Just the sight of her had put me in a great mood. Had I not run into her, I might have sat on my couch drinking and mourning the loss of my car all depressed, but instead I was just happy and grateful for another day of freedom and beer. That's the kind of high she would put me on, like nothing really mattered as long as she was there, existing somewhere, with a possibility that I might see her again.

That hit and run didn't come back to me for a long time. And when it did it was just a call from the police station asking me to go pay a fine, since the guy in the truck didn't want to press charges. No jail. No problem. Jail is a shitty place to be.

I forgot to mention the other time I went to jail. One night Cuauhtémoc, an old friend of mine from high school randomly came over to my house and we just sat around with nothing to drink and caught up on old times, which is kind of an unusual thing to do. In the morning we went to McDonald's and got pulled over for no reason. We both had warrants so we went to jail. They questioned me about Cuauhtémoc, asked me if I knew anything about any burglaries or car thefts and I told them I didn't know shit and I really didn't. I guess Cuauhtémoc had been on the run for a while now and maybe that was his reason for coming over to my house out of the blue like that. My warrants were just from unpaid traffic tickets. I got bailed out before I had to go upstairs. Cuauhtémoc ended up going to prison for two years. I still don't know what he did and I don't want to. The less I know about the crimes of my friends, the more impossible it is for them to suspect that I might be a snitch.

I got a court appointed lawyer. This guy was way better than the dumbass I couldn't afford. He got me a much lesser sentencing. They set a date for me to start my fifteen months of probation. It was going to be awhile.

This chick Audrey from high school started talking to me on facebook saying she wanted to hang out. The picture of her was of how she looked in high school, fine and gorgeous, pale skin, long reddish brown hair down to her big ass, beautiful slanted eyes, nice and thick with huge boobs. I had always wanted to fuck her. We met up at a bar and she had become fat. I wouldn't have even recognized her. Still, I had to fuck her. Besides I always liked fat chicks anyway, and she was so sweet, in that way that only a fat girl can be. But when I got to her house, my dick wouldn't get hard. I was too nervous or something. I ate her out, she sucked my dick, but it refused to perform. Then we smoked weed for some reason. I hadn't smoked in years. We fell asleep together. I woke up and found my way out of her house in the middle of the night. I hate not getting it up. What a shame it was.

My sister returned to my house, no longer with Mike. It was me, my mom and my sister again. One thing that makes me crazy sometimes is my sister. I was about to go crazy again and she was only a small factor in it. The wool that had been pulled over my eyes for so long was about to be ripped off like a band aid. I guess the best way to describe it would be a bad reaction to a sensory overload.

XXIV. THE DREAM SHATTERER

IT HAD STARTED one night when I was still crippled in my right arm and like a zombie on too much crazy pills, fresh out of the asylum, when my sister was living down the street with Valdo, some crazy epileptic dikey looking chick with a swastika tattooed on her neck, and an old man. My sister and this chick lived in constant fear of Valdo. She came to my mom's house all beat up one night. She claimed to have just fought the swastika chick. Later on, when Valdo was out of the picture and I was strong and healthy, she told me that he used to beat her up all the time.

More than a year after the night when I saw my sister all beat up I went to a coffee shop and got the numbers of three really hot girls. Then I went to a bar and couldn't stop talking to this fat chick who invited me to a party. This was a party in the street that you had to pay five bucks to get in. I thought I was all badass at Aikido and I wanted to fuck up Valdo if I saw him. Break his arms and shit. He just so happened to be there at this five dollar party. The more I thought about fighting him, the closer he would get;

the more I would chicken out the farther he would recede. There came a point when we were partying right next to each other, each of us hitting on different girls without acknowledging each other. Then I made the fatal mistake of offering him my hand to shake. He ignored me and then disappeared; I didn't see him again at the party after that.

It wasn't until my sister moved back in that it started to bother me so much that I had tried to shake his hand like a punk, when she started talking about him all the time and I became obsessed with revenge. I had this feeling that I knew exactly where he lived; I could just feel it. And later it was confirmed that my hunch was pretty close to his actual location. I started thinking evil thoughts of putting a pipe bomb in his house.

I knew I couldn't beat him hand to hand. I knew he had guns, and if you do beat him hand to hand he'll hunt you with a rifle for a while, like he did to Beto, who was the best fighter in the neighborhood and the only guy I ever knew to stand up to Valdo. Beto tackled him one time and dislocated his shoulder. After that, Valdo was laying in the ditch with the sniper rifle with my sister all night. He stalked Beto for days until finally he came to Valdo crying and begging for his forgiveness.

Because of my mental health record I was unable to buy a gun, also because I was broke, like we always are in the summer for some reason.

I guess I had told my sister that I blamed her for

my suicide attempt, for her betrayal that got me kicked out of the house to fall into the hands of an evil witch. One night I was riding in the bed of my mom's pickup truck, my mom and sister in the front seats. We were going to Burger King. My mom suddenly yelled out the window at me, "You told your sister you blame her for you trying to kill yourself?!"

"Yeah, I kinda do," I said. I totally did, and my mom too. I still hated them both for the way they acted back then. I had told my mom before many times when I was drunk that I would never forgive them. On our way home we stopped at a red light on the corner of Doniphan and Mesa. A guy in a Jeep came at me full speed, as I was sitting in the bed of the truck, and at the last minute swerved and hit the car next to us. I froze. I didn't even think to jump out of the bed. The Jeep would have killed or at least crippled me had he not swerved. I got a life or death adrenaline rush. I begged my mom to buy me some beer.

One day I was being so mean to everyone I knew, that I decided to stop drinking. This was three days without sleep, hearing weird noises and hallucinating, and when I finally fell asleep for a few minutes, I woke up having a seizure. It was scary as hell. My mom took me to the hospital. They put some IVs of nutrients in my arm and gave me a small supply of weak Ativan.

While I was fucked up on Ativan I did a tattoo on myself of the King Cobra logo, the old logo they used to have, like a tribal cobra on my left leg above the knee. This is the last tattoo I have gotten so far. There's a shark on my back smoking a joint, a skull with pot leaves and green smoke coming out of his cracked head done by Valdo himself for $20 on my belly long ago when he had just gotten out of prison, and the shape of Texas with a nautical star on my heart.

The Ativan ran out and I started going insane. I became constantly paranoid, like some Jeep might run me over or Valdo would come shoot me with a gun, having telepathically sensed that I wanted to bomb his house. I avoided anyone I knew, walked the back roads where I wouldn't be seen and was creeping around like a cowardly little mouse. I had accumulated too much bad karma by guilt tripping my family, impoverishing them with my alcoholism, treating girls badly and thinking badly of them, punking out in various ways, and generally being a cold-blooded, spoiled asshole, and I thought death was coming for me. I wanted a chance to change, to be a good person.

I decided never to back down again, from anyone, win, lose, or draw, even if it killed me. This was no way to live and most of my problems in life had been caused by backing down when I should have fought instead.

One night Dogoberto came to my door and asked me if I wanted to go to the bar with him. I said no, I was trying to quit drinking. He left without saying a word, but then texted me, "Dude, you're a bitch." I got angry. I sat on the couch for a long time listening for him to return from the bar, and as soon as I heard his voice in the street I went outside. I walked quickly up to him. "So you like talking shit, motherfucker?" I asked, then I bumrushed him swinging really fast, maybe five punches, and he leaned back and dodged them all like Muhammad Ali. It was sick.

Earlier in the year Dogoberto had gotten his jaw broken from a suckerpunch. He had to walk around with an extremely vulnerable jaw with screws in it. During this time he developed a heightened aware-ness for suckerpunches and bumrushes and practiced dodging any possible attack that could hit his jaw. When he was fully healed, he went out to the bars to test himself. He would walk around talking shit to anyone he felt like all night and stand in the middle of everyone until someone would finally get mad and try to bumrush or suckerpunch him. He was able to dodge every attempt made on him, usually without even spilling his beer. He wouldn't even fight his assailants back, just leave them with a feeling of shame and embarrassment at not being able to hit him. So it was no surprise to me, and in fact, I had expected that none of my punches would connect.

He got low and grabbed my leg to try to pick me up, just like I knew he would; my Aikido training kicked in and I knew how to think fast in an off balance position and fight while someone was trying to throw me. I clapped him on his ear with my right hand, stunning him and interrupting his throw. He lost his grip on my leg and my left index finger was in his mouth for some reason. I had been thinking about fish hooking a lot and how to rip a guy's mouth is probably why that happened so naturally, but instead of doing that to Dogoberto, I just got grossed out and pulled my finger out. Then we talked it out in the street.

He said he was worried about me, I just stayed in my house all day and didn't talk to anyone, and all he wanted to do was go to the bar with me and have a good time like we used to. I told him that maybe sometimes I just need a little time to myself and some privacy and if I don't feel like going to the bar with him, that's no reason to call me a bitch. And if he felt like calling me a bitch, he should say it to my face, not by a text message. He said that he was just joking, that we call each other bitches and faggots and all kinds of stupid shit all the time and we don't mean it. I said I knew all about that but it sounded to me like he meant it that time and I happened to take it personally. He said that if I had a problem with him I should have called him out like a man and not bumrushed him like someone I didn't even respect. Did he even take a swing at me? No, but he tried to throw me, and who knows what that could have led to? I told him if I ever had a problem with him, I'd come and call him out on it next time. He said there wasn't gonna be a next time. He was never gonna knock on my door again or call me, and he didn't want me to call him or knock on his door either. He said he felt like crying (and I did too) and he hated to have to do this but he verbally and physically turned his back on me and said he wasn't my homie anymore.

When I came back into my house, my dog, who had heard everything, jumped on me and licked my face like crazy. My sister, who had witnessed my fight with Silent, and had been sitting in her friend's car watching me while I fought Dogoberto (who was always able to easily beat Silent), remarked that I had gotten a lot faster.

After the seizure I hadn't been able to think about sex properly. Somehow it was intertwined with blood and guts and I was afraid that blood and guts might turn me on if I allowed it to and maybe I actually had the sexuality of some kind of serial killer. My thoughts were so mixed up and out of control that I could not be aroused by anything. When I tried to take refuge by thinking about Paloma from the convenience store I couldn't help but think of her with unintended hatred and imagine punching her in her pregnant belly. I hated this reflexive thought and I wished it would stop. I felt like thinking badly of her and her unborn child was something God would punish me for and that it was coming soon and it was going to hurt. It made me wish I was dead to think of someone I loved in such a terrible way.

Sometimes it would feel like a bolt of lightning would strike my brain, almost like a one second seizure, and "NO PRIDE!" would flash in my mind in shining 3-D letters made of chrome. I had so many fucked up images in my head all the time that I would keep making myself throw up for days and nights to try to make them go away, to display my disgust for what I saw, and what I believed everyone else could see too.

I also realized also that all my life, I had never really learned to give or receive affection from anyone, although it was what I desired more than anything in the world. There was always something disconnected and pragmatic in my relationships with everyone. I had been trying so hard to appear to be a normal person, to hide my emotional trauma from my suicide attempt, that I had created a cruel and cold façade to cover it and bury it so deep that nothing could reach it and heal it.

I had heard that oleander was one of the strongest poisons known to man. The plant is extremely common in El Paso and I had been tempted by it many times. I decided to walk along the canal eating oleander, make my way to the desert and keep walking until I was dead. I dropped my phone so that I would have no way of calling 911 on myself. Should have just left it at home; that was wasteful. I walked around eating the flowers and leaves, all the different colors of it. It would give me a really powerful headchange every time I swallowed the juice as I chewed it, similar to that chill you get down your spine when you take that first shot of liquor but a completely different poison. I walked along the canal parallel to Doniphan, the distance from Montoya to Country club. I had flowers and leaves all in my pockets. I wasn't sure if I was dying but I was definitely getting fucked up. It was a weird mixed up high. Not sure if it really felt good or bad. Made me throw up several times. I wandered into a desert, found a spot far away from everything and continued to eat and throw up until I was dry heaving and turning red in the face. This seemed like a peaceful place to die.

I could hear children playing in the distance, getting closer, and I didn't want them to stumble upon me and what I was doing, so I left, started walking along the Rio Grande back home. I was so thirsty I wanted to drink the nasty water from the river, but I couldn't get close enough to it without falling in. When I got home I wasn't dead at all, just dehydrated. The poison found in oleander is one of the deadliest known to man, but it has to be extracted and concentrated in order to be lethal. I was embarrassed.

Once again I was happy that I hadn't died and still had another chance. But I still felt so crazy that I took some of my old Risperdal and Lexapro. I thought maybe it would help but it only made me more insane, although it did put me to sleep for a little while.

When I woke up I looked in the bathroom mirror and my reflection horrified me so much that I went into my room, wrote a suicide note and gathered a bunch of shoelaces, ropes, and cords. I tied them around my neck, each one tighter than the last, with so many knots that there was no way I'd possibly be able to undo them. My eyes bulged out of my head; I couldn't see; blood was running out my nose; I was breathing through a tight little airhole in my throat. I kept waiting and waiting to die. I focused my out of control thoughts with all my will on only one pure thing, my happiest, most untainted memory, the time when I gave a bunch of roses to Paloma.

Sometimes all my senses would shut down and I'd feel a complete emptiness and blankness in my mind with no awareness of my body. These brief little explosions of nonexistence are the closest I have ever been to death, but they were few and far between. I had to hold my breath and force all my blood pressure into my brain to achieve them, which was counterintuitive while being choked, and I'd always end up gasping for air. I wasn't sure if I was killing myself, but I was definitely torturing myself. It was an unexpectedly slow and painful death that I was chasing.

After what seemed like about two hours, I decided that it was taking too long and the pain was too much. I didn't have the will to die by this method. I crawled out of my room blind and bloody for all to see, making a weird raspy hissing noise. My sister screamed, got the scissors, and with my mother's help cut me free. My sister stayed there hugging me and crying for a long time. It was the best hug I had ever had. If I had been alone in the house, I'm not sure if I would have been able to find something to cut myself free, and I wouldn't have been able to speak on the phone to call 911, and I might not have been able to find the keys to unlock the deadbolt on the front door. The ambulance arrived in just a few minutes.

XXV. WELCOME HOME

MY EYES WERE too bulged for me to open without pain, but strangely, I could see everyone around me. Not what they physically looked like, but who they were. A Policeman led me to a hospital bed. I sat in the bed with my eyes closed and sensed a nice older woman on the other side of the room in front of me and that she was a nurse. I said "Hi, are you a nurse?" She told me that her profession was a nurse, but she was a patient. She had called 911 on herself saying that she wanted to crash her car and commit suicide. I told her I had just tried to commit suicide too and explained why I couldn't open my eyes. She and I were about to go to El Paso Psychiatric Center together.

As soon as my eyes could open and the blood had been wiped off my face, I found that the cop had stolen my shoes. Why not just take the laces? I thought he had left them by my bed. I would never get them back and they were some good Nikes.

My roommate in EPPC was a middle aged white guy with grey hair named Hobbes who was bipolar. I would see him lose his temper sometimes with other people, but he and I never once had an argument. He was a real nice guy and the old woman I met at the hospital fell in love with him but he didn't really like her back.

I was afraid to leave my room at first, over-whelmed by all the people, and only went out when I had to. I stayed in there with all these colors floating around in my head, trying to put them in order and understand what they meant. It seemed to me that there was something sinister hiding in every color, something mixed up and confused, violence and rape all running through my mind. Also I had a feeling of gravity or magnetism pulling at my surroundings, desperately searching for someone to connect to.

I didn't sleep for five days. I refused to take any medication, since I figured medication was the thing that had driven me over the edge. I gradually started going outside more and talking to people. There were no pretty mental patients on the first floor, but there were a lot of pretty girls who worked there called "techs" and some beautiful nurses as well. It wasn't like this at all the last time I was in there. It was like a little vacation from my isolation with hot chicks all around to ease the pain. The most beautiful of them all was a tech named Sophia and she said she recognized me from before. I was surprised that I had no memory of such a gorgeous girl. She was also the nicest to talk to and the least stuck up, very empa-thetic. The other girls, you could try so hard with them but no matter what you did, they still regarded you as subhuman in the end. Maybe Sophia just hid her disgust better than the rest of them.

One beautiful tech, short with a perfect ass and tits, long black hair, would stand around me and get this sexy pouty expression on her face whenever she was near, and just stand there. It would make my dick hard. I would ask her what was wrong but she never wanted to talk to me. Just stand near me and look all pouty and sexy.

Another one, very thin and petit, beautiful like a Siamese cat, would go crazy around me. She would be drawn to me, then pushed away as if by an invisible force as my thoughts raced in confusion, and it would make her scream. She eventually got used to it and mostly avoided me.

The first time I sat down to eat at the table where the guys sat, I introduced myself and shook hands with everyone except one guy who I found to be repulsive. If there was one thing I had learned from all this, it's that there are some people whose hand you should never shake. He was one of those schizophrenic guys who talk mumbo jumbo all the time to themselves and he was begging everyone for leftover food from their trays. As soon as I saw him begging for scraps like a cockroach, I knew there was something wrong and couldn't bring myself to touch his hand to shake it. There was something disgusting and obscene about him. He didn't respect people's space. He smelled like shit and looked like he never bathed. I had no problem with anybody else.

It was important to me that I didn't accept any- thing offered to me by a mental patient or give anything, even something I didn't need, like a packet of salt. Better to throw it away than give it to someone.

By not shaking his hand I had inadvertently bound him to me. From then on he would follow me around and try to fuck up everything I would do. He would walk around muttering obscenities and threats at me, challenge me to fight, cock block me any time he saw me with a girl. He would walk by my door talking shit a lot.

I was not afraid of him. I knew I could easily whoop his ass. But I didn't want to fight him. He was schizophrenic to the point of being almost retarded and he was a little guy. He was chump change. I had just fought Dogoberto, a bad and dangerous dude. True, it was only a harmless scuffle with no damage done. He had plenty of chances to damage me but he didn't hit back. I only clapped him on the ear to disrupt his throw, but I could have torn the inside of his mouth by fishhooking it, gripping it tightly and ripping it with one quick, powerful motion, then controlled his head with that grip and hit him on the neck and throat, but because he wasn't fighting back, I couldn't do something so gruesome to him. It was a fight of principle. It was about respect. The fact is, although we were best friends, he had always kept an upper hand over me, subtly punking me every now and then based on an assumption that I was afraid of him. All I had meant to do with that scuffle was show that I wasn't.

The name of the parasitic little character whose hand I never shook, who reminded me of one of those little vampire fish that attach themselves to sharks, sucking their blood with no way for the sharks to get rid of them, was Juan, and I tried my best to avoid him. This made him mistakenly believe that I was afraid of him and only made him follow me more and disrupt my activities as best he could.

I pretty much stayed in my room most of the time except to get food, fucking around with those colors in my head, the electromagnetic brain waves that communicate between people. Sometimes I would think I had it just right and I'd leave my room to try to find a chick to talk to. But it wouldn't take long for something to go wrong again and I'd have to go back to my room and sort it out.

I had to figure out ways to regain my pride. I started hanging out in the lobbies more and getting to know people, becoming comfortable with them, purposely going anywhere that made me nervous. There were good people on the first floor. Regular people who were just going through some tough times all in their own ways, and we all improved slowly and helped each other out. I eventually got to where I was cool with everyone except Juan. After five days I finally was able to sleep. Not that much, but it got a little better every night.

My favorite part of each day was the indoor recreation in the evening because there was a pool table. The last time I was in there I wasn't able to play because my right arm was in a cast, but pool is one of my favorite things in the world. It usually came down to me and this one big guy who was in there because he was doing too much drugs, eventually had a bad crash and failed to hang himself. His wife would often come in to argue with him. We were always in friendly competition for the number one spot at the pool table. He had more of a soft touch style of play, and I was more into hard spinning shots. Somebody in there told me that I play "English" because of the tight backspin I tend to put on the cue ball.

On the day I finally went outside for recreation I saw that the yard had been improved. The ground which used to be dirt had been replaced with plastic green grass, which was always clean and much easier on the eyes. You could lie on the plastic grass if you wanted to, although I never did. The last time I was there during an unusually cold and icy winter, but now it was a beautiful hot summer. It was a lot nicer being in there with two working arms. I noticed how easy it would be to escape over the corner of the fence. No barbed wire for lunatics to throw themselves against. All you would need is a friend with a getaway car. I saw an old woman named Annabel who I recognized from the last time I was in there. I sat down at a table and talked to her. She was still the same, on the highest dose of the most powerful antipsychotic known to man, Clozapine. They would

give her an injection every month, which is pretty
much the point where you're screwed because there's
no way to quit. She had been in and out a few times
while I had been free.

I noticed a beautiful six foot tall girl standing by
the basketball court, nice long legs, wide hips and a
big gorgeous ass. Incredible ass. A pretty face kind of
like a Mexican Nathalie Portman. She wore no
makeup and had perfect teeth. She looked clean and
fresh, a natural beauty. She had light brown hair in a
long thick braid. I stared at her for a while until she
gave me a dirty look. She was the most beautiful girl I
had ever seen in a mental institution, a gorgeous girl,
even by the standards of the outside world. She was
standing next to a thin guy with a ponytail, a little
shorter than her. I sized them up. The guy didn't seem
like her boyfriend. There was nothing exciting going
on between them. I figured he must be either
medicated to the point of impotence or some kind of
eunuch to not be hitting on this hot girl standing next
to him. I didn't get the impression that he was gay
though, more like a weird guy with no game. I didn't
fall instantly in love with the girl or anything, but
filed her away for future reference and hoped that
she'd still be on the third floor by the time I got there.

It was the same psychiatrist I had last time, Ms.
Lara, a hot middle aged woman in a white lab coat, a
pale Mexican with long, jet black hair, big brown
eyes, and that icy personality, who was always trying
to seduce me into taking Abilify. I wondered what she

would be like if you could get her drunk. I wasn't about to let them medicate me and leave me impotent with all these hot chicks around and ruin my vacation. And my condition was definitely improving. It was the soberest time of my life since I had started getting high when I was fifteen. My only vice was a weak nicotine patch they would replace every morning.

At first I thought I was the only one who was harassed by Juan. I never complained about him to anyone. It was my own little problem I had to figure out, but I started hearing a lot of other people complaining. There was a young guy with a bad leg who used one of those walkers with tennis balls on the bottom like old people, and he was getting to be good friends with a nice female mental patient. One day he was talking to her and Juan came out of nowhere, backed the girl into a corner and did a weird humping, grinding type dance on her. Some big guy techs came and pulled him off. That was why lately whenever Juan would pass by my room talking shit, he would be accompanied by a big tech, who would usually give me a look like "Why haven't you fucked this guy up yet?" Or, looking back, maybe it was "Why don't you tell this guy something?" It never once crossed my mind to settle it with words.

There was a cool old white man on the floor, a hippy stoner type dude who mostly just talked about drugs all the time and I heard Juan punched him in the face. I never really heard why or how exactly it went down but Juan was never really reprimanded except by being given more of the same incompetent guards to follow him around and not really regulate any of his bad behavior. The old man was moved to the third floor.

There were also a few other girls who had complained of being cornered by Juan's obscene dance.

At this point most people either despised this dude and wanted to kick his ass but didn't have the balls to do it or just didn't really give a shit. Since I first met Juan, I had constantly been thinking of the best ways I could inflict the most damage on him before the techs intervened. It would have to be a sucker move and it would have to be done at just the right moment. I had used to think of waiting by my door casually and pulling him into my room by the neck in an Aikido style choke when he comes by to talk shit, barricading the door with my body in case anybody noticed, and putting him to sleep, followed by a stomping. It could have been done silently and without detection by the techs before he had them following him around, but now that would never work. It would have to be a suckerpunch, and a one hitter quitter.

I never found my real motivation until one day I saw him being disrespectful of Sophia's space. He was standing way too close to her while she was his guard, touching her, hugging her, and making her visibly uncomfortable but she didn't really know how to tell him to stop. I had had it with this fool. I had a mad crush on Sophia and I decided I was going to stay up all night until I had knocked him out. I told no one of my plans. I just put him in the simplest trap he had made for himself.

For no reason other than to disrespect me, if I was ever watching TV, Juan would walk back and forth from his room to the balcony, in front of the TV every time. This was something nobody else ever did to anybody else. You see people watching TV, you walk behind the couch, just good manners. He did this specifically to me. At first it annoyed me, but it didn't take long for me to realize that this repetitive habit of his was his greatest vulnerability. So I actually enjoyed it every time he walked in front of the TV, my eyes pointed at the TV but focusing on Juan peripherally, thinking about how to fuck him up while he was walking around back in forth in front of me like clockwork. That joy that I felt was like a cloaking device; it made it look like I was just enjoying watching TV with no violent intentions, not even bothered by this guy at all. Over time this had caused a false sense of security among his guards.

On the night when I decided to make my move, everyone was in their rooms sleeping except me, Juan, and his big guard. I sat in a relaxed position, my adrenaline increasing every time he passed by. I hoped that this big guard was not perceptive enough to detect this rise in adrenaline or notice anything unusual going on. If he came from his room, he'd get hit with my left hook, which was pretty good but might not knock him out, so it would have to be a combination of punches. If he came from the balcony he'd get hit with my overhand right, my most dangerous punch that I had plenty of faith in.

The guards switched. The big guy was replaced by a small woman. I would have to be careful not to harm the woman, but other than that, this was great because I didn't have to worry about a big guy intercepting me if he was fast enough and knew what he was doing. They walked to the balcony, the woman following closely behind him. Then they walked back from the balcony and the lady walked behind the couch while he was about to walk in front of me. It was automatic. In a split second I went from sitting down, to quickly rising and throwing the fastest, hardest, most adrenaline filled overhand right I'd ever thrown. I hit him perfect on the jaw in the little cleft between the lower lip and the chin, slightly on the left hand side of it and felt it give. I knocked him off his feet and he landed on his back, his glasses flying off to his right. I started to pursue him for the stomping, but the lady screamed, jumped over the couch, got behind me and wrapped her arms around me. That was confusing. I didn't want to do any harm to the woman, even the slight pain that may have been caused by escaping from her weak grip on me.

Juan woke up and shook his head, quickly got to his feet, and rushed at me with his head down. The lady saw him coming and let go, ran off screaming. His head painlessly hit me in the stomach and I allowed myself to be pushed back onto the side of a couch. I leaned back and wrapped my legs around his torso. He threw a slow, weak, girl's punch that hit me on the ear, not even with his knuckles and I trapped his right arm there with my left and grabbed his wrist. I started banging on his temple with right hooks so fast that his left hand couldn't get through. A bunch of big dudes came and pulled us apart. I released him from my legs, but tried to take a cruel grip on his ear with my left hand. He was so unwashed and greasy that my fingers slipped right off.

The night I beat Juan, I had a dream that I was standing with my paternal grandfather. We were listening to a preacher who thumped his bible as he spoke, but the things he was saying were evil and untrue. I looked at my grandpa and said "Is this guy full of shit or what?" He nodded and narrowed his eyes at the preacher. Slowly, we watched little black horns grow out of the preacher's head and his skin turn red. I walked around him and gave him a nasty blindside punch, knocking him to the ground on his belly. I fell down with all my weight behind my fist, slamming it into the back of his head, and continued hitting him, faster and faster, trying to beat him to death. I woke up in the middle of the night swinging wildly, tangled in my bed sheets.

The next day I had to go explain myself to Ms. Lara and some other people. I told them "This guy has been harassing me since I first got here, walking by my room talking shit to me, challenging me to fight him. I was never scared of him, and I didn't want to fight him so I tried my best to avoid him. Because I avoided him, he thought I was afraid of him and followed me around even more, talking even more shit and muttering threats to me. Not only that but he goes around sexually harassing women and he even hit an old man and you don't do anything about it. Had this been the street or a bar or anywhere but here, where he's followed around by guards all the time, I would have beat his ass the first time he challenged me. I tried to avoid it as best I could, but he wouldn't stop bugging me so finally I checked him. I don't think there's anything crazy about that at all. That's normal human behavior."

What it came down to was, if he pressed charges I would have to go to court, but he didn't want to so there were no repercussions. I think they wanted me to check him, because maybe they didn't even really have the power to. The worst thing they could have done to him was put him in the all male unit, Adult 2 where he would wind up being some guy's bitch right away, the way he acts. And he didn't deserve that. He didn't have the mental faculties to defend himself at all from whatever goes on in there. It would not be a healing experience for him and they're supposed to be trying to heal people.

Turns out all this guy needed was a little ass whooping to straighten him out. After that night he behaved, stopped harassing people, avoided me, or at least gave me my space, because he could see I was always keeping a tab on him. If he ever walked into the room he was always in my peripheral vision, just in case he had any plans to suckerpunch me back for revenge. And I never said anything to him or harassed him in any way. I just let him do his thing, which was often talking to an imaginary girlfriend on his mp3 player as if it was a phone.

The thing about that punch was, I threw it so hard and fast that every muscle in my arm was sore for a week afterwards, and when the soreness died down, I felt a permanent lightness of my right arm, like it would always be faster, stronger and more likely to throw an overhand right for the rest of my life. The way I wrapped my legs around him, trapped his arm and hit him in the head was some poor man's Brazilian Jiu Jitsu that I must have picked up from watching countless episodes of UFC where guys won from the bottom while mounted. Ever since I got scrapped by Silent I struggled to learn every way that I could to fight from the bottom, which to me was the scariest position to be in.

In the morning everyone had heard about what I had done and they all respected me for it, or at least thought it was funny. I felt like a new man. I now had another shred of pride to cling to. I felt a mixture of pride and shame for my scuffle with Dogoberto, because although I had stood up to him, I had bumrushed him instead of calling him out in a more manly way. I felt no shame in suckerpunching Juan though, because it was the only way I could get him with his guards following around all the time.

XXVI. LET'S WAIT AWHILE

AFTER ABOUT TWO weeks of being in there Ms. Lara told me that if I didn't take her low dose of Abilify, she would make a phone call and a bunch of big guys would come into her office, hold me down and inject me with something strong that would last a month. I decided that it was in my best interest to humor her. They started giving me a pill every night that I would hide in my cheek and spit out in the toilet, then rinse my mouth of any residue. When I was called to her office and she asked me how I liked my new medicine, I said it was nice, kind of like I was on a really low dose of heroin all the time.

They moved me and the big pool player to the third floor. Up there was a beautiful tech named Maritza. She was thin and petit, a light skinned Mexican with natural red hair and green eyes. First thing I did after I saw her was go masturbate in the bathroom. The rooms on the third floor were filled almost entirely with females. The only men were me, the big pool player, a huge Mexican guy who was my new roommate, and Rob, the thin guy with the ponytail who was always hanging around the tall chick. Maritza said that Rob would be happy to have some guys to hang out with since he only had girls to play cards and pool against, and they were all too easy to beat.

The tall girl was named Reina, and I decided to detach her from Rob. Although he didn't seem like a bad guy, I didn't like the way he constantly made fun of her or his attitude of trying to stay in there as long as he could. He had been in there for months, telling them how crazy he was and not even trying to get out. He had definitely done something serious though, because the scar on his neck was twice as long as mine and still swollen and pink. He seemed to have a weak but negative influence over Reina.

During my time in the mental institution I had taken up my old hobby of drawing. Since my hand had been damaged by my first suicide attempt, I had given it up, believing that I wouldn't be any good, but after a little practice I found that I was even better than before. I had made a detailed, depressing looking drawing of my unmade bed one morning, several 3D looking pictures of the empty chairs in the lobby at night, each one better than the last, a drawing of the face of Jesus Christ I had copied from a Jehovah's Witness pamphlet, and a crucifix from a National Geographic Magazine. It was from a photo of a little South American kid in the jungle carrying a little homemade cross of cylindrical twigs tied together with a hand carved and painted Jesus. These last two religious drawings I had made after my dream of beating on the devil. I showed my drawings to the people at the table and said that I was having a hard time figuring out what I should draw next. Reina suggested that I draw the water fountain, and I did, quickly and accurately.

We went to play pool and I was determined to win, since the final victor's reward was to get to play with Reina and be in a little room all alone with her and Maritza for a while. First I beat the big guy mercilessly. I suspect that he may have subtly let me win. Rob came next and did everything he could to disrupt my play, made loud noises and whistled every time it was my turn to shoot, but because he had been playing only with women for so long, he totally sucked and I beat him easily.

When it came my turn to play against Reina, I told her that I would only take the most difficult shots available to me so I'd get some good practice and she'd have a chance at beating me. This was also a strategy to make the game and my time spent alone with her last as long as possible. I also made sure to let her win. I offered the big guy his turn against her since I lost, but he seemed amused by what was going on between Reina and me and let me go another round with her. Once again I made it last as long as possible and let her win. Then it was time to go back upstairs.

Before bedtime they give you hot chocolate and a little snack, as well as some medication. Everybody sits at the tables and a tech comes individually to each person and punches holes in the card you get every morning. If you bathed, a hole is punched for hygiene. A hole is punched for every group meeting you attended that day, things like that. Those points add up as you save your cards, which can be redeemed for sodas or worthless items from the little store in the rec room.

As Maritza punched my card I noticed that Reina couldn't stand for me to look at another girl and was fidgeting nervously.

The next day I woke up and got my breakfast, then went back to bed to sleep a little more and missed the group meetings, as was my usual habit, since it has always been easier for me to sleep in the morning than at night. At lunch time, Reina sat next to me and offered me the things she didn't want to eat, her chicken soup and crackers. I asked her if she was sure she didn't want them and she said that if I didn't eat them she would throw them away. Instinctively I knew that it was alright to accept food from this beautiful girl but no one else. We stayed on the balcony talking after everyone else had left.

She was twenty one and I was twenty three. She had ended up in here because she had lost her job as the manager of Pollo Town at the Sunland Park Mall and become depressed, then her fiancé who she had been living with dumped her and completely disappeared, changed his number, and transferred to a job somewhere else. She moved back in with her parents, who were always arguing, in the process of getting divorced, and giving her a hard time. She attempted suicide by swallowing many bottles of pills. She had been in here before and was released, but had to be readmitted because she wasn't doing well. She asked me why I was in here and I said that it was hard to explain. I had become isolated, started hallucinating a lot, and one night I tied a bunch of cords around my neck to try to choke myself to death.

"So, loneliness?" she asked me.

"Yeah, I guess that's pretty much why. Since I've been here around people I feel much better every day."

My roving gravitational pull had found what it was looking for, a girl to firmly attach itself to and for the next couple of weeks she and I were inseparable and constantly magnetized to each other. She would wake me up every morning for breakfast; I would follow her to the balcony and watch that beautiful ass switching back and forth in front of me, eat breakfast with her, giving her all my sugar packets, since I never put sugar in my coffee (which is decaffeinated in there), and then go with her to every group meeting. I had always found these group meetings to be tedious and useless before, but now they were a nice excuse to spend time with Reina.

I did learn something important from one meeting though. They should have told me this a long time ago. In fact, they should teach you this in high school and advertise it on TV. If you ever feel suicidal, you can call 911. Merely feeling suicidal is not enough for them to come and take you to the asylum; you have to tell them what instrument of suicide you have in your possession in order for them to take you in. This instrument can be anything, a rope to hang yourself, a razor blade, a car to crash. You can even say that you're out standing next to the highway to jump in front of a moving car to make them come get you. So before you ever harm yourself, you should always call the cops and give yourself a chance to get help.

Reina and I liked to play basketball. She was much better than me; I have always sucked at the game, but I had a goofy way of having fun and flirting with her as we played. One day the biggest mental patient in the whole looney bin from Adult 2 came onto the court, shoulder checked her, and made a two point shot. I recognized him from the last time I had been in there. His name was Martinez and he was so heavy that when he tried to hang himself he broke his house. I also recognized that although he was big and strong, there was something of a bitch and a coward in him, and he had only pushed Reina counting on an assumption that I would be afraid of him and back down.

My hands went numb and icy, like I could infinitely beat Martinez with them and feel no pain in my knuckles no matter how hard I hit. My right arm felt light as a feather and was hanging low behind me, cocked back where he couldn't see it. I stepped to him at an advantageous angle with my left foot forward, prepared to make quick, evasive movements to get behind him and choke him out before he could get a chance to put his weight on me. I glared into his eyes, simultaneously watching his whole body peripherally. He looked down like Starvin Martín had before. The fingers of my right hand straightened and spread out into four spines that might have gouged at his downcast eyes, but he whined in an effeminate voice like he was about to cry, "Why you wanna step to me like that?"

"You pushed a female. That's not cool. Apologize to her."

"I'm sorry," he said to her, "It won't happen again."

Reina and I walked away and left the court to him. We sat at a table with an old woman who taught arts and crafts there and worked on a puzzle with her. One of the craziest old ladies in the whole place passed by us and said "Ya casi. Ya casi." I asked Reina what it meant and she said that the lady was telling us to get married. (That was a lie, or maybe she heard it wrong. "Ya casi" means "almost"; "casar" means "to marry", but "casi" is not a conjugation of "casar")

There was an old man who spoke incoherent nonsense and wore sunglasses all the time. I had played pool with him before and he was pretty good but a sore loser. Reina had told me that he had once whipped out his dick to her and gotten in trouble for it and she was afraid of him. He came to the table where we were sitting side by side, sat down in front of me and started staring at her. She gave me a look that expressed her discomfort and I told the old man calmly, "I can tell that you're making this girl uncomfortable by the way you stare at her and it's making me uncomfortable too. Would you mind sitting somewhere else?" He looked surprised, got up, and never bothered her again.

I felt so close to her that day. The mutual gravity between us was so strong and intense, sitting next to each other so calmly but with a desire to bang and slap against each other as hard as we could. That night I kissed Reina on the patio for a long time before a lookout detected someone coming who could have caught us.

I had started drawing her, not so well at first, but one night, as she sat in a chair crocheting in a short little nightgown, I made an excellent drawing of her whole figure. It was not completely accurate in the way she looked, although it captured her beauty, and the expression on the face of the drawing, which didn't seem to make sense at the time, accurately expressed her bossiness and dissatisfaction that I would later get to know. She liked the drawing. It was sexy.

"What's that in my hands? A bacon?" she asked.

"No, it's that shit you were crocheting." It wasn't perfect.

Reina's family came to visit her often, different relatives every day. First came her older sister, who was my age and very beautiful. She was the same height as Reina, with the same big ass and long brown hair, big breasts, darker skin and a different face that I would later find out resembled her father and younger brother. I thought to myself that although Reina had smaller breasts, I had still gotten the prettier of the two. The visit with her sister had a positive effect on her.

The mother came next. She was short, chunky, dressed in loud, shiny clothes and with something angry and stuck up in her demeanor that I didn't like. A petty woman who believed her trashiness to be some sort of class. She spent about 20 minutes or so with Reina and then stormed out angrily. Reina came out of the room crying and shaking. I tried my best to console her. The staff of the mental institution had already caught on to our developing relationship and forbade us from hugging or any type of physical affection. They had told me that I was to stay at least fifteen feet away from her at all times, and I always followed her at exactly fifteen feet. We were allowed to sit at a table together but only facing each other, never next to each other. That night, they made an exception and allowed me to walk beside her. I told her I loved her that night; she needed to hear it. She said she loved me too; I gave her a hug and she kissed my neck. Then we were separated again.

I sincerely and desperately did love Reina and depended on her more than anything. Had we not crossed paths exactly when we did, I don't know what would have become of me.

Reina's grandmother was a tiny old woman who

seemed pleasant and to love her very much. She told Reina that she looked like a boy and gave her some makeup and nice clothes. She began to look even hotter after that with pink lipstick and some skin tight white jeans.

Reina's father was a slim giant, standing at 6'8". The combination of him and Reina's short mother averaged out to create two gorgeous six foot tall daughters. The father carried himself with a humble dignity that I admired. I got the impression that he was a good man and respected him. Also, I feared his judgment, for his would be the least petty, the most objective and severe, able to detect any true weakness or strength in my character. His opinion mattered to me and I wanted to earn his respect. The mother's opinion I didn't really care about because she did not strike me as a good judge of character. She would always hate me for being a mental patient no matter what I did, while pretending to be nice to me. Reina's father came in with her little brother who must have been about nine years old. Their visit with Reina also was a positive one and I figured that her mother was probably the only abusive force in her family.

Reina and I would find any way to touch each other, occasionally getting to hold hands secretly in a dark room while watching a movie under the supervision of someone who had not yet been informed about us, or sneaking a kiss in the hall when the security was lax. We were always writing notes to each other and passing them across the table. A guy came once as we were writing these notes at night and told us he had nothing against our romance in there, in fact he even gave us his blessing, but it was against the rules, and we had to be careful, especially with those notes, and never allow them to be discovered. He said that it would be wise to destroy them every night, and then he told us to go to bed. If they didn't put us to bed like that every night we would have probably stayed up all night talking and passing notes and playing cards across the table.

We would write about love and sex and anything that was on our minds that we couldn't say out loud. I kept all of the notes hidden but never destroyed any of them. One main feature of our conversations was that we wanted to get out of there and fuck, whereas when she had been hanging around Rob all the time, he had been convincing her to stay in there with him. We had even contemplated elaborate schemes of how to escape together, but only hypothetically, because I explained to her how to get out of there.

One night I had this dream. I was in a ghetto apartment complex at the top of a staircase. At the bottom was a young, gorgeous Janet Jackson dressed in '80s clothing. She was my girlfriend and a virgin, looking up at me, singing a beautiful song, "Let's Wait Awhile". The dream was so vivid. When I woke up it dawned on me how great it was to have all this time to spend getting to know a girl and strengthen our bond, and how much more intimate and intense it would be when we finally got to have sex. I had never had such a chance in my life, mostly just a bunch of one night stands and brief relationships that quickly ended at the first sign of turbulence.

It sounds nice, but it was far from perfect and filled with all kinds of insecurities and jealousy. For one thing, I couldn't so much as glance at a woman, even an old unattractive woman or a professional woman who was giving me my medicine without provoking jealous insecurity from Reina, which could manifest itself either as depression and hurt feelings or vindictive wrath. I pretty much had to not even look any female in the eyes at all in order to appease her.

There was this scary fat goth chick who really wanted my nuts. One time, while Reina was being visited by a family member, I played pool with her. She asked me if I wanted to fuck and I said nah, I'm good. Reina came down, saw me playing pool with her and became enraged with me.

That night I snuck into her room and tried to give her a kiss, but she wouldn't let me, and I got caught and sent back to my bed. Later on two big guys came in and said that I should never do that again, that I was lucky that the girl didn't press charges against me or get mad, and that I was forbidden to speak to her or go near her. Just stay as far away from her as possible from now on.

After that she attached herself to a new guy, some sleazy little cholo dude with the fingernail of his pinky overgrown to show everyone that he was a cokehead. She followed him around for about five days until he left. Was it just to torture me? Or was it because she always had to have a guy by her side? She had told me that before me there was a guy who she had been getting close to and they sent him to Adult 2. I got depressed and rarely left my room because I couldn't stand to see her with another man. We still saw each other at meals and did our usual exchanges of food when we could get away with it but barely spoke. This guy was allowed to sit next to her and do as he pleased but I was forbidden to go near her or even acknowledge her except by avoiding her. The authorities of the mental institution were getting on our case so bad that they were threatening to send me to Adult 2 any time I even looked at her.

I remembered telling her once that an old friend of mine had told me that love is when you let someone eat all your fries and you don't mind that you get none for yourself. On Fridays for lunch we would get burgers and fries. I walked up to her, dropped my fries on her plate, smiled at her, and walked away. She blushed and smiled back at me.

XXVII. NUMB

DURING MY TIME away from her, I tried to hang out with the other people, but I had to avoid women if I wanted any chance with this chick. And it wasn't a big deal. The only hot chicks besides her were employees anyway. I tried to learn how to slam dunk during recreation time. I got a little closer every day, and a couple of times I even made it. I read some books. I mostly just kept to myself and bided my time. Most other mental patients had formed their own symbiotic relationships with each other and divided into little cliques and I wanted no part in that. Soon enough they told us when we were leaving. I had two weeks left and she had one.

We slowly tested the boundaries and started getting closer to each other. They allowed us to hang out again with the fifteen foot rule loosely enforced. They didn't really care so much anymore. They just wanted us gone. Any threats of sending me to Adult 2 were empty and they knew it. A few times we even made out right in front of everybody when the techs had their backs turned for a second, and when it came Reina's time to leave she gave me a long, slow goodbye kiss with a lot of tongue right in front of their faces and there was nothing they could do about it.

She came to visit me the same day right after she left, shaking and scared, saying she couldn't make it out there without me. She asked me if I'd go out with her and be her boyfriend. Of course I said yes. I had asked her out a million times and she had never been sure yet. I only had a week to wait before I could be with her. She would come and visit me every day and bring me melted Snickers bars hidden in her bra. It's not really one of my favorite candy bars normally, but that was the candy bar I craved the most in there, I guess because there's something filling about a Snickers. We would hold hands across the table and talk for half an hour every day about what we were going to do when I got out. Basically the idea was that we were going to my Granny's house, since we could have the whole place to ourselves while she was having surgery on her hip.

We talked on the phone and sent text messages throughout the day. I was allowed to have my cell phone in there since it didn't have a camera. One night she said she was going out to party with her friends at a club. That made me nervous, and it got even worse when she stopped texting me back at two in the morning and didn't come visit me the next day. Some spiteful people who didn't like the idea of us were a little too happy to see me suffering. It had restored their faith in a cruel world. Then the next day she came back all beat up with her wrist in a brace.

A guy friend of hers had publicly urinated outside of a nightclub, attracting the attention of the police. A sheriff felt her up indecently. What could she possibly be hiding in a skin tight dress? He touched her pussy and she kicked him in the nuts. Then he beat her up and took her to jail. Had to admire the fighting spirit of this girl. She was charged with resisting arrest. Her parents bailed her out. She was supposed to go on the news and talk about it, and to go to court and sue the sheriff but she was too shy to go through with it.

She had bruises on her arms and legs and her wrist was sprained. At least the guy hadn't fucked up her face or raped her. She still looked great. She always did. Every time she came in there she was dolled up for me, had on a nice dress and her hair done, smelled like expensive perfume. I never had a girl like that before. Homicidal thoughts of revenge and cop killing tormented me for the next couple of days and then I got out.

Reina wanted it to be done a certain way, so when my mom picked me up she brought me my nicest clothes so I could get dressed up for her. We stopped at the store and bought the candles she had requested, a big box of condoms which we had agreed to use (but I doubted seriously that we would), and some nicotine patches that were stronger than the ones I had been using. I intended to stay off cigarettes, and now that I was free the temptation to smoke would be all around me. I'd use the stronger ones and then taper down to the weaker ones step by step until I was free of those too.

At my Granny's house, I had set everything up, but I couldn't get ahold of Reina. I started to panic. After all we'd been through was she really going to stand me up? Was I ever gonna catch a break? It wasn't until much later that night that she finally texted me that she was in jail again! She wanted me to bail her out but I didn't have that kind of money and neither did my mom. I had my Granny's Discover card though and I went to a bunch of stores and got out as much cash as I could, which came to about sixty bucks. Then I walked around for hours looking for people to beat up and rob but I couldn't really find anybody walking around where there were no security cameras.

In the end her publicly urinating friend was the one who put up the bail money; I just had to go pick her up. I took a taxi to the county jail and waited there for hours, watching people get released, every now and then seeing a girl with long brown hair and thinking it was Reina. Finally she got out, wearing a red dress with roses all over it. It was the first time I had ever seen her without some type of authority restricting us.

As I stood hugging her from behind while we waited for the cab, she explained that she had been shopping with a friend who, unbeknownst to her, was shoplifting the whole time, and when her friend got caught, she was considered guilty by association and hauled off to jail. The cab came, we got in and made out in the backseat all the way to Kholl's, where her truck had been left when she got arrested. Then she drove us to my Granny's house.

The candles were lit, the room was ready; we took off our clothes in a hurry. I was kissing her, sucking on her, leaving hickeys all over her breasts. She told me to put it in but to my shame it wasn't hard. She asked me if I didn't find her attractive without her clothes on, if I thought she was fat. I told her that she was beautiful and perfect and I didn't know why my dick wasn't hard. She lay down next to me with a sigh. I held her in my arms and stroked her long brown hair, felt her softness against me, relaxed and felt like I never wanted to let her go. I would never let anyone come between us, never let anyone tell me not to touch her again. She was mine now, my most precious possession that I had to take care of and nurture and protect with my life. I finally had a girl on my side. We were breathing slowly and heavily as we clung tightly to each other. My dick was hard as a rock.

I turned her onto her back. Her big brown eyes locked onto mine. She spread her long legs, and I eased slowly into her. She was hot, wet, and soft. I made love to her as slowly as I possibly could, never allowing myself to go too fast, yet still very gradually increasing my speed and force as she moaned and begged for me to fuck her harder. Her body's response to my careful self control was to become gradually wetter, softer, and looser, giving me some slack to pound her hard, then she would tighten around me a little and I'd have to go slow again, or even pull out for a few seconds and make her beg for me to put it back in.

I wanted to make this last forever, and we continued acclimating to each other until I was pounding her as hard as I could, flexing my dick and making her scream and dig her nails into my back, her pussy spazzing out, rapidly twitching and contracting. I wrapped my arms around her, squeezing her and flexing all my muscles to make my whole body hard against hers as she screamed, "I'm cumming! I'm cumming! Cum inside me!"

I pulled out and shot fat loads of sperm all over her belly and breasts. I had not masturbated in three days and we had just fucked for about an hour. I would have loved to cum inside her, to spend the whole night impregnating her. Our children would have been extremely tall, beautiful and strong, had she not been taking Zoloft, Abilify, and Klonopin, which almost guaranteed that they would also have been anything from retarded to stillborn.

XXVIII. SWEETHEARTS TOGETHER

WE FUCKED GREEDILY all night long until we had no strength left in our bodies and fell asleep in each other's arms as the sun started to rise. When I woke up around noon I had scratches all over my back and my legs were sore. We did it a few more times and lay around in bed lazily. I had to report to the MHMR (Mental Health Mental Retardation) office and go get the medicine I was pretending to take by court order. She loaned me her big white Toyota truck and I drove out there. The chick I had to report to was so hot, I wanted to bend her right over the desk, lift up that tight little skirt, and pound the living shit out of her until she was dead. But I didn't flirt with her at all. I had no intentions of being disloyal to my fragile love who was waiting for me sleepily back at my Granny's house.

We took a shower together and washed each other. Because she was so tall and her ass was so big, the only way to fuck her doggystyle without getting down on her hands and knees was for her to bend all the way over and put her head down. She disliked doggystyle, but would submit to it as a reward for me only if I had truly pleased her or if we had no other alternative but to do it standing up. She was also grossed out by oral sex, giving or receiving it. She just liked raw dick in her pussy and that was it. We had a ways to go. This chick had only ever been fucked by one guy other than me and he hadn't made her into a freak the way I intended to. She definitely had an unlimited appetite for sex and so did I. Being forced to hang out platonically in the mental institution for two weeks had left us unable to keep our hands off each other now that we were free. When we were together we didn't really feel comfortable unless we were touching each other somehow, constantly, every-where we went.

She let me drive us to Subway, which was right across the street. We were wobbly, drowsy, and exhausted. When it was time to pay for the sand-wiches I came up a couple bucks short. I had spent most of my money on the cab fare the night before. The nice guy who worked there spotted me. I was grateful but ashamed. I needed to get a job. Within the week that Reina had been out of EPPC she had already arranged for a job at a different Pollo Town location at the Cielo Vista Mall and to go back to UTEP for the fall semester. She had a few days left without any obligations to hang out with me as much as she wanted.

Whenever she would come to my house, she would call me on the phone when she arrived so I could go outside and walk her to my door. Whenever she would leave, I would walk her to her truck, kiss her goodbye, and watch her disappear down the street before going back inside. I had arranged for it to be like this because I had a lot of neighbors who might whistle or yell some drunken catcall to her if I was not with her. Every time I walked her in or out of my house I was prepared to fight to the death over any slight act of disrespect to my girl. I had decided long ago in the mental institution to hide Reina from my neighbors as best I could so they wouldn't start acting funny with me.

The place where I lived was a volatile little neighborhood where everyone was constantly fucking around with each other's wives and looking for any weakness or advantage they could take over each other. Although it deceptively didn't look so bad, within the seven years I had lived there, there had been several drive by shootings and even a couple of gun fights right in the middle of the street, and although it had definitely calmed down a lot in recent years, it was still better to always keep your eyes and ears open in there. I didn't want to make Reina scared to come to my house, so I never told her about any of that stuff, and the walks I took with her to and from her car were just something that appeared to her to be merely gentlemanly. I noticed that Reina didn't really seem to like being in her own house and she spent as much time at mine as she could. I kept the same room I had attempted suicide in, with a rug to cover up the stain from my nosebleed. We would always have to try our best to have sex quietly in there so my mom wouldn't hear it in the next room.

We drove to the other side of the river, which is like a big park, and had a nice long romantic walk together. We stopped at a little concrete bridge in the shade of a pecan tree and stayed there holding each other and making out for a long time, sometimes breaking pecans open on the cement and eating them. We were tempted to have sex there but people would occasionally pass by on bikes or jogging and see us, so we decided it wasn't a good idea. Reina declared, "This will be 'our spot' now." I really liked that day when we took that walk. I had always wanted to take a girl there, but we never did that again or went back to "our spot".

In my house, one night as we sat in the kitchen eating dinner, I noticed that Reina had bad posture and was always hunched over, how some tall girls do. I mentioned this to her as politely as I could and she told me that she had noticed the same thing about me. We both made a conscious effort to sit, stand, and walk with good posture after that. It made us look good and feel much better about ourselves.

Reina had a shopping addiction. She didn't even like to wear the same outfit twice. I didn't mind shopping with her most of the time, until it would come to that point when I thought she was being excessive, buying frivolous crappy things as fast as she could in a frenzy, and I'd have to persuade her to stop. I liked walking around hand in hand with her at the mall and showing her off. I was proud to be seen with such a beautiful girl. I liked watching her try on clothes, telling her what looked good on her and having a say in how my girl dressed. She was insecure about her looks. She was by no means fat, just perfectly thick in a way that any man could appreciate and desire, even had a flat stomach. She used to be really thin before she went to EPPC and got on the meds that made her gain a little weight and that was the reason for her unrealistic body image. She had no idea how hot she was.

She didn't like the way I dressed, said I looked like a cholo. She quickly bought me a bunch of trendy clothing that no self respecting man would ever choose and dressed me up like the other guys who had girlfriends. I always wondered why a lot of guys with hot girlfriends dressed so badly; now I knew and was one of them. She wanted me to look like some fresa guy. Tight jeans, tight, flamboyantly colored shirts. I honestly thought that the clothes she was putting me in looked a little gay, and it was only barely tolerable. When I wasn't with her I would wear my normal clothes. Although her taste in casual menswear was awful and embarrassing, she had good taste in formal clothing and she bought me some nice slacks and button down shirts to look for a job. Once again I had that gigolo pimp feeling of a girl paying for me, and this was a girl I loved and didn't want to take advantage of, so I felt indebted to her.

She started going back to work, so I got dressed

up, took the bus and went out looking for a job. I started around my Granny's neighborhood since there were a lot of businesses around there and I could work my way down Mesa Street applying everywhere. I noticed Sheldon's Jewelry and before I applied anywhere it crossed my mind that I might marry this girl, why not? So for the first time in my life, I went inside a jewelry store, browsed around and looked at some engagement rings.

Then I walked next door to a Chinese restaurant called Moon Dragon and instantly got a job there as a waiter. The guy asked me what my availability was like and I told him I could work anytime, but I would prefer it if I could have Sundays off to go to church with my girlfriend (since Sunday was her day off).

"What church do you go to?" he asked.

"I don't know yet," I grinned, "New girlfriend." He laughed and told me to come in the next day in the morning, and gave me a menu to study. Not even a week had passed since I got sprung from the looney bin and already I had a job and a hot girlfriend who liked to fuck every chance she got. I wasn't smoking cigarettes either, was eating tons of food, working out, and getting big.

After Reina heard how easily I had gotten a job at the first place I applied, she came to my house looking fine as hell, in a little black dress with a black bow in her long, pinned back hair, so shiny, straight, and perfectly arranged. She had a pale glow around her; her eyes looked especially big and her lips were hot pink. She looked like she had spent a long time and paid a lot of attention to detail to make herself look so strikingly beautiful for me. She looked immaculately hot. I wanted to vandalize her. I had been lifting weights and my shirt was off, but I had showered before she arrived. We made out and I pushed her head down a little. She got down on her knees, pulled my pants down and gave me head. She didn't really know how, and at first was scraping me with her teeth, but she soon became competent and was able to take it down her throat. I skullfucked her. She was behaving so submissively that I couldn't help but choke her during sex until I saw fear in her eyes. I almost wanted to slap her. I grabbed her, turned her over, fucked her hard from the back and spanked her, wrapped her hair around my hand and pulled her up by it so her back arched. I tilted her head back and whispered roughly in her ear, "Are you a fucking little whore?"

"Yes!" she moaned.

"Say it! Say you're my fucking little whore!"

"I'm you're little whore!" She whined. I kept pounding her harder and harder, making her repeat it, her big ass slapping against me and jiggling all over the place. Then I pulled out and shot a load all over her back and ass crack. I released her hair to tumble down, the little black bow and bobby pins dangling crookedly and pointing all over the place in different directions. I wiped her off and that night I taught her to ride me like Angelica the prostitute. It turned out that that was actually the position that made her cum most easily of all and we did it, not so rough, now I was talking sweet to her and telling her how much I loved her, until two in the morning when she had to go home.

My job at Moon Dragon was alright. I didn't get to keep the tips and was paid minimum wage by the hour, which sucked, but they paid me every day under the table as soon as I was done, so at least I always came out of there with some cash in my pocket so I could take my girl out to eat or to the movies after work. The people I worked for were nice enough, but there was a bad language barrier. The guy who hired me could speak English well, but he wasn't there most of the time, and the Chinese woman who ran the place while he was gone could barely communicate with me.

Moon Dragon was right next to my Granny's house. She had recovered from her hip replacement surgery and I could go visit her on my lunch break and make some food from her fridge. I told her about my new girlfriend I had met at the grocery store and she was eager to meet her.

I had never introduced a girl to my Granny, my great grandmother, before, and it had always been a little dream of mine to take a respectable girl to her and give her a little bouquet of roses from her garden. When Reina met Granny, she whispered to me, "I can't understand her..." My Granny had a thick Texas accent and I thought it was funny that Reina was the first person I had ever met who couldn't understand it. My Granny liked Reina and said she had "a very shiny, sparkly personality". She would later tell my mom on the phone that she was worried that a girl like Reina might put too much pressure on me. She was sweet and respectful to Granny, asked if there was anything she could do to help her. Granny asked if we could go across the street to Walgreens and get her prescription filled. We did that for her, then I picked the best rose from every bush, cut the thorns off them with a kitchen knife, wrapped them in a paper towel and presented them to Reina. We said goodbye and went to the mall.

Reina was on her period that day, which was great because it meant I hadn't gotten her pregnant. She amused herself by getting me to do my Granny impersonation, which she thought was funny as hell, and it was in no way disrespectful to my Granny, but just accurate from knowing her since I was born. Every time we went to the mall we would stop at Tuxedo Palace, where her mother and beautiful sister Elena worked and talk to them. I always found her mother to be unpleasant and insincere. She was polite to me and nice in a double edged kind of way, and every time I was in her presence I couldn't wait to leave.

Elena was cool though and I enjoyed her company. I couldn't help but wonder how her pussy felt compared to her sister's. She was so nice to talk to that I always had to restrain a natural urge to flirt with her. Reina would get insecure and confused when I was around her older sister and berate and make fun of me if I talked to Elena too much, but then get mad and take it as a sign of disrespect if I didn't talk to her enough. Elena was my age and more mature than the high schoolish Reina and seemed to understand her sister's ridiculous little controlling game and find it amusing. She was so attractive to me that I had to make a conscious effort not to become infatuated with her every time I was around her.

XXIX. A THIN RED DEVIL

THE NIGHT BEFORE Elena's birthday we got dressed up and went to Club Lotus on the Eastside. Reina had some high heels on and her hair was pinned back in a way that gave her the illusion of even more height. She appeared to be much taller than me and there was something sexy about it. On the way I got a phone call from a girl I used to like who lived somewhere else. It was not a good time to talk to her and I let it ring until it stopped. Reina saw the name on my phone and asked me, "Who's Melody?"

"Oh, she's just an old friend of mine. She doesn't even live here."

"Did you ever hook up with her?"

"No." I lied. It didn't feel like a lie as I said it, because the words "hook up" sounded to me like "fuck", and although I had made out with Melody once, I never fucked her. I corrected myself. "Well, I never had sex with her, we just made out one time and that was it." Reina was enraged.

"You lied to me!"

"I lied to you by accident and then told you the truth immediately afterwards. Does that really count as a lie?"

"Yes, it does count as a lie! I don't want a boy-friend who tells me lies."

For the rest of the night she showed me her wrath by ignoring me and treating me like a stranger in the club, refusing to speak to me, dancing with her guy friends, but without touching them. That made me feel violent. I hadn't had a drink in almost two months. We had bottle service and I sat at a table drinking Buchannan's and soda (the trademark drink of fresas in the club), glaring at these guys she was dancing with, prepared to rip their fucking heads off if they came too close to her. These guys could see me watching them, studying their anatomy, considering the possibilities of how to disfigure them. The drunker I got, the more creative my thoughts became. I felt like a wolf watching a bunch of little bunny rabbits. I wanted one of them to fuck up so I could take out my anger on him. They looked a little uncomfortable under the scrutiny of this deranged mental patient, but what could they do if she was right in front of them dancing like that?

One of Reina's many beautiful friends, a married one, came up and asked me what was wrong. I told her Reina was giving me a hard time. She laughed and told me that's what the whiskey was for. A rose salesman came in. One brave guy bought a rose and was walking towards Reina with it. I got up from my table, stood between them, slapped the rose out of his hand and glared into his eyes. He winced. I crushed the rose under my foot without taking my eyes off him. I had half a mind to grab this punk by the collar and smack him around the place. Some girls came and broke us apart before any violence could occur. After that, no guy would dance with Reina and she just danced with her girlfriends for the rest of the night. The same one who had asked me what was wrong before came up to me and laughed, "You're gonna marry that girl! I can tell. You have my blessing. Cheers!"

"If I don't murder her first," I smiled and said not loud enough for her to hear over the music. I knocked my glass against hers.

Reina continued to ignore me all night, no matter how much I tried to apologize to her. She wouldn't dance with me either. She even slapped me once in front of everyone. Then out of nowhere she said she was sleepy, took my hand and we went to the backseat of her sister's Nissan Xterra. She had nothing to say to me and quickly fell asleep with her head in my lap. Looking down on her trusting neck, I felt like a guillotine and thought about how easy it would be to strangle her to death with no one to stop me. When her sister was done partying she drove me home.

The next day I had to wake up early to go to church with Reina, where I would meet her aunt and grandmother. After that we were supposed to eat lunch for Elena's birthday. She had stressed me out so badly the night before that I started smoking again that morning. I chainsmoked about a half a pack of cigarettes, then took a shower, shaved, brushed my teeth and got dressed in some black slacks and a light blue button down shirt. She came to pick me up, looking beautiful in a light blue dress with matching high heels. What a coincidence that our clothes matched that day. She was smiling and acting like nothing had happened the night before and everything was normal between us. As I stood next to her truck, I sized her up. I wanted to open that door, yank her out of that truck and hit her with my belt right there in the street for all the neighbors to see.

"Did you have fun last night?" I asked her. Send her to church with two black eyes and drink myself to death.

"Yeah. Did you?"

"No. It was fucking horrible. You treated me like shit in front of all your friends, like I wasn't even your boyfriend. If that's your idea of fun I don't wanna go to church with you. I don't think I wanna go anywhere with you. Are you gonna treat me like shit in front of your family too?"

"I don't see what the problem is. You lied to me so that was your punishment."

"I told the truth to you! I didn't deserve that. I would never treat you like that! Don't ever fucking treat me like that again or we're through! No. You know what? Fuck it. We're through right now. Get the fuck out of here! I can't even stand to look at you." She started crying.

"No! Please! I'm sorry! I promise I won't do it again! Please, just come to church with me. My family's all waiting to meet you today! You have to come!" I didn't want to make her cry and I didn't really want to break up with her.

"You better be real fucking nice to me from now on," I said and got in the truck with her. On the way to church I held her hand as she drove, feeling its trusting softness and how easily I could break its delicate bones with one crushing grip. I was so angry that I didn't have anything to say to her. I was going to have to hide this anger from her family. It was going to be another stressful day.

"I'm going to have to confess to the priest today," she said.

"What are you going to tell him?"

"That I treated my boyfriend bad." All at once I forgave her and my anger completely dissipated. Now I just felt worn out and abused, a feeling that was going to last. I was always going to feel insecure around her people after what she had done. If our relationship was a planet, it was slightly lopsided now, spinning with a bias, slowly deviating from whatever stable axis it had seemed to be on before.

I had gone into many churches to pray by myself in an empty room, or on the doorsteps in the middle of the night, but I couldn't remember the last time I had actually attended the Sunday mass. Reina's Catholic church was modern and expensive. I thought it was funny that the Jesus in the stained glass windows at the Stations of the Cross was all buff, in contrast to his usual scrawny depiction. I sat down and glanced around at the people. I definitely had the hottest girl in the church.

When I looked behind me, I saw a thin red devil prance into the church through its big wooden doors and seem to take off his hat and give a little bow to me as if to say, "at your service". Was I evil? I shook my head to make the hallucination go away and put it out of my mind. I saw other men with their arms around their women, so I figured it was acceptable in church for me to do the same. Elena looked hung over as fuck, sitting next to her little brother on a bench in front of us and to the right. To our left was Reina's aunt, who was much prettier than her mother. Her tiny grandmother was there as well.

Reina whispered to me that I was doing the sign of the cross wrong; it was supposed to end on the right, not the left. I said I had been doing it that way because I thought it was supposed to end with my hand on my heart. I was the only person in the church who was not Mexican and could not under-stand much of the sermon that was given in Spanish, but I listened attentively and tried my best. Then everyone started singing while someone played the guitar. The mingled voices of the adults and children sounded so innocent and heavenly. The image of my slashed and bloody arms flashed in my mind for a second. I thought of all I had been through and had to push down a momentary urge to cry. The donation plate came and I put $20 in it. Reina was surprised and impressed.

Reina looked hot as we walked hand in hand through the parking lot. There was something so sexy about the drowsy, medicated sway of her long legs in those high heels. I met her grandma and we took a liking to each other right away. I called her "abuelita" and she said that Reina and I were "una pareja muy bonita", a very beautiful couple. She linked her arm in mine; I walked her to her car, opened the door for her, gave her a hug and helped her in.

At El Corralito Steakhouse, which was right by my house, I made the mistake of ordering fish. I have a tendency to eat seafood every chance I get. Not that the fish wasn't delicious, but it didn't compare to the unexpectedly awesome steaks everyone else got. Everyone gave a gift to Elena except me. We ate some birthday cake. I was experimenting with how much I could touch Reina in front of her family without offending them. They had no problem with her holding my hand, leaning drowsily on me with my arm around her or even giving me a little kiss.

They dropped us off at my house; the stress was finally over and I got what I had been waiting for. We had sex all day and most of the evening. She was generous with herself and apologetic, trying her best to heal the wounds she had left me the night before. She would sometimes hold me in her arms almost maternally, soothing me and stroking my hair, promising she would never do anything like that to me again. We only occasionally left the room to drink some water, and finally to eat dinner, before my mom drove us to her house. I walked her to her door, kissed her goodnight and felt completely satisfied. That was the closest I ever went to her house and I never went that close again.

The next day I spent waiting tables, lifting weights when I got home, and that night I went to a party at Hermán's house. This time, just out of the mental institution, I looked better than I did before I went in, and had the confident, laid back attitude of the sexually active. Reina, insecure, afraid that I might make eye contact with a woman or something, wanted to come, so I gave her the address. I really just wanted to have a little night off from her to hang out with my friends, but I didn't mind and was excited to show off my new girl. As soon as she got off work she drove to the party.

She was dressed conservatively in some jeans and a T shirt and her hair was tied back elaborately in a braid that was wrapped up as a bun. She looked fresh, clean and innocent. I had never before introduced a girlfriend to Hermán's family, who were like family to me. His mom and dad were respectful, surprised and happy to see me with such a decent looking and beautiful girl. Hermán on the other hand, with all his experience with women, didn't trust her for shit or even seem to like her. Clearly, I was in love and blindly pussywhipped, but he saw right through her and noticed something about her that wasn't quite right for me. His advice to me was, "Just take it for what it's worth." It angered me that Hermán didn't like my girl. I wanted everyone to approve of her and see her as I did. But what could I do?

She thought all my friends were dumbasses with our drunken, intentionally comedic dance moves, didn't get the joke, and didn't feel comfortable at such an informal backyard family party like this. She nagged at me, angry that I had been smoking cigarettes, extracted me from the party prematurely, took me back to my house and was even more pissed off when we got to my bed and I was too drunk and sleepy to perform and passed out in her arms.

My job at Moon Dragon didn't last much longer than a week and a half before the language barrier became too much of a problem and they realized they were better off without me. I had a little money saved up and Reina had arranged to take a few days off work so we could go on a little romantic getaway in Ruidoso. I had never been there before.

On our way there we stopped in Alamogordo where her best friend Yesenia lived. First we went to the Little Caesar's where Yesenia's boyfriend was the manager. He and Reina spoke Spanish rapidly to each other and I couldn't understand any of it. He offered us a free pizza and at first I politely declined, still with my prison style attitude of not accepting food from people, but Reina convinced me and he gave us the pizza with a smile of victory over me. In the truck Reina asked me why I hadn't talked to the guy and had just stood there silently. I said that they were speaking Spanish so fast that I couldn't understand them and I didn't know what to say. He didn't talk to me either.

We went to Yesenia's apartment. This girl was hot. She was tiny, with a fine body, an enormous ass (which Reina would later tell me was fake; she had ass implants), a great rack that was real, pale skin, long jet black hair and a beautiful face. She and Reina were shockingly foul-mouthed when they were together. I had never seen this side of her before and they cracked me up. I liked this friend of hers. She said she wanted to buy Reina a boob job, and I protested against it, said I liked her just the way she was.

"I bet you like her hairless vajayjay too, don't you? She's had every hair on her body permanently removed by lasers."

"Wow! I didn't know that. I always just thought she was just and expert at shaving it and that's why there's never any stubble."

They continued babbling in that indecipherable high speed Spanish to each other, playfully insulting and calling each other names. One thing I was able to pick up from their conversation was Reina asking her in Spanish, "Why does he choke me?" Her friend was unable to come up with an answer. Obviously she had no idea why her own boyfriend probably strangled her every night. Reina had tried to choke me back one time, and I didn't particularly like or dislike it, I just thought it was funny. I couldn't help but laugh at the angry look on her face and she stopped, confused. I had considered the possibility of seriously choking her out during the approach of an orgasm to see if I could make her achieve some sort of terrified erotic asphyxiation super orgasm but I never acted on it or discussed it with her. It was a purely hypothetical thought.

Reina's friend approved of me, gave us her blessing, and we left for Ruidoso.

XXX. LESS THAN TWO YEARS

WE ARRIVED AT night and got the cheapest motel room we could find. I paid the smaller half of the bill. We had cable and Reina got mad at me for being distracted momentarily by a UFC fight on TV during sex. By now she had learned how to ride dick like a pro and it was her favorite way to fuck. As she rocked back and forth, I would grab her by the hips and rock her even faster. With all the combined strength in our bodies she would rock as fast as we could make her go and this would give her the best orgasms.

When I would feel those spasms and contractions, I would lift up off the bed, wrap my arms around her, squeeze her tight, and have to try as hard as I could not to cum inside her before her orgasm was complete, then push her off and let myself go. We had planned to get her on birth control as soon as possible so we could enjoy the pleasure of simultaneous orgasms and she could walk around all day with her pussy full of my sperm. In the meantime, I just had to try not to get her pregnant.

We lay on the bed and I told her my story of how a witch had put a hex on me, given me the evil eye and driven me to my first suicide attempt. The story didn't make her afraid. Without me asking her to, she kissed all my scars tenderly, like a mother would kiss a child's booboo. She had no idea how much I had longed for a woman to finally do that to me.

She showed me all the pictures on her laptop, pictures of her before she had ever gone to the mental institution, when she was thinner, more confident, and engaged to a guy who was thirty. There were pictures of her modeling many of the flashy dresses from the Tuxedo Palace when they had a fashion show, pictures of her on dates with her ex-fiancé, with the excitement in her eyes of a girl who had just lost her virginity at the late age of twenty. She told me that he had started by going to Pollo Town every day for lunch just to see her and talk to her a little bit, then taking her out on dates a lot, then one day he proposed to her with a big diamond ring. She accepted and he moved her into his house and finally took her virginity.

I thought he looked just a little bit gay. She seemed to read my mind and said that after being with me, she thought that he might have been gay because he didn't like to have sex a lot. She would have to beg him for it sometimes and he wasn't usually in the mood. She would buy all kinds of sexy lingerie and walk around his house in it to try to get him to fuck her, and usually he'd rather just watch TV. What he really liked to do was take her out on dates all the time and show her off.

She explained the complicated circumstances of how she had been unjustly fired from her job, became depressed, and her fiancé lost interest in her and vanished into thin air as quickly as he could. She had given him back his ring, and curiously, he had taken all her lingerie with him for some reason. To sniff her panties forever? To try it on himself? I thought. Who knows?

I told her that this guy was just a sleazy flake who took advantage of her and didn't have the right idea about marriage. You're supposed to stay together through thick and thin and support each other no matter what, 'til death do you part. A marriage is a sacred promise before God. Too many people marry the wrong person for the wrong reasons and end up giving up on it. You should only marry your true love, you should expect for there to be problems some- where down the line, maybe horrible ones, and be prepared to work through them. You shouldn't marry someone too fast; you should be together for a long time first, spend years getting to know each other.

She disagreed. She said that all the women on her mother's side of the family had a rule that if a guy is with one of them for two years without proposing to her, she has to dump him because he must not really be serious. She told me the story of how her mother's cousin had rejected a man's proposal because the diamonds on the ring he offered weren't big enough, then when he came back with a better ring, she rejected him again and the guy had to take out a loan to get the third ring with a huge diamond on it that finally made her say yes. She said that I had a little bit less than two years to come up with a ring, and it had to be bigger than the one her ex-fiancé had given her. I did not like the sound of this at all but I agreed to it, as I would have probably agreed to almost any ridiculous whim of hers in order to make her happy and continue having sex with her.

The more I got to know about her mother's side of the family, the less I liked them, especially the mother herself, who was cheating on her father. The aunt and grandmother seemed nice so far, but they had to be some shrewd bitches if they lived by such an unromantic tradition of marrying with haste and for convenience. Maybe it was practical for people like them and necessary for their survival. I suspected that it must have been a safety precaution to ensure marriage before they lost their good looks. Reina's mom sure was ugly, although her aunt wasn't bad.

Reina could seem like the best girl in the world most of the time, and I really did love her, but the negative and shockingly petty qualities that sometimes came to her surface I attributed to her mother's bad blood. Did I want some of that blood to be coursing through the veins of my future children? How much of it was blood and how much was influence?

We watched a terrible movie on Netflix called *Crazy Love*. I hated that tacky movie but she loved it. She said that guy was me and she was the girl. I laughed at her, "You got it the other way around, baby. Whatever you do, don't stop taking your meds and we'll be fine."

"Asshole!" She threw a pillow over my face and started smothering me to death with it until it turned into sex.

In the morning, we ate the motel's complimentary breakfast of muffins and cereal, then walked around the little touristy part of the town. We happened to be there during a huge biker convention. There were mobs of friendly bikers everywhere, all over the place, the most bikers I had ever seen, and we had fun checking out all the bikes and deciding which ones looked the coolest. We went shopping and Reina tried on a bunch of dresses in front of me. She was looking for the one she would wear on her upcoming birthday and decided on a nice green one. Her birthday was more than a month away, but she wanted to get the dress from this particular store in Ruidoso that she liked so much. Our birthdays were about two weeks apart, both in October.

We had a little fight in the afternoon. I don't remember what it was about, probably money. I left her in the bed in the dark room and took a walk to clear my head. I wanted to go into the woods, but I could find no way in; they were meticulously fenced off. I noticed the huge black crows, three times the size of the ones we have in El Paso. I found a cool spot at the top of a hill with a really nice view and relaxed there. I thought it would be nice to take her there but she really didn't like long, uphill hikes so she probably wouldn't enjoy it as much as I did. I must have been searching for some kind of romantic gesture to snap her out of her depression, but couldn't find anything, couldn't afford anything, and went back into the room to cuddle with her. Sometimes she just needed to be smothered with physical affection and held for a really long time.

XXXI. RUIDOSO

BY NIGHT TIME Reina was wearing my clothes. I had some royal blue Nike breakaway pants that I let her wear and a dark red Nike hooded sweatshirt. I wore a black Nike hood and black Adidas sweatpants. We took a long walk, doggystyle, how cholos do with their girlfriends sometimes. She told me that the only reason she was letting me walk with her that way was because we weren't in El Paso and nobody we knew would see us. It must have been a guilty pleasure for her, but for me it was a pleasure without shame. I would have probably walked doggystyle with her everywhere we went for the rest of our lives if she would have let me, but that was the only time.

It was a beautiful night and cold, but we were dressed for it and the closeness of our body heat added to our comfort. I remember it as pure bliss walking with her like that all over the dimly lit streets of Ruidoso, having pleasant conversation and not running into a single person, like we had the whole world to ourselves. We were looking for a place to have sex outside and settled on a clean, dark little back alley. I unsnapped the breakaway pants; she bent all the way over; I pulled her panties to the side and slid it in. My dick had been hard for a long time while we were walking like that. She was quiet at first, but then she got a little thrill of exhibitionism and moaned exaggeratedly into the dark for anyone to hear.

When we got back to the motel she opened the blinds and windows, letting a chilly breeze into the room, took off all her clothes, sat on the counter of the bathroom sink, spread her legs wide open and said, "Fuck me hard. I want everyone to hear it!" The bathroom mirror was shaking and banging against the wall, she was screaming with no restraint. Maybe everyone in the motel or out in the street could hear and wanted to fuck my girl now, even though probably nobody could even hear us except maybe the people in the next room and there was nobody in the street. A feeling almost like I was jealous of my own self? We looked out the window as we fucked steadily, casually, all over the hotel room, just in case somebody should pass by and catch a glimpse, and nobody ever did. Soon we felt ridiculous about what we were doing and started laughing at each other, closed the windows and had a more intimate kind of sex until we fell asleep.

In the morning we ate some muffins and cereal, pocketed some for the road, got in our truck and started on our way home.

On the way we stopped at a lake and got someone to take a few pictures of us together. I made a drawing of her with a ballpoint pen on notebook paper as she sat on a big rock by the water looking so cute. I captured the sweetness of her smile in that drawing, and I wished I could have kept it for myself, but she really liked it and wouldn't let me have it. The drawing I had made of her in the mental institution, a striking image, was in a new wooden frame against a mat of pink construction paper, hanging on the wall in front of my bed so that it was the first thing I would see every morning when I woke up. My drawing of the crucifix was in a dark old wooden frame, passed down from generations of my mother's side of the family, on the wall behind my bed to ward off evil, the two of them at about the same level and facing each other.

When we got to my house, I felt so close to her that I had conflicting desires. I wanted never to be apart from her again and at the same time a little bit suffocated by this overwhelming joy, like when you eat too many sweets, a need to be completely alone. We ate some of my mom's cooking and she went home.

I felt great. I needed to get a job though. I felt guilty that she had to pay for most of our vacation and we hadn't really gotten to eat much. It would have been nicer if I could have taken her out to dinner while we were there. I had been spending all my time with my girl and it had been a while since I had hung out with any of my guy friends. I felt an old pang to go have some drinks at a bar with Dogoberto like we used to, but I wasn't really sure if we were friends anymore. I had talked to him briefly a few times since I had gotten out and he was cool but it seemed like he was still mad about my bumrush and we had some unfinished business. He always made a point to cut the conversation short and exaggeratedly turn his back on me before he walked away to remind me of it. I wasn't sure to what extent I had damaged our friendship. Did he now think of me inimically?

XXXII. SHE WAS FULL

REINA AND I had a little pregnancy scare and avoided sex, waiting for her period. She pissed on many different pregnancy tests and they all showed negative, but I had gotten carried away one night and shot a serious load in her and we really weren't sure. She told me what kind of birth control she liked. It was called Diane. My mom gave me some money and I went on a mission to Juarez. I had some other things to do that day as well and was dressed up to look for jobs along the way.

Juarez was crazy. A guy in a taxi cab offered to take me to some "putas calientes" right when I got off the bridge. Who knows what little heaven or hell on earth he was really inviting me to. A little kid jumped in front of me and did some undeniably sick breakdancing moves, then took off his hat. I dropped a dollar in it. I wanted to get the hell out of there as fast as I could before anybody else could ask me for shit. I went to the first pharmacy, closest to the border and told the lady, "Buscando pastillas Diane." She gave me a small pink rectangular box for fifteen bucks. I noticed two hot, strung out, junky looking chicks waiting for me to leave so they could try to buy some good shit. I contemplated the kind of sleepy limp dick adventures with them that could be bought from the pharmacy if you had a little money. Thank God I had a girl of my own who didn't even know the Klonopin she was taking was drugs. They gave me no trouble at the border when I showed them the birth control and one mission was complete.

I went to MHMR and talked to my new therapist lady. It wasn't the hot one from the first time who had been there as her substitute. This was a cute little rocker chick with thick glasses who was nice to talk to. I would later burden her with all my relationship problems every time I had to come in, but now I just told her everything was going good, I liked my medication, etc. and tried to leave as fast as I could.

I went to pick up some more of the Abilify I had to pretend to take and threw it in the trash can right outside the pharmacy. As I was walking back to the bus station, I saw a little restaurant called La Planeta Café with a HELP WANTED sign in the window. I went inside and filled out their informal hand made job application, which had at the bottom a little section where you could make a drawing if you wanted to. What kind of hippy suckers were these? I drew a proportionally accurate cartoon of my view of the inside of the room that included some of the cheesy decorations I suspected the boss lady must be fond of, like a little statue of a giraffe with a fedora on its head. I left the application with a waitress and continued on my way.

I stopped at a women's jewelry store to buy Reina's birthday present. Reina was a member of a Catholic Church group called ACTS. They meet up once a week to talk about religion and every now and then go on little retreats. The female members of the group like to wear fancy charm bracelets. Reina owned one, a simple one with plastic beads. She had told me that her father was going to buy her a really nice one made of silver for her birthday. I went in there with $60 and walked out with two little 10k gold charms for her bracelet, a gold cross with a white gold dove on it, representing the Holy Spirit and a fish that said Jesus on it. Those were the best things I could come up with.

Reina got her period and started taking Diane. Also she was going to school now. We waited two weeks before deciding it was safe for me to pump her full of my cum every night. I wanted to shoot that cum into her as hard as I could. I remember a guy in my Aikido class who said that Morihei Uyeshiba, the creator of Aikido, who went through many spiritual, religious, and idealistic changes in his philosophy as his martial art developed, at one point told his pupils to masturbate in their spare time until they could pierce the paper of Japanese walls with the force of their ejaculation, as part of their conditioning.

One Saturday, I woke up early in the morning and masturbated until I was empty. Then Reina showed up at my house unexpectedly to get some before school. I couldn't get it up for her. I apologized and explained that it was because I thought I wasn't going to see her that day, so I had been hanging out with Manoela all morning and there was none left for her.

"I hate Manoela!" she said. "If you can't please me, I'm going to find a man who will. I'm going out tonight with my friends with no panties on!"

"Oh you better not! Just come back to my house when you get out of the club and I promise I'll fuck your brains out like never before."

"We'll see…" she said with narrowed eyes, and stormed out of my house. Little did she know how true to my word I would keep.

Her threat of going to the club with no panties inspired a wild, jealous horniness in me. I drank coffee and lifted weights all day while thinking about sex, keeping my dick hard as much as I could, my balls steadily gathering sperm for her as I sent her dirty text messages about what I was going to do to her when she got back from the club. A few times I came close to priapism in my meditations. She was gonna get it tonight.

I barraged her with text messages while she was at the club, giving her no chance to look away from her phone to talk to a guy or something, and at two in the morning when she pulled up to my house, I was more than ready for her, shirtless, and freeballing in my breakaway pants.

I opened the door of her truck. She had a tight grey mini skirt that accentuated the enormity of her ass and a black button down shirt with short sleeves. Her hair was pinned back in that way that gave her height and with a long ponytail in the back. She smelled like sweet sugar.

"Did you fuck anybody?" I asked.

"No."

"Did you dance with any guys?"

"A lot of guys kept asking me to dance but I told them all no."

"Are you sure?"

"Yes. I promise."

"Show me your pussy." She leaned back in her big truck, lifted her skirt, and spread her legs. She had no panties and her pussy showed no signs of having been tampered with under the yellow glow of the streetlight. It was dry and it parted slowly, like a woman's lips blowing me a sideways kiss.

I pulled down my pants and pounced on her, fucked her right there in the truck with the door open. If a neighbor comes out, fuck it; let 'em see. Then I took her in the house and we continued like rabbits, with no regard for her orgasm, just fucking her as hard as I could, bashing our pubic bones together painfully, busting off nut after nut without pulling out or getting soft.

A guy walks into a whorehouse. The doorman tells him, "We got a dead bitch upstairs. You could hit it for $20 if you want."

"Alright, why not?" He goes upstairs for a while. When he comes back down the doorman asks him,

"How was it?"

"It was alright I guess. Something weird though, her nose kept running for some reason."

The doorman shrugs and says, "She was full."

We kept on going well into the afternoon. We had been keeping count and by now I had fucked her nine times, and busted way more than nine nuts. We decided to set a record that day. When we got to twelve we were so dirty and sweaty that I told her to go home, take a shower, and come back; let me rest for a moment before we continue.

When she came back she was glowing and smiling, her hair was flowing, her eyes were huge, and she looked like the sweetest girl in the world with half of her big ass hanging out of some tiny cutoff jeans. She took me to the grocery store Mando's where you could get some of the best burritos in town. Everyone was staring at her. Her body seemed to be singing. We walked out by the river and had a little picnic under the bridge. There were people on the other side of the river, which was dry at that time. They seemed to sense something obscene about us and left.

I broke my pants apart, spread them on the ground like a blanket for her to lie down on; she pulled her little shorts down to her ankles and opened her knees. I stepped into the diamond of her legs, got down on top of her with my knees in the dirt, made out with her for a while and stuck it in her. It was hard for me to cum outside and we did it for a long time under the bridge, my knees getting scratched up in the dirt. Some guys on dirtbikes came riding through the dry riverbed and practiced popping wheelies under the bridge without noticing us. After they left I made Reina just a little more full. We finished our burritos and went back to my house. Before number eighteen, we were so tired we could barely walk and it took a long time and a lot of head for me to get it up, and then about an hour and a half for me to finish. We decided to call it a night and she went home.

I remember feeling like I was retarded after she left, stupid, unable to make simple calculations, empty headed, like some kind of Neanderthal man. I sat on my bed and stared at the wall, slackjawed, and thought of nothing. There was nothing to think about. What a perfect silence. I was as peacefully empty as she was full.

XXXIII. SILVER AND GOLD

I GOT THAT job at La Planeta Café. I knew it wouldn't last. The people who ran the place certainly were nice and good people, but they were hippies. Their kitchen was the cleanest I had ever seen, their ingredients the freshest and most organic, but how long could I last making and peddling sandwiches called "paninis" for a living? It was degrading to a man like me. I was sorry to have to rip them off by never showing up to work again by surprise one day, but I couldn't stand those people. I'd rather dig ditches for a living or be a janitor. I had worked for them for a little more than two weeks, just enough time for them to train me, and then I abandoned them. What goes around comes around. I'd pay for it later.

I quickly got another job at Redcats, a call center that sells plus size clothing for women. This was acceptable to me, and I enjoyed the constant fat jokes. During my training I noticed a hot girl named Maricela who I was tempted to cheat on my girlfriend with. She was short with huge breasts, a tiny waist, a nice round ass, and great legs. Her eyes were big with long lashes; she had a perfect smile and shoulder length brown hair. There was a magnetism between us. We were always bumping into each other. We sat together and talked during our lunch break every day and played pool during our little recess. She knew I had a girlfriend, had seen Reina drop me off at work and kiss me goodbye, and that only made her want me more.

I could see her frustration at my indecision. She had dropped plenty of hints that she wanted me to ask for her number, told me how close she lived to my house, and had even offered to give me a ride home any time if I wanted. What more could a girl do? I knew that if I let her drive me home I would automatically fuck her when we got there. I could fuck Maricela every day and Reina every night. But I stayed strong and took the bus home every day. I was keeping her on reserve, waiting for Reina to treat me bad again, like she had that night at Club Lotus, a constant fear of mine. But Reina was behaving like an angel and treating me like a king, so I remained faithful to her and resisted Maricela's temptations while making sure to keep her close by just in case.

On the night before Reina's birthday we went to some club downtown. Her sister, aunt and best friend Yesenia from Alamogordo parked in the same lot as us and walked with us to the place. Inside the club was a mob of beautiful girls who were all Reina's friends. Reina stayed close to me all night, frequently displayed her affection for me clearly in front of her friends and did everything she could to make up for what she had done at Club Lotus.

I took her downstairs to the lower level of the club, away from everybody else, and taught her to dance dirty with me. She had never danced the way I was making her, the only way I really know how to dance with girls when dirty rap songs come on. The song by Jeremih ft, 50 Cent – Down on Me was playing while we made out on the couch. I found a door that led to a staircase and tried to convince her to have sex with me in there but she wouldn't.

Afterwards we had breakfast at Village Inn. We had a little fight in there. She was holding it over my head that she had to pay for my meal and drive me home, showing off in front of Yesenia. I said, "Well who says I was even hungry? And who says I need a ride home? When you give someone something, it's not supposed to be because you want to guilt trip them about it or expect something in return. It's supposed to be out of the goodness of your heart." I walked out of the Village Inn.

It's not like I had never taken her out to way more expensive dinners than that before. I might have been broke but I would get paid in two days and take her out to eat. Plus I still hadn't picked up my check from La Planeta yet. Why was she always trying to make me look like such a broke ass motherfucker? Before I met her, I never gave a fuck about money a day in my life as long as I had enough to get drunk or high, and never cared for fancy formal places. Now it was going to be a constant job of trying to prove to her family that I was good enough for her by throwing all my money at her and buying frivolous crap. And it wouldn't have felt frivolous and crappy at all if they hadn't put that pressure on us.

Girls are innately inclined to fall in love and fuck the guy they have naturally selected for their own pleasure, but their mothers make them to charge you for it, pimping their daughters out to the highest bidder, teaching them to feel anxious and worthless when not on the arm of a man with money. Too many people deny themselves true love when they see the smug, jaded face of practicality laughing at their heart's desires.

I held my head high as I walked home, enjoying the cool night air and planning to bang Maricela as soon as possible. I felt like a fool for not having already gotten her number, but Reina stopped me in the street, begged me to get in her truck, then drove me to a dark place and changed my mind before dropping me off at home.

The next night my mom dropped me off at Pacifico, a good Mexican seafood restaurant, for Reina's birthday dinner. I was introduced to her giant father, who I had long suspected to be a descendent of the ancient Nephilim of biblical times. It was the first and only time I saw her mother and father together. They generally avoided each other and stayed at opposite ends of the party. There was a tense, invisible hatred between their straight faces, and they never once acknowledged each other's presence.

Reina's father put his enormous, heavy hands on my shoulders and whispered in my ear a promise to murder me if I didn't treat his daughter right, then turned away, smiling at me, to talk to his son. He was thin and not a muscular guy, but he had a little bit less than a foot of reach on me and I'm sure he knew how to use it. The thought of fighting a guy built like that seemed ridiculous and inconceivable by the standards of combat I was accustomed to. The image of Kareem Abdul Jabbar's giant footprint on Bruce Lee's chest came to mind. I made a mental note to watch *The Game of Death* and pay attention to what Bruce Lee did to beat him, and then I remembered that he was getting his ass kicked and had to poke holes in the paper walls to illuminate the dim room and take advantage of Jabbar's unusual sensitivity to sunlight to win.

I wasn't scared of him, and sensed hollowness in his threat, the kind that all fathers must feel obligated to say to their daughters' suitors, a lie he had to tell to distract himself from the impotence that must have been gnawing at him. I felt like we were on the same side for some reason, although to him I may have been just another problem on his long list, a questionable brand of glue holding something together for him. I sympathized with him. He had to deal with Reina's mom and I had to deal with the half of Reina that was like her mom. Hopefully there was enough of him in her that I wouldn't end up like him, cuckolded, defeated, and possibly about to be robbed by his divorce. The fact that he was so big and his wife's sancho wasn't dead or beaten halfway there suggested to me a lack of the kind of passion that would have been necessary to murder me.

It was one of those tense nights with her family that I was going to have to get used to, but the food was good and I kept it cool. We all gave our presents to Reina. My small gift of gold was well received by Reina, who got her father to pry the little clasps on the ACTS bracelet he had gotten her and add the charms to it. He had also given her a Jesus fish and cross almost the same as mine but made of silver. It seemed to me like my gift was being looked upon like a threat, to the part of Reina's family that was rooting against me, that I might stick around, and also an exposed weakness, a chance to exploit me for all I was worth and see how much more gold they could wring out of me before I was discarded. But maybe they didn't see it that way at all and it was all in my head?

I was glad when the whole thing was over, glad that she was happy, and glad to be alone with her in my room again. She told me that her tiny grandmother, when she saw the way I looked at her, warned her to watch out for a guy like me, because all I wanted was sex. I was insulted. It was a lot more than just sex. Reina and I were emotionally dependent on each other. And besides, Reina wanted it just as bad. I wasn't quite sure, but I got the feeling that her family was setting everything up to really put the screws to me. But hey fuck them. I was about to bang their daughter and they knew it and what could they do about it right now except condone it grudgingly?

What happened next is something I still don't quite understand. It was, in its own way, more terrifying than my experience with the witch and it brought me once again close to the edge of death. I believe it all came about from a weakness in my pride, which was the only thing I had been surviving on, and had been built on a foundation that was mostly genuine, but was also held together by just a few little fallacies and paradoxes, that caused it to eventually transform into a cocky hubris, which is a dangerous weakness that can be exploited, should the wrong "entity" pick up on it.

XXXIV. THE DEVIL OUTSIDE MY HOUSE

I FUCKED REINA slowly, gently, and respectfully, like she was an angel, working our way up routinely to the simultaneous climaxes we had learned to create. I remember feeling something religious about what we did, like a holy cross of energy running through her body. She fell asleep in my arms, and I lay there awake. I sensed something outside my house. It was a red devil with hooves, kicking up dust like he wanted to charge at me like a bull, jumping around cagily with the footwork of an excellent and cruel boxer, showing off to me. I wondered what it would be like to fuck my girl like the devil. Why not?

He rushed into my house through the walls and was now a part of me. I felt like I had horns and hooves and a long red tail. I snatched up my sleeping girl by the hair like a ragdoll. She gave a little scream. I rammed my dick into her dry pussy and felt it surge with wetness instantly. I pounded her barbarically like I never had before, like she was not someone I knew but some common object that I hated and wanted to beat to death as she screamed and scratched up my back. I went faster and faster, busting three nuts without any decrease in acceleration or hardness, and then stopped suddenly, out of breath. I had an infinite amount of that hatred that pleased her so much and was only withholding it from her out of sheer dominance and control. I could rape her again even more brutally than that any time I felt like it.

"Whooo! I needed that!" she said, and drifted back to sleep. Had she not been on birth control, I'm sure that those three nuts would have created the spawn of Satan.

As she slept in my arms, I could feel that macho diabolical energy within me, like I was someone else entirely, a cruel, wicked man. I could feel her soft energy bonding to this new persona and falling submissively in love with it, completely seduced by its raw evil power. Then the devil's energy seemed to leave my body, hand in hand with the energy of my girl, the two of them walking away into the distance until they disappeared. I could feel her body beside me now, but there was no spiritual connection, like she was a stranger in my bed.

I tried to fall asleep, but when I closed my eyes I was barraged by horrifying images of upside down crosses with twisted skeletons on them, like they had been writhing in pain before they died. They were dripping with blood, fields of them against a red sky with lightning bolts storming against it. Black clouds rolled over the horizon ominously, twisting into tornadoes of red blood that lashed at my face. The deep voice of the devil in my head was cackling as he danced among the upside down crosses that hung the remains of the many people that had fallen for his persuasion. Then he showed me an empty cross in the middle of it all, and pranced around it with a mallet in one hand and railroad spikes in the other, overjoyed and cackling at the prospect of nailing me to it. That put a chill down my spine and a quick shiver of fear ran through my body, unnoticed by Reina. What had I done?

The alarm on her phone went off fifteen minutes before midnight, which was her curfew.

"I couldn't feel you while I slept just now. Did you get up and leave?" she asked.

"No. I didn't get up. I was here with you the whole time. Did it feel like you were with someone else?" I hid the nervousness I felt asking this question.

"No. It just felt like I was alone. You didn't leave me to smoke?" She smelled me. "You didn't. Are you sure you were sleeping with me?"

"I was holding you the whole time but I wasn't asleep. Maybe that's why you didn't notice me."

"I don't know," she said, "That's pretty weird..."

I walked her out to her truck and kissed her good-bye, a hollow kiss, like a stranger I had never met before.

The rest of the night, I tried to fall asleep but was tormented by vivid satanic imagery every time my eyes closed. I got on my knees and prayed to Jesus, unintentionally visualizing myself stabbing his living body on the cross with a spear. His face looked down at me calmly, disappointed in me but completely unfazed by the cruelty I was inflicting on Him, with an understanding and endless forgiveness in his eyes but also an intense expression warning me of the severe the danger I was in. Something was very wrong now. I stayed up all night.

In the morning, I made a quick breakfast, drank some coffee, showered, shaved, dressed up in my sharpest clothes, because today they had requested for all of us to do that, although it wasn't mandatory, and my mom drove me to work. I got paid weekly, with the first check withheld, so today I would be picking up a check, but they also owed me another one that I could only get by quitting my job.

As I walked into work, I felt like my legs were not quite my own and I was doing a subtle, devilish strut, almost violent, suggestive of boxing. In the training room, Maricela would stare at me intently from time to time, sensing that today might be her chance. She looked sexy in a tight blue business jacket with a short matching skirt, showing a lot of leg. Her hair was straightened and looked longer that way. She was wearing a little more makeup than usual and her lips and eyes looked nice and big. We sat close together at lunchtime, touching each other as we talked. When work was over, I walked with her all the way to her car, feeling like the devil himself. She asked me, a little bit shyly, "Do you want a ride?"

"Not today. My girlfriend is coming to pick me up.

But maybe on Monday?" We had weekends off.

I hugged her goodbye for the first time, slowly, gently, and close. We stayed there like that, my arms around her waist and hers around my neck, until my dick got hard against her body. Had Reina seen that, she would have killed me, or maybe herself. Maricela parted from my embrace, narrowed her eyes, looked down at my erection, then into my eyes and smiled mischievously.

"You're bad," she said, "I'll see you on Monday." She got in her car and left.

Reina picked me up from work, looking ridiculously hot. She had these black pants that made her ass look bigger than I had ever seen it and a red sleeveless button down shirt. Her hair was done elaborately, pinned all sorts of ways and in a huge bun. She wore red lipstick. We held hands on the way to my house. I had just gotten paid and we had planned to go out to a late birthday dinner for her that night.

"Do you talk to any of those little sluts at your work?" she asked me, taking her eyes off the road to look me over suspiciously.

"No, I see them stare at me sometimes, but I keep to myself," I lied.

"Promise?" she looked so vulnerable.

"I swear to God. You're the only girl for me. I pay them no attention at all. And you look so hot today by the way."

"Thank you," she said, and looked at me hungrily,

"So do you."

When we got to my room, I summoned all of that swollen diabolical machismo I could find and fucked her very dominantly. She wiped my dick off with my boxers and got a little bit of sperm on her finger, looked at me, laughed and touched my mouth with that finger. I grabbed her roughly by the wrist and growled at her, "What the fuck are you doing, bitch! Putting jizz in my mouth? You think that's funny?" My hand was gripping her wrist tightly. She started crying and struggled to break free. I let go suddenly.

"I was just trying to wipe the lipstick off your mouth," she said, with tears and a look in her eyes so hurt and scared that it made me afraid that what I had done was irreparable.

"I'm so sorry. I don't know what came over me. Please forgive me. It'll never happen again. I promise!"

"No! I'm never coming back to you!" She quickly put her clothes back on, ignoring my apologies, and ran out of my house to her truck. I chased her, she slammed her door in my face and sped recklessly down the street.

XXXV. CASTRATED

EVERY SWEET SHORTCUT the devil offered came with a horrible price afterwards. I had to get it off me, but how? It seemed to come and go as it pleased. I tried calling Reina many times but she wouldn't answer. We eventually got to texting and I calmed her down and convinced her to let me take her out to dinner tomorrow. I stayed up all night again worrying for the fate of my soul.

In the morning I went outside to check the mail. Dogoberto was in his front yard and he whistled to me. I looked up, friendly, ready to make some conversation. He smiled and turned his back on me. I went back into my house confused. Then I got angry. So this guy still wants to turn his back on me and insult my pride? He wants to act like I'm a coward because I bumrushed him instead of calling him out? Well, I'll call him out today then and beat the shit out of him if that's the way he wants it.

He outweighed me by maybe 20 pounds, but he had a lot of fat on him and I was made of nothing but muscle. He did have that natural, genetically endowed knockout power in the structure of his bones, but I'm almost impossible to knockout. He could hit harder than me, but his hands weren't nearly as fast as mine. He could probably break my jaw, but it would take much less power for me to rebreak his, since it was only held together by screws. He had his dodginess, but I had already figured out what I would do if he ever leaned back again. It would only take the slightest, sweeping kick to his front leg to make him fall down while he was off balance like that, and that might be his greatest weakness, should I choose to hit him while he's down. I had my own type of dodginess too, which he was also slightly familiar with, the entangling, bone-breaking evasiveness of Aikido. I had shown him the basics of it, and he had developed a slight immunity to it, but I had plenty of deadly moves up my sleeve that he didn't know about, and I'm sure he had plenty of his own too. We both had equally crappy stamina from smoking too much and liked to think of ways to end fights as quickly as possible. One thing was for sure; I would not give up. He would either have to kill me or give up first. It would be a closely matched and bloody fight.

As I was hitting the bag in preparation for him, my legs were not my own and neither were my hands. There was an unusual cruelty in the way I was moving. I was boxing with the devil's moves and I didn't feel like myself at all. I stopped before my knuckles could start hurting, then I lifted weights, but stopped before I could get sore. I ate a big meal, gave it some time to digest, then called Dogoberto's house on the phone. There was no answer. I went outside; he wasn't in his yard and his truck was gone.

I still had a fear leftover from my fight with Silent that I might be abandoned by everyone I loved if I lost a fight. When Reina came over that night, with the bruises I had left on her wrist, I asked her, "If I got in a fight and lost, would you stay by my side, or would you leave me?"

"Why?"

"I'm about to fight my neighbor. I fought him once before and it was a tie, but today he insulted me so now I have to fight him again."

"How did he insult you?"

"It's hard to explain. But he definitely challenged me to a fight today and I can't back down from a fight. I'd rather lose or be dead than back down. Would you leave me and go with my enemy if I lost?"

"Don't fight him. Why do you have to fight over nothing? My ex-fiancé never had to fight anyone." Your ex-fiancé was a faggot.

"This is something I have to do. Would you promise me to stay by my side whether I win or lose?"

"No. I promise that I will break up with you if you fight anyone. You have to promise me not to fight or I'm leaving right now and you can fight all you want and never see me again."

I should have known better than to involve my girl in this. She had little understanding of the ways of men. It would have been better to just go out to eat with her and fight Dogoberto in my spare time without telling her, but it was that little fear of abandonment that made me ask her for a declaration of loyalty. At the same time, I knew that it was the devil who wanted me to fight Dogoberto even more badly than I wanted to fight him, and I wanted to get the devil off my back more than anything. I had already figured out that my little suspicion that she was on the devil's side the night before had only been brought about by his deception, and although it was counterintuitive, I knew I had to listen to this devoutly religious girl if I wanted to escape his clutches. Also I was a pussywhipped pushover and what was one more emasculating compromise in order to continue getting laid? I was about to find the threshold.

"Fine. I promise not to fight." Instantly something changed all around me. I had given my word not to fight, some precise words, so now, if I broke my promise, my word of honor which was entirely mine and no one else's, and fought anyone, no matter who it was, I would be surrendering a little more of myself to the devil. So now I would be a defenseless man when I walked in the streets. I would have to rely only on authoritative posture and words to fend off potential assailants, and hope than no one would see through my bluff.

We went out to the restaurant Crave by Cincinnati Bar. Sitting across from the gorgeous girl dressed in yellow, who kept her right arm hidden under the table to hide its bruises whenever the waiter came, I felt no devil within me, and also a complete absence of my own pride. I felt deeply ashamed at having laid hands on my girl like that and like an empty shell of a man. I had to make an effort to keep my head up and not let it droop morosely. I found it hard to concentrate on Reina, who seemed like some stranger who I had allowed to convince me to castrate myself.

Normally I would have had a huge appetite after a day's workout, but when the food came I could barely bring myself to eat it. Why had I been working out all day if not to fight? Just to look pretty for her? I was nothing and no one. I forced myself to finish my big meal of fried chicken and waffles. Then we walked around and windowshopped at some women's clothing stores, before driving back to my house.

When we got into my neighborhood, I was almost trembling with fear now that I couldn't fight and unable to concentrate on my girl. She would often have to repeat herself several times before I could hear what she was saying. In my living room she asked me, "Do you really like me?"

"I love you more than anything," I said, "but I know what you're talking about. It's hard for me to concentrate tonight. I'm distracted."

"By what?"

"I can't say." I couldn't admit to her the fear and paranoia I felt, bound by my word, the only thing I had left, not to fight anyone.

In the bedroom, something interesting happened. Reina had now gained control over the contractions of her pussy and could squeeze me tightly at her command.

"Whoah! When did you learn to do that?"

"I just thought about it today and decided to try it. It kind of hurts me but it feels good."

"Squeeze me when I pull and relax when I push."

It took us a little while to get the rhythm, but soon we had it perfect to where I would flex my dick and she would tighten around it at the same time and it felt crazy, like I was stuck in her. This mechanical sex we had devised was to make up for the lack of the spiritual connection that used to thrill us so much and make her pussy do that kind of stuff when it felt like it, and when we were finished, I felt like I had just had unprotected sex with a very skilled prostitute.

"Thank you for lending me your body," she sighed. I knew exactly what she meant. We lay in bed and I didn't know who the fuck we were or who we belonged to.

After she left, I decided that I didn't want her around me anymore. Only danger could befall her in my company. The devil had succeeded, maybe not in actually stealing my girl from me, because she would never join him, but he had taken us apart and I had signed away my power to rid myself of him. He didn't have my soul, or any use for me anymore. We had parted ways in a stalemate, or so I thought.

I imagined that, had it been a game of chess, the devil would have already taken most of my pieces away from me, including my queen, and I, not many of his; none of his pawns would have made it to my side for him to gain control of my queen and use her against me, but the pieces on the board would have been arranged in such a way that the game was over and nobody had officially won, although he had a victory by points.

I would later find out that it was one of those games where it looks like it's over, but then you notice that there are still some good pieces you forgot about that you can move to get out of check and the game continues.

XXXVI. WASTING AWAY

FROM THE MOMENT I promised not to fight, I slowly began to lose my will to live. I didn't sleep, I barely ate, and barely drank water. I would try to eat, but the food was flavorless and my mouth would produce no saliva. I could drink water, but it was a real job just to make myself get up off the couch and do it. Of course, I never went back to work on Monday. Mostly I just lay around in a catatonic stupor and slowly wasted away.

Reina was safe if she was away from me. I wanted her to move on and find a better guy who wasn't a fucking lunatic. She would call me every day and I would tell her I wanted to break up with her, not because I didn't love her, but because I wanted her to be happy, and then I would frantically warn her not to come near me because if she did, she would be in great danger. She didn't understand what was going on at all and refused to break up with me. Nobody understood what was going on. I told nobody about the devil. Reina would threaten to come to my house sometimes and I would beg her not to, beg her to leave me and find another man. She would refuse and say she was on her way over and I would have to yell at her to stay the fuck away from me if she knew what was good for her and that would make her cry.

I would hear Dogoberto outside sometimes and then a homicidal gravitational pull would take hold of me, the devil would try to possess me, and I would get all pumped up with adrenaline and want to run outside and kill that motherfucker for playing such a dirty trick on me, but I wouldn't do anything. I had to keep my word or I would burn in hell. I would hear him go back into his house and then be able to resume my catatonic stupor. Every time that happened I'd end up feeling more burnt out and exhausted. I remember my mom trying to talk to me, but barely being able to understand English sometimes, and when I spoke, she often couldn't understand me either.

After about a week of this, Reina showed up at my house one night. By now I looked sickly and had dark circles under my eyes. I hadn't slept a wink since I last saw her. Walking out to her car to meet her was the first time I had even left my house. Dogoberto happened to be outside across the street in a parked car with a friend. A smiling devil appeared in a puff of smoke and pranced along behind Reina and me as we walked into my house. He was so happy to see her. He wanted me to beat her and hold her in my arms and say sorry afterwards and convince her to sell her body and give me the money. This was completely preposterous to me and in my mind I laughed at his bullshit proposition. He seemed to shrug and say that if I would only work together with him we could easily make it happen. Look how much she cares for you. She would do anything for you if you only had the balls to make her. You underestimate yourself. You let her treat you like shit sometimes you fucking simp, but she could be putty in your hands...

"SHUT THE FUCK UP!" I looked behind me and roared out loud in my house. Reina jumped.

"Who are you talking to?" she asked me. Her eyes were so scared, worried, sad, confused, and neglected. It almost made me cry to look into them. She sure did look hot though. She was wearing some loose grey pants of a thin fabric that clung nicely to her body, with a matching top. Was she dressing for someone else? For the devil? Anybody but the devil, I hoped. Anybody but me.

"I wasn't talking to you," I said wearily.

In my room she sat on my bed and I kneeled on the floor with my arms wrapped around her waist, clinging to her and breathing heavily as the devil tried to drag me by my legs out into the street to fight Dogoberto. And I would lose now. I was in no shape to fight.

"What's wrong? Why are you acting this way? I thought you loved me. I just want everything to be how it was before..."

I couldn't hear her so well over the devil's deep voice laughing in my head.

"You don't understand, Reina. Something bad is

happening to me. You need to get out of here. You're in danger just by being near me." I spoke rapidly and my eyes were wide and terrified. She suddenly looked in the invisible direction that I was being dragged. "Please get out of here, get out of this neighborhood and stay far away from me. I'm going to try to get help, but for now just forget about me because I'll only take you to hell if you stay with me. I'm going crazy again. I need to go back to the looney bin. Don't even wait for me to get out. Find yourself a good man, one who is not cruel or evil or devilish in any way."

"But you are a good man! You're the best man I've ever met! Why can't you see that? Don't go back to the psych center. Don't leave me all alone!" She was crying now. The mixture of the sound of her crying and the devil's laughter in my head was the creepiest sound I had ever heard. I couldn't stand it. I gathered all of the strength I could find within me, stood up straight, wiped the tears from her eyes, kissed her forehead, took her by the hand and walked her out of my house to her truck.

Dogoberto was standing against his wall now, smoking a cigarette and watching us. Maybe he had heard me yell "SHUT THE FUCK UP!" and suspected me of domestic violence. She quickly turned her head and glared at him sharply, like a mother protecting her child. I opened her door for her, she got in, and I told her, "Don't ever come back to this evil place. I never want to see you again." She was about to say something to me but I closed her door. I stood there and waited for her to leave. When her car disappeared around the corner, my strength suddenly left my body and I got weak in the knees. I got a headrush and felt like I was about to faint. I stumbled into my house and fell down on my couch, out of breath. I hadn't eaten in a long time and the whole thing had taken a lot of energy out of me.

XXXVII. SHADOWDODGING

I KNEW THAT if I kept on like this I would die, but at least I wouldn't go to hell, and I was starting to warm up to the idea of death again. Shit, I had experienced enough pleasure and pain to be satisfied. But now I had told Reina that I would get help, and although it wasn't a formal promise, it was still another word that I had to keep, and it slightly renewed my will to live to have a commitment to honor. In order to get help I would have to leave my home and walk around paranoid and defenseless.

Then a crazy idea struck me of how I might survive and also escape damnation. I had surrendered my pride to the devil, but fighting Dogoberto wasn't the only way to get it back. There was a better way. I remembered the scene from *Enter the Dragon* where Bruce Lee told the bully on the boat what his style was, and tricked the guy into getting into a little boat that was cast off from the main ship and nobody ever saw him again.

If I would not allow myself to fight back, I could still develop a perfect attackless defense and learn to dodge any possible assault from any direction. If I could induce someone to bumrush me and dodge every attack without fighting back in any way, or using the devil's footwork, my own genuine pride would be restored. Would my failed attacker then be afflicted with my same devil's curse after that? It seemed highly possible by the deranged standards of rationalization I was operating on that maybe the curse would continue forever, men bumrushing and dodging each other, losing and gaining their pride, passing it on until the end of time, or until someone either figured out another way to get rid of it, died, or submitted to the devil's will.

As soon as I came up with this plan, I got a voracious appetite and could now feel my body's starvation and malnutrition. I ate as much food as I could stomach, rested until I was hungry again, and repeated this process several times until I felt somewhat healthy again. Then I began my training. Shadowdodging. This was difficult, because the devil already had plenty of easy ways for me to do this, and I knew that if I used them it wouldn't count and I would still be damned. I had to jump around constantly and be sure that I was the one controlling my legs. Should one offensive move slip out as a reflex, my pride would not be restored and I would still be damned, so I kept my hands behind my back and walked around like a shackled prisoner. I decided that the only circumstance by which I would allow myself to use any offensive move would be as a last resort to protect someone else, and that could not possibly be damnable in the eyes of God or the devil, and if it was, so be it.

The funny thing about all of this was that I wasn't even Catholic, wasn't even sure if I was a Christian, wasn't a member of any organized religion, and wasn't sure if I even believed in an afterlife. But I had gone to a strict Catholic school as a child, so it would always be deeply ingrained in my way of thinking no matter what I tried to believe in throughout my life. The imagery of Catholicism always provided me with comfort or the fear of its particular brand of God whenever I needed it.

I continued eating, drinking water, and shadow-dodging for days without sleeping. I wasn't sure if I could get Reina back and was sure that I was unworthy of her, so I was determined to drive her as far away from me as possible with my words whenever she would call or text me. One day I experienced a powerful loss of faith in what I was doing and searched my house for implements of suicide. The best I could come up with were a hammer and a long nail to drive into my heart. What a dramatic way to go out, and difficult to pull off. Chances are I would only end up with another non-fatal wound. But the suicidal impulse and the gathering of the instruments, I had been told, were enough to have me committed, at least briefly, to a mental institution, which was where I needed to be.

So now I was ready to get help. I was satisfied with my training enough to feel confident anywhere I would have to go, and was eager to induce someone to attack me and rid myself of the curse. I told my mom that I needed to go back to the looney bin, and the long and drawn out process of getting me in there began. If you're not half dead or standing on a ledge, it's actually pretty hard to get in there.

My mom drove me to MHMR and on the way I noticed that the devil was in everyone, some people more than others. Some people appeared to have a complete absence of him. Some people appeared slightly tormented by him, and others satisfied at their union with him. One guy in particular, a tall skinny vaquero looking dude with a cowboy hat, might have been the devil himself for all I knew, he had so much devil in him. So it was more complicated and simple than I had thought before. It was not a man who I had to induce to attack me, but the devil within the man, who would use him like a puppet. I had to challenge the devil himself and beat him with my hands tied behind my back.

When we got to MHMR and I talked to my therapist chick, I burst into tears and told her about how I had laid hands on my girl, lost my will to live, had been awake for about two weeks now, and was feeling suicidal, but I wanted to get help rather than harm myself. Somehow this chick couldn't get it through her thick skull what an emergency this was, and the soothing effect of her simple femininity and psychology calmed me down enough to convince me that all of this was normal. She got me to sign a contract stating that I would not harm myself or anybody else.

As soon as I got out of there, I realized the stupidity of what I had done, and that this contract I had signed would only make it harder for me to get help. My mom was fucking pissed at me and this therapist chick. I had been worrying her to death for the past couple of weeks and she had to take time off work just to drive me around back and forth as I would change my mind between the two extremes of total confidence in myself and complete helplessness with uncontrollable crying spells. Eventually we settled on just going back home.

That night I firmly decided to go to EPPC and demand that they let me in. My worn out, pissed off mom drove me there. In the waiting room, with all those people, I didn't feel right at all. I couldn't sit still in my chair. I was unintentionally sending off random homicidal vibes to innocent people, trying to induce them to attack me and this was the wrong place to do that. There was a lot of paperwork to fill out and it was going to take a long time. The devil was back and he was desperate now. I was writhing in my chair as he tried to possess me and make me murder the people in the room, men, women, children; it didn't matter to him who it would be. He wanted to use me as an instrument of indiscriminant violence toward humanity and prevent me from getting help at any cost. My eyes were trying to roll back into my head as I squirmed in my chair. Everyone was staring at me and whispering to each other. As soon as my mom's back turned, I ran out of there as fast as I could with my hands behind my back.

XXXVIII. THE STONE GARDEN

EL PASO PSYCHIATRIC Center is right next to the graveyard. From the balcony on the third floor, you can see the whole graveyard and just past it is Chico's Tacos. The graveyard is where you would be if you had succeeded and you're so hungry that Chico's Tacos is where you wish you were. That's how standing on the balcony gives you some will to live on.

I felt much better walking the streets by this graveyard with my hands behind my back, every now and then dodging around like a boxer to regain control of my legs as they tried to walk in a direction I didn't want to go. Eventually I got lost, which is what I wanted to do. I walked along a railroad track, crossed a highway, but only when I was sure I was ready to do it without throwing myself into a car, and wound up in a bad looking neighborhood. Surely in here I could find a devil to challenge.

A tough looking dude about my age was walking angrily on the other side of the street. Curiously, there was no devil to be found in him and although he looked violent, I suspected that he must have been on some sort of righteous mission of his own. I kept walking and some hot chick pulled up in a convertible. There was a row of small, connected apartments with bars on their windows to my left. The girl told me, "Hey, would you knock on that door for me?" and pointed in some general direction of those apartments, then she seemed to see something in my eyes that terrified her and drove off. I knocked on the door that looked the most like what she had pointed to and put my hands behind my back again. An old, skinny, balding man with a pot belly, a moustache and glasses answered. I must have gotten the wrong house. What could she have to do with this guy?

"Sorry to bother you so late, man, but some chick in a convertible stopped her car and asked me to knock on your door."

"Oh yeah? What'd she look like?" he took off his glasses and wiped the sleep out of his eyes. For some reason, I wasn't sure if it was me or the devil who wanted my hands to wring his scrawny neck.

"She was pretty hot. I think she was white. She had black hair."

"What are you doing out here so late?"

"Oh, I've been awake for about two weeks now, I'm going insane. I tried to get into the mental institution just now but I felt too claustrophobic in the waiting room so I went for a walk and that's how I ended up here."

He didn't seem too interested in my story and was only standing on his little stoop talking to a lunatic who wanted to murder him just in case that hot chick might come by again. And then she did. She must have just circled the block and come back around. She stopped her car, said, "Meet me at the Howdy's!" and drove away.

"Okay I'll meet you there!" I and the old guy said at the same time.

"I think she was talking to me," I said.

"No, she was talking to me. I know her. She's my friend." He sounded completely full of shit. What a creep.

"Well, let's go together then and wait for her and see who she was really talking to," I said and turned around, walking in the direction of the convenience store. He didn't walk with me.

"Are you wearing handcuffs?" he asked me, now looking a little scared for the first time.

"No, I'm just keeping my hands behind my back because the devil wants me to murder you but I promised my girlfriend I wouldn't fight." He quickly closed his metal door and locked it, then closed the wooden door behind it and locked it too.

I waited at the Howdy's, which was closed but illuminated on the outside, for about an hour smoking cigarettes. She never showed up so I continued wandering around looking for devils. I got a call from my mom and told her I was ok, that I was just walking around because I felt claustrophobic in the waiting room. Then I got a call from a police officer, the coolest cop I have ever met. I explained to him that I was feeling suicidal but I did not want to harm myself and wanted to get help from a mental institution instead. I found a bench to sit on and told him my location based on the street signs around me. He drove up and let me into the backseat without handcuffing me, and took me to UBH (University Behavioral Health), a private psychiatric hospital, and made sure that the people running the place would let me in. My mom was there waiting for me, and as soon as she saw that I was safe in their hands she left. It was morning now.

When the cute nurse came to take my vitals she commented that my hands were ice cold. When she took my temperature it was dangerously low, although I didn't feel particularly cold or warm. She was shocked when I gave her a sample of dark brown opaque urine with just a little bit of blood in it that came out at the end, like a little splash of grenadine in some kind of rotten tequila sunrise. She said that I needed to go to the hospital before I could be admitted into UBH and called for an ambulance. This was the sweetest nurse I have ever met, so genuinely concerned for me that she looked like she was about to cry.

A gay male nurse came with a plate of food for me, bacon, eggs and biscuits. He sat across from me at the table and watched me try to eat it. My mouth would create no saliva for this food. I chewed the first bite as best I could and tried to swallow it, but ended up choking on its dryness and coughing it up onto the plate. I gave it back to him.

"Thanks for the food, man, but it looks like my body doesn't want to eat it," I said. He threw it in the trash and left me alone. Some paramedics came, strapped me to a stretcher, and put me in the back of an ambulance.

At the hospital, the nurse who initially checked my vitals was the same red headed lady who had come to my room to say a prayer for me the last time I was in there. As soon as I saw her I burst into tears and told her that the devil was after me. He was following me and trying to possess me to make me do evil. I felt like I had to fight him but the only way I could win was with my hands behind my back, so I was always jumping around trying to dodge him. Everyone in the room was staring at me with wide eyed religious superstition. I told her that I let the devil possess me by accident one night and now I couldn't get rid of him and he was ruining my life. I had laid hands on my girl and I wanted to fight my best friend who seemed like my enemy now.

"He's your friend," she said, "What is happening to you is real. Jesus can save you." She put her hand on my forehead and said the craziest prayer I've ever heard anyone say, like an exorcist. She seemed to be possessed by some divine force and spoke rapidly. The only words I can remember of it are "...I send confusion into the house of my enemy..." It was one of those scary prayers from The Bible that people said against their enemies in times of war. Maybe a psalm, or something from David, I thought, since he liked to pray against his enemies a lot. Personally, I have never prayed against anyone in my whole life. She got me to say some things about accepting Jesus as my savior and protector, and I said those things sincerely. This lady sure did make me feel better, just having admitted my real problem to someone who believed me and tried to help.

They diagnosed me with a urinary tract infection, an electrolyte imbalance and some other things I can't remember. I lay in a hospital bed, numb and in my own world, occasionally jumping out of bed in terror to do some shadowdodging in the confined space beside my bed. Never know, it might go down in just such a confined space. The sneaky devil was most likely waiting to catch me off guard. It could be anyone. They were suspicious that I might try to hurt myself and assigned me two guards who were cool and mostly just flirted with the pretty nurses who would pass by from time to time, unconcerned with my shadowdodging. A lady, who seemed to be very scared of me, kept bringing me water and food until my body temperature and urine became normal and they decided that my condition was stable enough for me to be admitted to UBH.

XXXIX. PITCH BLACK

UBH WAS DIFFERENT from EPPC. I liked it better right away. It had its own funny system of rules. There was a little station in the middle of everything operated mainly by three black guys. One was an enormous and serious guy with the slightest vestige of an accent from somewhere in Africa, I estimate 300 pounds of muscle, the other an equally built and jolly guy with a strong accent from the some part of the Caribbean, and the third a tiny little gay guy with glasses who was American. They confiscate your phone, but you are allowed to make calls from a landline at this station that are always overheard by someone behind the desk. The only way to get water is by asking someone behind the desk for it. They give it to you one tiny cup at a time. This is so they can take a good look at you periodically and see how you're doing every time you get thirsty. With my urinary tract infection I had to spend a lot of time there drinking little cups of water quickly. I remember the big African guy saying something like "pseudohydrative something or other" and explaining to him that although I wasn't particularly thirsty, I was making myself drink all this water because I had been dehydrated for a long time and had a urinary tract infection.

He took me into an office to explain myself. I told him that my girlfriend had tried something in the bedroom that I didn't like and I grabbed her by the wrist really hard and left bruises on her arm; then I felt so guilty that I lost my will to live and was unable to eat or sleep for two weeks.

"Two weeks without sleep? That's got to be a world record or something," he said. Sarcastically? It must have been, because how many sleepless mental patients had he come across? But the guy had said it with such a straight face and neutral tone of his voice that it was impossible to tell.

"Not even. I've heard that there is a man in China who hasn't slept in years and he's perfectly healthy," I said and something all around me seemed to change by my accurate measuring of myself against an infinity. He asked me what medications I was on and I explained to him how I was not taking anything, but pretending to because of my court order. I also made it clear that I refused to take any medication. He seemed to have heard enough and made some automatic decisions. He closed the binder he had been writing in and showed me to my room. This was a big room with no door and three beds in it. Mine was closest to the doorway. I was told that three times a day I would get to eat a meal from an all you can eat cafeteria for 45 minutes, and twice a day I would get a

20 minute smoke break outside. This sounded great to me. Much more conducive to healing than the smokeless starvation of EPPC.

There were people of all ages in UBH, a bunch of funny people and little kids, and none of them seemed bad at all, just troubled in their own ways. I tried hard not to intimidate anybody with my posture, but somehow it had the opposite effect, and I gave everyone the impression that I was withholding violent intentions. There were no devils here, and there was no devil in me. He had been absent from me ever since my little exorcism in the hospital, but I knew he was around here somewhere, trying to leave me with a false sense of security before the inevitable showdown, so I still kept my guard up mentally and was ready to dodge anything.

When the smoke break came I went outside and sat at an unoccupied table. There was plenty of space around it so I would be able to see any attacker coming and be ready for him. I lit a cigarette, put my hands behind my back, and kept my feet on the ground ready to dodge. At this point I could probably dodge faster than I could swing. I was confident in my abilities.

Then the old man you might remember from EPPC, the one who had exposed himself to Reina and was asked to sit somewhere else by me, walked out. To say he was old is not quite accurate. He may have been in his thirties. He had shoulder length black hair, a beard and moustache, and always wore sunglasses. I had never seen his eyes before. The darkness of his skin and the wrinkles on his face suggested the premature aging of occasional vagrancy. This guy had plenty of devil in him and he walked into the smoking area cockily. When he saw me, he spat on the ground, then gave me a second glance and studied me curiously for a moment. He was completely insane and seemed to know exactly what was going on.

The smoking area was enclosed by four three story walls. He picked up a small rock. He would look up at certain windows of the rooms on the upper levels, then back at me, and scratch a line into the concrete ground between me and each of the windows that he carefully chose. He walked around me, doing this, until he had made a rough, broken circle of scratches on the ground around my table. Then he laughed at me, sat down at a table so that he was facing the right side of me, pulled out one of those little orange, abridged pocket Bibles that are often distributed for free, and started reading it. I did not look at him directly but stared ahead of me, seeing him peripherally.

I could see the devil in him and for a second I definitely smelled fear. So, motherfucker, you're the one who's been caught off guard. I've been ready for you every second of every day and night, ready for any possible opponent you might control, and this is the pawn you bring for me? I could see the devil in him swelling with anger, trying to make himself look bigger to intimidate me. Give this man all your strength, all your power, rage, speed and stamina and make him attack me. Make him fight dirty. I dare you, you little chickenshit motherfucker. You won't win and you won't put a scratch on me. I can dodge this guy for as long as it takes for him to tire out and give up. The man began to breathe heavily. He hunched over and growled at me, building his rage as I sat and stared calmly ahead of me, making no visible acknowledgement of him. I'll even up the ante, you punk bitch. Not only will I beat you with my hands behind my back, I'm gonna keep this cigarette in my mouth the whole time and it won't fall out.

The man suddenly stood up, threw his Bible on the floor, and ran, not at me but at nothing, roared and swung wildly into thin air, punching and kicking and snarling until he was out of breath. Then he turned and stared at me, afraid of something. Me? Himself? Something unknown that had taken control of him? I looked calmly through him at the devil, who knew that I knew he was afraid of me. I won. I had punked the devil. I had even controlled him in a way. It was finally over. The man picked up his bible, went back to his table and read with his back to me. I took the imaginary cuffs off my hands, relaxed, and finished my cigarette.

The devil had been unable to break my will, unable to make me break my word, unable to control me, and had shown that he was not even powerful enough to make someone attack me. Was it the man's will not to attack me, or was it the devil's own cowardice and knowledge that he would lose that made him run in another direction instead of at me? Either way he had shown his impotence. I had won on my own terms and he would never be able to fuck with me again. I was very sure of that. I stood up and once again, I felt like a new man, surging with vitality and stronger than I had ever been before in my entire life, although physically I was in pretty bad shape.

I went back into my room and sat on my bed, watching the people pass by and interact with each other in front of my doorway. Although they were talking to each other they seemed to be speaking for other people and trying to tell me something. I was interested in their conversations and body language. It all somehow reminded me of Reina and me. How was I going to get her back after all of this? Had she already found someone else? I knew I could trust myself not to hurt her again, but after what I had put her through, did I even deserve her? Had I ever even deserved her in the first place?...

My thoughts were interrupted by a group of men who walked into my room. They were the three black guys who operated the little station and two regular sized Mexicans. The African, the obvious leader of the group, had a syringe in his hand. He told me that it was time to take my medicine and we could do it the easy way or the hard way. I said that I refused to take the medicine, and like I had told the cops who drew my blood, I said I wasn't going to swing on them, but I would defend myself. "All I want to do is go take a little walk through the halls. I'm not going to hurt anyone. I just want to go socialize a little bit. I'm feeling much better. Why don't you just let me take a walk?"

"Sure, go ahead, take a walk. We'll just be here watching you to make sure nothing bad happens. We saw that guy get mad at you in the smoking area and we wouldn't want anything bad to happen; that's all," said the African.

"You promise you won't inject me against my will? What's in that needle anyway?"

"It's Ativan and Haldol."

"Well, that does sound pretty good right about now... Why don't you just let me take a little walk, and then inject me with it later when I agree to it? I'll take the shot later. Just not right now." Maybe I would have been a good man if I would have had someone to shoot me in the arm with Haldol and Ativan every day of my life.

"Sure, go for your walk. We won't stop you."

As I slowly walked towards the door, they slowly surrounded me and I knew that I was trapped. "Now!" said the African. The Caribbean guy wrapped his arms around me from behind and lifted me off the ground. I automatically stomped the Mexican guy standing against the wall in the nuts, and with the same leg stomped his chin so I felt his jaw give when his head hit the wall, two quick, precise kicks that broke my promise not to fight, but that shit was out the window now. The Caribbean guy threw me onto my bed and once again I was in a wrestling match with five guys. I heard one of them laugh and say, "This one's got a lot of fight in him." Eventually we were all tangled up so that I couldn't move but I had the Caribbean guy by the thumb in such a way that I was slowly applying pressure that could easily break it and he couldn't escape.

"I got this guy by the thumb! If you don't let me go I'm gonna break his fucking thumb!" I yelled.

"It's true! He has it good! He could break it!" said the panicking Caribbean man. The African grabbed my right arm, turned it over and braced my elbow against the sharp, wooden edge of the bedframe.

"His thumb for your elbow?" he asked, "Either way you are getting a shot. One way you get a broken arm and a lawsuit."

"Fuck," I said and let go of the thumb. The African let go of my arm, pulled my pants down and injected my left butt cheek. I suddenly felt sleepy and weak, but I feigned more of it than was actually there and stopped resisting so they'd get off me.

"Are you done?" somebody asked.

"Yeah, I'm done. I just wanna go to bed now."

"Well, we're going to take you to a chair and re-strain you. Come on, we'll help you walk." I put my arms around two guys who walked me like a drunk man to the chair with the straps. I sat down and allowed myself to be strapped, pretended to fall asleep, and rotated my wrists so that the widest parts would get strapped and I'd have a little room to escape if I turned them the other way. I never got to find out if my Houdini shit would have worked or not because they did a half assed job of strapping my right arm, and as soon as their backs turned I easily and quietly escaped the chair.

They were all laughing in the hallway about our little wrestling match. The Caribbean guy's back was turned to me, and he was so wide that he obscured anyone's view through the doorway of me creeping up on him. I had nothing against the Caribbean guy. I would have done the same to any of them. He just happened to be the one standing there with his back to me, and maybe I did have a slight bias against him for being physically the strongest of them all. The shot had gotten me high, but I still had plenty of strength left in me when I jumped on his back, caught him in a tight rear naked choke, and hooked my legs into his torso. He slammed my back against the wall three times but I couldn't feel pain or let go. He turned around to let somebody pull down my pants and give me another shot.

Next thing I knew I was waking up in my bed. I didn't know how long I had slept, but it wasn't enough. I needed some more of that good shit. I walked drowsily to the little station. There was the Mexican guy who I had kicked in the nuts and jaw. I smiled at him, slapped him on the back and said, "Hey, I'm sorry I kicked you in the nuts last night, man." He laughed and slapped me on the back harder so I slumped forward.

"Don't worry about it. It's just part of my job. It was fun. Best fight we've had in here in a while." The jolly Carribean guy was laughing at me too from behind the desk.

"I'll be careful not to turn my back on you again," he said.

"Nah, you don't gotta worry about it. No more fighting for me in here. All I wanna do is sleep. Can I get another shot of that good shit?"

"Of course!" He went and got an old white doctor with grey hair in a lab coat.

"Give me as much of that shit as I'm allowed to have," I told him, "I have a lot of sleep to catch up on."

"No problem." He smiled, and seemed to take pleasure in pulling the liquid from the little bottles; he looked like he wanted to show off and really knock me on my ass with this dose. He gave me a shot in my left shoulder. It was so strong that I almost fell down when it hit me. The psychiatrist was pleased at my reaction and laughed. I dragged myself back to bed and slept some more, that perfect, dreamless, pitch black sleep. Thank God all this madness was finally over.

XL. CHRIST THE KING

I ATE IN the cafeteria that night. What a cafeteria. Sometimes I think I should eat there every day. Just enough time to wolf down a big meal and come back for seconds. Then I spoke to a psychiatrist lady who prescribed me an antipsychotic Zyprexa. She gave me a little purple one that dissolved under my tongue and tasted like Juicy Fruit chewing gum. It made me really sleepy and hungry in a pleasant way. She asked me if I had anxiety. I said I had plenty. She prescribed me 1mg of Klonopin twice a day. Hell yeah. I finally had some real drugs. At EPPC they would never give me anything good because I had told them of my history of drug abuse. I took a drowsy smoke break and went back to sleep again.

The next day was my birthday. What a shame to have to be institutionalized on my birthday, but it wasn't so bad. It meant that every subsequent birthday would be a celebration not only of my birth but of another year without getting locked up. Reina came to visit me with her mom, looking gorgeous in a long blue dress, her hair perfectly straight with a metal clip in the back, smelling so sweet. She sat on my lap and I squeezed her tightly and made out with her. My dick was perfectly hard, poking against her through the thin dress, and I knew that I could trust this Zyprexa not to put a damper on my sex drive. If anything it seemed to make it even more natural and easy to concentrate on my girl, even in the midst of all these wierdos in the visiting room. Before, my every thought had always been tainted at least by some slight shred of paranoia. For the first time in years I felt totally relaxed.

I had about $450 in unclaimed paychecks and I told Reina I was going to buy her a nice gold chain with a cross on it with that money. What a gal to stick by me through all this. She deserved it. She told me she could not accept a chain from me unless I bought myself one of equal value too. I really wasn't the type of guy who liked to wear jewelry of any kind, so it disappointed me that my girl's chain would be cut in half, but on second thought it wasn't a bad idea, after doing battle with the devil himself, that I should walk with a Jesus around my neck too. I didn't want my girl to leave but when her time was up she had to go. It was ok, they were going to release me the next day and she was coming to pick me up.

She gave me a nice black DKNY sweater and two embarrassingly tight V-neck T-shirts, one white and one black, for my birthday. Reina's mom gave me a silver ring that fit on my index finger. It was a stress ring. It had a ring around it that you could spin when you're stressed out. Reina told me that her dad had one too and that he was always spinning it. Poor guy. Reina's mom. She'll cheat on her husband, stress him the fuck out and give him a silver ring to spin. Was I any better with the gold chain I was about to buy?

My mom came to visit me too and didn't have much time, because I had spent most of it with my girl. She gave me some nice fuzzy slippers that I didn't particularly like, but I didn't even care or have any desire for a birthday present from her. She had done enough just by all I had put her through. I was glad to see some relief in her that I was finally ok and that was the real gift.

I slept well that night. The next day I felt perfectly sane among a group of friendly lunatics. Everything that had happened over the past two weeks didn't make any sense to me. How did I make that guy run up and fight against nothing? That was crazy. I could no longer see galloping devils and I never wanted to see them again. Had I really been in the grip of some sort of demonic possession or did I have some kind of evil split personality within me that had tried to take control? It was too much to think about. The satisfying peace and clarity in my mind was much better. Zyprexa was a miracle drug. Only time would tell, but it seemed like we were made for each other. Not like that cheap ass Risperdal that made me twice as crazy. This stuff was clean.

I skipped all the smoking breaks that day just to prove to myself that I could, and so that I would smell good for my girl. I ate my meals and kept to myself.

Right before I was released that night, on my way out, I noticed a worn out, skinny, tattooed, white man with a shaved head walking funny through the hall.

"Hey, man, your shoes are too big for you, huh?" I asked him.

"Yeah, they are. Somebody gave them to me and they're all I got," he said. I don't remember exactly how it came about through our conversation, but he mentioned to me that he was a homeless Satan worshipper.

"Try on these slippers. They're brand new but I've got plenty of shoes at home and I don't want them." He put them on.

"They fit perfect. Thanks a lot, man!"

"No problem. And good luck." Anybody doing business with that shady ripoff artist needed all the help he could get.

Reina was waiting for me outside. We stopped in a dark neighborhood and did it in her truck. She seemed wounded, starved of sex and affection; the way I made her cum several times so easily and greedily was enough evidence for me to back up her word that she had not been with another man during our time apart. I didn't want to know. We went to my house and continued until it was time for her to go home. Everything was right again, or even better now than it was before. I took my Zyprexa, in solid, undissolving form (two 5mg at night and one in the morning), and went to sleep.

The next day, while Reina was at school, I took

the bus and collected my checks from La Planeta Café and Redcats, cashed them at Wal-Mart, then went downtown and browsed the Jewelry stores looking for the right chains. I got a thin, feminine 10k gold rope with a plain 18k cross with no Jesus hanging from it for Reina and a unisex looking 10k chain for myself. The cross I chose was hollow in the back, so it appeared to be made of more material than it actually was, and had a white gold Jesus nailed to it. Not that I like the idea of Him suffering like that, but I wanted to make sure He was on there to protect me. I didn't like the hollowness of the back but it was the only one with Jesus on it that I could afford. Reina's chain was about $50 more expensive than mine but I didn't tell her. She was very happy with it when I gave it to her and full of religious pride that we should have matching crosses.

Coincidentally, the very next day was a Catholic holiday where people make a pilgrimage to the top of Mt. Cristo Rey. I went with Reina, her father, her sister, her brother, and her aunt. Even though her mother's sister was there, Reina's mother was absent, suggesting that Reina's mother and father couldn't stand to be around each other so badly that they alternated religious holidays. Did they even live together? Looking back, he must have had a woman of his own on the side, but had the decency not to expose her to his children.

Mt. Cristo Rey is a mountain in Sunland Park, New Mexico that is lined with little hiking trails that lead to various shrines of different saints, which you can choose to skip by route of a direct shortcut to the top, where you can meet the giant Jesus on the cross, Who you may have seen a million times from a distance but never met in person.

The mountain is a beautiful work of art and nature. We chose to take the long way with no shortcuts and visit every shrine. Reina's aunt had something interesting to say about each of the obscure saints and virgins that I had never heard of along the way. I saw many people taking the entire journey barefoot, many with old wooden crosses, or plastic rosaries around their necks. Everyone had something, and the wooden ones on the barefoot people made mine feel cheap around my neck.

When we finally got to the top, we stayed there for a long time praying to that huge statue of Jesus. This was the Jesus of El Paso; although He resides in New Mexico, it's us He faces. The Jesus at the top of Mt. Cristo Rey is not a crucifixion because He is not nailed to the cross and his palms face downward in a gesture of blessing. He has long straight hair, is not naked at all but fully robed. He is not thin, and has plenty of meat on his bones. He is racially ambiguous. His face is serious, because every day, from his view, He can see all of the things people do in our wicked city. He looks strong and tough and well fed.

XLI. WIN, LOSE, OR DRAW

ONE DAY I came out in the street and said what's up to Dogoberto. He walked up to me with his arms hanging widely, an unconscious posture to appear bigger when threatened. My arms were relaxed.

"Hey, that was fucking sick how you dodged my whole bumrush that night!" I said. We reenacted our scuffle in slow motion, sparring friends again. The red headed lady was right. We went to the bar and on the way I told him how I had wanted to call him out and fight him again so bad that I went insane and had to go to UBH and now I was taking crazy pills again. I also told him that one of the reasons I had bumrushed him that night was because I didn't like how he had been hitting on my sister when she moved back in and even treating her disrespectfully. I never hit on his sister or treated her with disrespect, or anyone in his family. But I should have talked to him about it rather than build up rage and distrust against him until it blew up into violence.

This seemed to make him angry, and for a moment in the silence I knew we were both contemplating stopping the car to throw down, but changed our minds and decided it would be better if we stayed on the same side. We went to Texas T's and talked about fighting and how we liked to fuck our girlfriends. We talked about our enemies and guys from the bars who we didn't like and wanted to fuck up, the usual stuff.

It was good to have my friend back, and as is often the case when two men who are like brothers fight each other, it only strengthened our friendship after we talked it out. In the case of Silent, it was not like that. He would remain unforgiven for his act of disrespect (although I had found out that it probably wasn't even my sister in that picture anyway; I'd never know for sure), and although we would not be enemies, we would never be friends again. We would even shake hands when we saw each other and he would treat me with exaggerated politeness, knowing that one slight remark would result in a rematch that I wanted more than he did.

His brother, Valdo, I would always consider my mortal enemy, and although I would not pursue revenge against him, I would eternally be preparing and arming myself just in case he should ever rear his ugly head and take another strike at my family. If I ever saw him I would call him out, win, lose, or draw. I would never fully relax until he was dead. I knew that I would outlive him, no matter how he would die, because he was already getting old and many people wanted him dead. At this time, I believe he was locked up, to my satisfaction.

XLII. BEAST OF BURDEN

I REMEMBER SHE was so verbally abusive to me one night that I tried to break up with her, then she came to my house crying and begging me to stay with her, pulled a knife from the kitchen and looked like she was about to use it on herself before I gently disarmed her, took her to bed and promised never to leave her. When I told my mom what had happened, it made her cry that I would allow a girl to treat me so bad and then keep her.

I applied for a job at the Seashell Oyster Bar. I told Reina about it and she said that her friend's dad owned the place and she could pull some strings to ensure my employment there, but I had better do a good job or it would make her look bad. I would have preferred to get the job from my own merits, but she insisted on doing it her way. I got the probationary under the table period of the job and I enjoyed it. This was my kind of place. A kitchen full of only guys where we could talk as dirty as we wanted to without any women to offend.

The main chef said I was doing a good job and quickly mastering the food, which was good and easy to make. I had to do one hell of a job to clean up their filthy kitchen though, which was not up to my standards at all. It turned out that the boss had only hired me to put some of his slacker employees on edge and make them work harder with fear that they might be replaced, and as soon as he had accomplished that, he fired me out of the blue, on the basis that the kitchen was too small for that many workers. That caused Reina to be so abusive to me that I had to break up with her.

I called my paternal grandmother one day and told her about it, and I broke down and cried to her over the phone about how badly I missed my girl. I collected my small check from the oyster bar, got back together with her after three days of being apart, and spent all my money on her. Her family was very angry at me now for breaking up with their prized daughter and I would have to do a lot to redeem myself. They were the type of people who verbally abused each other frequently and lowered each other's self esteem at the drop of a hat just to make sure that nobody ever got too happy or confident unless they had lived up to each other's unreasonable expectations, and they didn't understand my rejection of that philosophy.

Thanksgiving, my favorite holiday, was spent in my usual way: excessive, gluttonous partying. Turkey and wine and sex and too much Klonopin. I'd fuck my girl, leave her in the bedroom to eat and party some more, then fuck her again, and repeat this process over and over. All she wanted to do was cuddle and I wanted to party. She said she had a dream that I hit her with a beer bottle. When she left, sad and neglected, I smoked some chronic. I could feel her presence, so far away from me, this delicate and beautiful creature who was so devoted to me and desired to procreate with me with all her natural instincts. I sat on the couch drooling over her for the rest of the night, thinking over and over, "I love my girlfriend so much…"

Christmas time came around and I had to do something in her family's eyes to make up for my unforgivable act of breaking up with her. I had to hustle up some money to buy her a present. I used the Christmas money sent by my father's side of the family to buy some chronic and rode the bus for days, selling weed right there on the bus to people who looked to me like potheads. I barely broke even before my mom found out what I was doing and got mad, so I said Merry Christmas and distributed the remaining weed to her, my sister, and Dogoberto. I went over to his house and gave him some weed, which I didn't want to smoke; it was a rare thing for me to do. Then he bought a bunch of beer and I busted out with the Klonopin and we crushed a bunch of them up, snorted them and got retarded.

The Christmas present I ended up buying for Reina was a silver ring with cubic zirconia all over it and a big sapphire in the middle for about sixty bucks. She wore it on her marriage finger as a symbol that I was her boyfriend, and it slightly mollified her impossible family, who would continue to resent me, probably for the rest of our lives.

By now I was on probation, and although it was a violation for me to leave town, Reina convinced me to go to Las Vegas with her, her mom, sister, and little brother to celebrate New Year's Eve. I really didn't want to, because I was almost broke and would be relying on her to feed me. But somehow she made me do it. Her mother left her own truck in my yard, and we drove out to Las Vegas in her sancho's big ass truck. The nature of her sancho was still a mystery to me. Reina's aunt and her husband and little son went with us in their own vehicle.

Our time in Las Vegas was spent mostly walking around as drunken tourists with giant beer bongs full of piña colada, since you can drink anywhere you want in Las Vegas and the crime of public intoxication doesn't exist there as far as I know. Reina and I had a lot of fun doing a little prank where we would go in front of a crowd of people, I'd get down on bended knee and say to her in front of everyone, "Reina, I have always loved you since the moment I first saw you and I want to be with you forever!" Then I'd pull out the ring I gave her for Christmas and present it to her, "Will you marry me?"

"Yes! Of course I will!" Then we would kiss and I'd pick her up and spin her around in my arms and the crowd of people we were performing for would say "Awwww!" We really got a kick out of that sarcastic proposal of ours and I think we must have done it about five times. So technically was she my fiancée? We passed by one of those places where you can get married by a justice of the peace Elvis impersonator, and Reina and I were so drunk that I took her by the arm in that direction, but her family all saw what we were trying to do and ran up and stopped us, shocked and terrified at the thought of such an improper wedding, or maybe at the thought of us getting married at all.

It was a sexless and exhausting vacation of windowshopping at the fanciest malls and hotels I had ever seen. Gambling was forbidden and it was all I wanted to do. Smoking was forbidden and I wore nicotine patches to ward off grumpiness. When the New Year was only minutes away and the countdown was drawing near, the streets were so packed that we had to make a ring around the children and brace our bodies together with all our combined strength against the pressure of the crowd that could have otherwise crushed them.

The countdown was chanted, the fireworks went off, and we went on the journey through the anarchic and vomit encrusted streets of the Las Vegas strip back to the cheapest hotel with the giant clown on it where we stayed. There, we were presented with handwritten bills from Reina's mother stating that we owed her $240 each for our stay. I made no agreement to pay this bill, nor did I say I wasn't going to pay it, but I crumpled it up and threw it in the trash as soon as I was out of her sight. Reina's mom would never get that money from me. Never.

When we got back to El Paso, Reina's mom got me a job at Freedom Taxes. She wanted me to work there and pay her back the money I "owed" her. This was a degrading and physically demanding job where I had to dress up like the Statue of Liberty in the icy weather of January and February and wave at cars and spin a sign pointing to the office. I would come home with stiffness in my joints for chump change. I'm sure you've seen these wavers before. I lost no favor in Reina's eyes by taking up such a crappy profession. To her, "a job was a job," and she was proud of me just for working.

I used the money I got from this job to take her out on expensive dinners mostly, and when February came around, I had to save up to buy her a Valentine's Day gift. She wanted a Michael Kors watch, a specific one, which was tacky and ugly to me. She would leave little ads from the mall on my counter with watches in them circled. "Hint hint" I hated everything made by that brand, trendy, worthless items that depreciated in value instantly the moment the newer ones came out, not like things made of diamonds and gold and silver. I quit my job as a waver, just plain sick of the bullshit, and when I got paid I was $40 short of a Michael Kors watch. So I went to J. Edwards Diamonds and spent $200 on some beautiful earrings made of silver with real diamonds in them. Each one had a big purple amethyst heart in it, representing the month of February and Valentine's Day in general. It also came with a bouquet of half a dozen red roses that I had to pick up from a flower shop far away. I ended up miscalculating the address, taking the bus way too far, having to run about a mile in the cold and barely made it before the deadline to pick up those roses.

When she heard she was not going to get her Michael Kors watch, she got pissed and didn't come to see me on Valentine's Day. She didn't act like she was pissed but she was and her lame excuse for not seeing me that night was that she was on probation (for her resisting arrest conviction that she never protested against) and that it was unsafe to violate it by coming to my house after her curfew, even though she had violated that curfew a million times to come to my house and get fucked. I should have given her NOTHING.

Once again, even with a girlfriend, I didn't get laid on Valentine's Day and spent it the usual way, with King Cobras. I decided that Valentine's Day was not a day for romance at all, and I would never try to spend it that way again. It was a day strictly for the drowning of sorrows. Reina's mom and dad had gotten married on Valentine's Day. It must be bad luck.

The next day she came to collect her gifts and still didn't put out, just picked up her shit and went home. Then she called me and told me that her tiny grandmother had said that the earrings were nice, but she needed to find a man with more stability, money, and education if she wanted to have a happy future. I was so insulted. I called my aunt, my mom's sister, and told her about all this and she said that no guy had ever bought her anything so nice for Valentine's Day and that my girlfriend was a stupid, ungrateful little bitch. It felt good to hear someone say it for me.

I took her out to dinner. She wore a purple dress to match the earrings. And only after that dinner did she belatedly and selfishly put out in honor of Valentine's Day. I decided that I would never marry this girl, or any girl who refused to put out on Valentine's Day. If I would have had any balls at all, I should have broken up with her right there, once and for all for being such a spoiled little bitch, but I decided to set my mind on finding a replacement for her first. (Not to mention the fact that Reina couldn't even cook. I'll never marry a woman who can't cook.)

Valentine's Day is a day when men emasculate themselves and dress in pink shirts, spray cologne until they smell like Pepe Le Pew, and walk around with heart shaped balloons hanging out of their asses just so that a girl can have the pleasure of putting her special pussy that is like no other up on an unreachable pedestal and deny it to the man who tried so hard in vain to satiate her materialistic whims, as if to say "My priceless pussy can't be bought. How dare you insult me with those expensive gifts?" But who knows? Maybe if I would have put up the extra $40 for the stupid watch she would have sucked me off all day, and then her grandma sucked me off all night. Fucking whores. They should be dickslapped to death.

I think Valentine's Day should be a special, intimate day, where you permit yourself the rare indulgence of feeling sorry for yourself and getting drunk and high and fucked up out of your mind on the best shit you can find. Save up your money in advance, not to buy some stupid shit for a girl, but so you can afford to sniff coke all day until your heart explodes with joy. That's the way to do it. My Valentine's Day spirit has been broken. I've never even heard a story about that day that had a happy ending. The happy ending is the one where you don't stick a gun in your mouth and blow your brains out.

XLIII. MOST DEEPEST THROAT

IF YOU THOUGHT the story of Shameless James coming out of the closet and inviting me to a bisexual clusterfuck was awful, and if you thought the story of pimping out Rosie for a dollar was ruthless, that's nothing compared to my blackest tale of Most Deepest Throat.

Reina went out of town on one of those ACTS retreats for two weeks. During this time, I was determined to find a replacement, substitute, or long term side chick, so Dogoberto and I went to the bars as much as we could looking to pick up chicks. One night we did a bunch of coke and went to Botellas. As we played pool, I got a text message on my phone from a number I didn't recognize, something like, "Hi."

"Who's this?"

"Missy."

"Do I know you from somewhere?"

"We met at a bar one time." It was possible that I had met some weird chick named "Missy" at a bar one time and didn't remember her, but it was sketchy.

"What do you look like?"

"5'2", long black hair" Could be any bitch.

"What are you doing tonight?"

"I wanna get fucked." I showed this to Dogoberto. We agreed that this was very sketchy. Could be a guy, could be anything. We decided to go together and investigate this mystery. And it only got deeper.

"Where do you live?"

"Email me a picture of you first. mostdeepestthroat@iforgot.com" I showed this to Dogoberto and we laughed uncontrollably. Had to be bullshit. So I sent a picture of myself. Most Deepest Throat was satisfied and gave us the address.

"How about I bring my friend and we tag team the shit out of you tonight?"

"Is he handsome?"

"Almost as handsome as me."

"Sounds good to me."

"Ok. We're on our way. We're gonna bring beer." We did some more coke in the car, bought a twelve pack of Budweiser, and mentally armed ourselves for whatever danger we might be stepping into, prepared to take guns or knives away from people, prepared to beat the shit out of them and rob them for their deception. Whatever it was, we were pretty sure it wasn't a girl, but why not make sure just in case? Never know, there are all kinds of horny freaks out there. We pulled up to the house, which was near the bar, only a few blocks away, a nice two story house in a little cul de sac. I called Most Deepest Throat, "We're here."

"The door's open. Just let yourself in. I'll be waiting." The voice sounded like an older woman, but it could easily have been a man impersonating one. We walked into a filthy, dark living room, beer cans all over the floor everywhere. I felt like I was in a horror movie. A naked, terrified, white man suddenly ran out of a room to our right, holding his clothes in his arms, and said, "It's a guy!" He ran out the door without even putting his clothes on inside the house. Someone was crawling on the floor in the dark. He came near me and took a swipe at my dick, but I saw it coming and I jumped back and dodged it. Dogoberto and I quickly stepped way back towards the door.

"We know you're a guy. Turn on the fucking lights," I said.

"Don't worry, we're not gonna hurt you. Don't be scared. Just turn on the lights," said Dogoberto.

"Yeah, come on. Just turn on the lights. We're not gonna have sex with you but we can still kick it and drink some beers," I said. He crawled up the stairs and turned on the lights. Then we were howling with laughter. I laughed so hard that my side hurt. The worst parody of a woman I'd ever seen. Some short, balding, wretched little middle aged guy in a bad wig and some crappy lingerie.

"Come here," Dogoberto told him, "Let me feel your tits." He walked obediently to Dogoberto, who pulled down Most Deepest Throat's brazier and pinched his sorry excuses for tits. He laughed, "Hey, come feel his tits. Tell me what you think." I walked up to the guy and pinched his weird, flabby pectoral muscle.

"These titties ain't shit, man. You need to get some implants or something if you ever plan on fooling anyone," I said.

"I'm taking hormones," he said.

"Well, they must have not kicked in yet, cuz you still look like a fucking dude."

"Come on, sit down. Let's drink some beers," said Dogoberto. We sat down on the guy's nice couches. I suddenly felt like I wanted to take a shower. There was probably shit and sperm and all kinds of hepatitis on these couches. We all opened up some beers and were quiet for a minute. Then we burst out laughing again at this ridiculous guy and this ridiculous situation. Then we got serious all of a sudden.

"Dude... What happened to you?" I asked.

"Yeah, how the fuck did you get like this?" asked Dogoberto.

"Nothing bad ever happened to me. Ever since I was a little kid I always wanted to be a girl. So this is what I do," said Most Deepest Throat, "Guys come to me because I do things their wives won't. I take it in the ass, and I give the best head."

"Guys come to you because they're fucking faggots," I said. "Does your dick even get hard? Are you just like a walking wannabe pussy?"

"My dick never gets hard. My ass is better than a vagina," said Most Deepest Throat.

"You can't say that if you've never had pussy

before. Girls got three holes, and you only got two," said Dogoberto.

Most Deepest Throat asked us if we had ever heard of Morrissey. I said I had. He's a musician who claims to be asexual.

"What's that?" asked Dogoberto.

"It means he don't like chicks or dudes, or any kind of sex at all."

"That's fucking weird."

"Yeah, it is." Most Deepest Throat went and came back with his most prized possession, a book of Morrissey autographed by the whole band, who he had met in person after their concert. He sat next to me and showed me a picture of the guy.

"What do you think of him?"

"I dunno. Looks like a fag," I said. Most Deepest Throat touched my hand. "I don't mean to be homophobic or anything, but you need to stop touching me and go back over there or I'll be quick to fuck you up right here in your own house." He scurried back to his chair.

"Come with me, let me show you something," he said. Dogoberto and I looked at each other uneasily, then followed him to a bedroom. He got on the bed and pulled out the biggest, fattest, longest white dildo I've ever seen, double sided with two dick-like heads, about six inches in diameter and three feet long.

"Holy shit!" said Dogoberto. Most Deepest Throat pulled down his panties. I turned away, gagging.

"Dude, you need to put that shit away or I'm gonna fucking puke. Please don't do that, man," I said.

"Ok. I see you guys are really not into it. That's cool. Wanna go upstairs and do some coke?"

"Yeah that sounds much better," I said, relieved as soon as he put his giant dildo away. We went into a little dark room with a little set of drawers. Most Deepest Throat opened one of them and took out a dub, chopped it up, and divided it into three equal lines. He had a little straw, did his line through it, offered it to me, but I refused and did my line without any kind of straw, as was my custom. Dogoberto did the same. We went back downstairs and drank some more beer from a 30 pack in Most Deepest Throat's fridge. Dogoberto had fixed a weird stare on Most Deepest Throat.

"Dude. I wanna piss on you," he told Most Deepest Throat.

"No, don't do that! I don't want to," he said and got all bashful like a little schoolgirl. I started laughing my ass off. This was too fucking ridiculous.

"Come on. Just let me piss on you," he was staring harder at him, more dominantly now.

"No." He shook his head.

"Come on, dude. Obviously you got no fucking self respect. You'll probably like it," I said, "Take a golden shower!" We all busted out laughing this time, even Most Deepest Throat. He was warming up to the idea.

"Just go upstairs. Get in the bathtub. And I'm gonna piss on you," Dogoberto said, calmly and authoritatively. Most Deepest Throat responded to this tone of voice.

"Ok," he said. We walked up the stairs. I stopped in the hallway near the room with the set of drawers we did coke off. I watched Most Deepest Throat get on his knees in the bathtub and pull the shower curtain to the side. Dogoberto whipped out his dick and started pissing all over him. Most Deepest Throat made a grab at Dogoberto's dick, but he pushed his hand away and aimed his stream of piss upwards so that it made an arc into Most Deepest Throat's mouth. To this day, the image of that piss going into the dude's mouth is still the funniest thing I've ever seen in my life. It pops into my head from time to time and I end up laughing to myself for no reason.

I quickly stepped into the coke room and started opening the drawers. Dildos, a set of graduated metal butt plugs, all kinds of disgusting instruments of sodomy covered with invisible fecal matter, then I found the right drawer that contained six dubs of coke! I put them in my pocket and went back to where I had been standing before. Most Deepest Throat didn't even know I jacked him! They were done. Dogoberto and I walked down the stairs as Most Deepest Throat dried himself with a towel. Dogoberto ran to the guy's fridge and jacked most of a 30 pack of Budweiser from it. I took the remainder of our twelve pack. We made a break for it. All I heard was "My beer!" from behind us. We got in the van and drove back to our neighborhood.

We stayed up all night and into the afternoon doing coke and drinking beer. Dogoberto had even jacked the dude's cigarettes, so plus the ones we already had, we had everything we needed. If you would have been in my neighborhood all you would have heard was two guys howling with laughter and snickering. We contemplated little schemes of going back to his house and punishing him even more, duck taping him to a chair and stealing his TV and computers and all his furniture, but decided it wouldn't work because he knew my phone number, had a picture of me, and my email address, so it would be easy for him to get the cops on me.

The next day Dogoberto told me that he went to work and told all his coworkers about how he had pissed on Most Deepest Throat and said, "So if any of you guys are gay, you might wanna keep it to yourselves, because I piss on faggots now!"

I still have no idea where Most Deepest Throat got my number, but for the next few days he would keep texting me, asking me to come over and do coke with him again. Then I'd tell him "Stop texting this number you fucking faggot!" and he'd ask what about the other guy? If I gave him Dogoberto's number, he might go and do coke with Most Deepest Throat every time he had to take a piss. After a couple of days Most Deepest Throat gave up and I never heard from him again. He was the saddest character I have ever met, a guy whose sexuality was so ruined and distorted that the man he admired most in the world was one who claimed to have no sexual desires at all.

XLIV. DON MAGNÍFICO

MY RELATIONSHIP WITH Reina wasn't all bad. There was plenty of goodness in it that kept us together. One thing I really liked was her sexy lingerie that she was always buying. She'd make me wait in the next room while she put it on, and then I'd walk in to a nice surprise. She'd leave that stuff at my house, so when she was gone, a lot of times I'd sniff her panties and jerk off. I loved the smell of her pussy.

We had a little role playing game that we had developed. It had started way back in the mental institution. One night she passed me a note asking me if I had a big dick. I wrote back to her that it was magnificent. She looked up at me skeptically, put her hands together and slowly took them apart.

"Tell me when to stop," she said. I stopped her at about seven inches. She was disappointed.

"Hey I never said it was big, I just said it was magnificent." Then I passed her a note asking how big her nipples were. I made a little circle with my thumb and index finger and let it slowly expand until it was a big circle made with two hands, since she never stopped me. "Really?! They're that big? Wow! It's ok,

I'm sure I'll love them just the way they are."

"They're not really that big!" she said and showed me with her hands two circles that represented some average sized nipples.

Since then she would call my dick "Magnífico". Sometimes she would say, "I want Magnífico tonight," or "Bring me Magnífico!" Then I started calling myself Don Magnífico. This was a guy who spoke Spanish badly and with a rough voice like some bad guy in a telenovela. I would say things like, "¡Dámelo tu panocha, puta, porque soy El Don Magnífico!"

"¡Ay, por favor, Señor Don Magnífico!" She would beg exaggeratedly, "¡Dime más tiempo!"

"¡No!" and it would lead to rough sex.

One time I went with her to one of her ACTS meetings. On the way, for some reason she kept looking at me with narrowed eyes and calling me "white meat!" under her breath. It took me a few minutes to come up with a comeback for this.

"If you're gonna call me White Meat, I'm gonna call you Colitas de Pavo from now on."

"No!" she said but she was laughing and I could tell she liked it. When we got to church for the ACTS meeting she went around with her big ass crying to everyone, "My boyfriend calls me Colitas de Pavo!" just to make everybody laugh at us.

One time she came to my house to pick me up; when I tried to get in the truck she drove away a little bit so I'd have to walk a little more and try again. I shrugged like I could care less about going wherever we were about to go and acted like I was walking back into my house. Then she drove off. I turned around and chased her truck, jumped into its bed, and at the same time she hit the brakes so I crashed into the back of the truck's cab and hurt myself a little bit but didn't care. I slid open the little window at the back of the cab and squeezed myself through it. We were laughing.

"You should keep that window locked or some guy could crawl in like I just did and rape you," I said.

"Oh no! Please don't rape me!" She threw her hands up with sarcastic fear.

"Too late. This is what I do to girls who leave their window open!" and I fucked her right there in the middle of my street in broad daylight, the truck bouncing up and down on its suspension.

Sometimes we would get all dressed up to go on some fancy date, like to a play at UTEP, or a little concert, or to a nightclub, and just get bored in the middle and go do it in the truck. It's safe to say that a big part of what kept us together was that no matter how bad we would fight and argue, the sex was almost always great.

There came a day when I finally mastered her. It was an idea that had been floating around in my head for some time. I had noticed that after I would make her cum, if I didn't cum inside her, the texture of her pussy would change. It would no longer feel so watery, but more oily. That new oily liquid she would make, I hypothesized, was some form of female cum.

It gave me an idea.

My granny had been moved to a nursing home where people could take care of her, so her house was empty again and I would sometimes use it as a fuck pad. There was a blister sheet full of Tramadol, a synthetic opiate painkiller, on the counter, so I'd take like six of those and be secretly high while I kicked it with my girl.

I took Reina there one night, made her cum, felt that oily stuff come down and refused to let myself inseminate her. As long as that oily stuff was there, it was ten times easier to make her cum, and I stubbornly gave her sixteen screaming orgasms in a row that night. Then she begged me to cum inside her, like a cherry on top, so I did.

"How did you do that?" she asked me, all out of breath. I explained to her about the oily female cum and how I could use it to create infinite orgasms in her as long as I didn't cum inside. "Wow!" she said, staring wide eyed ahead of her, "Wow." Then she went on my Granny's laptop and started looking at engagement rings and telling me which ones she liked. I guess I must have fucked her so good she wanted to get married as soon as possible now. We did it a few more times, more for me than for her, because after the sperm was inside I couldn't really do the multiple screaming orgasm thing to her, but I still had to get my rocks off.

We had a little fight about something, I can't remember what it was, something stupid I said that hurt her feelings. We stayed obstinately silent. I wanted a cigarette. I was high as fuck off Tramadol. Then I got an idea. I told her I'd be right back. I ran to Tortillas Diaz, a little tortilleria near my Granny's house. On the side of the building there is a little shrine of the Virgin Mary with candles and plastic flowers. I stole some plastic flowers, ran back and gave them to her. That made her happy and we did it again. She returned to the computer, looking at rings again.

I remember lying there on the bed, high as fuck, feeling so good, and thinking, "This is perfect. This is the best day of my life," then questioning it, "This is great, but, is that it? There has to be something better than this. There's something missing. Do I even really love this girl? I know I love her in many ways, but I sure as hell don't want to marry her. I've been leading her on like I do just to keep having sex with her and I don't know where I'm going to come up with four grand for the kind of engagement ring she wants. There are so many better ways I'd like to spend four grand if I had it. Even a nice vacation with her somewhere in the Caribbean would be better. There has to be a better love than this hollow pleasure I feel. I don't mean to be ungrateful; this is awesome, really awesome, but I have to be honest with myself. It's just sex and drugs and I know it. This is not true love."

I had decided long ago that I would only marry for true love, not for convenience, not for practicality or out of desperation, not for anything less, not even for my child if I didn't truly love its mother. I'd rather die a bachelor. After that night, our relationship, which had had its ups and downs before, began its rapid and final decline.

XLV. GOOD TIMES, BAD TIMES

FIRST, SHE BECAME selfish in bed. I had to do the multiple orgasm thing to her every night and I'd only get one nut off and then she'd go to sleep. I'd lie awake in bed with a boner, fully capable of doing it like five more times like I was used to. Sometimes I'd jack off. Sometimes I'd try to fuck her in her sleep but it never worked. One time I squeezed her butt cheeks around my dick like a hotdog bun, fucked that, and left sperm all over the inside of her ass crack. She acted like she was asleep for that one, but there's no way she wasn't awake. All in all, I was walking around sexually frustrated, and a man with a girl-friend shouldn't have to be.

I got a job at Wal-Mart as a cashier. This was a job that I really enjoyed. It was not like working in a kitchen where you're stuck in a little room with the same people day in, day out. I got to meet tons of people every day and make smalltalk with them. And I was good at it. I quickly became the fastest cashier in the place. I could get rid of big lines during a rush with ease.

Reina went on a diet and off her meds at the same

time. This was a type of diet that allowed her to eat very little food. So her starvation mixed with the stress of going off meds made her really grumpy and weird. We would get into fights over the most stupid shit. Like she was saying that she was jealous of her friend, whose boyfriend had bought her one of those cheap costume jewelry necklaces from Forever 21 in honor of their two month anniversary, and how I needed to buy her necklaces from Forever 21. In my mind I'm thinking, "Bitch, you're walking around with a gold chain around your neck that you got after two months, jealous of a fucking plastic one!" but I told it to her in a much more reasonable way. She was saying I needed to write her letters; I needed to take her out to eat more; I wasn't romantic. I took her out to eat as much as I could, but she couldn't even eat anything so she would find no pleasure in it other than dressing up for the date and being seen. True, maybe I could have written her some love letters every now and then, but I didn't know how to handle her like this.

Was I romantic? I thought so, but we had two different ideas of romance. Mine was taking a nice walk together with a good view. Hers was doing formal expensive things.

Sometimes she'd be totally nice to me, and then all of a sudden she'd have an explosion of rage and vicious verbal abuse, a snarling voice that would echo in my head for days. I picked up on the pattern and realized that it was only when she would see me feeling happy and confident that she would get this rage and have to belittle me. And all this time I thought it was money! No, it was worse, because I had money now (not that much, but a steady full time minimum wage job's worth) and she was treating me worse than ever. And I never belittled her. I was always nice to her. I would always shower her with compliments and try my best to make her feel good about herself, because she was so sensitive. Just one mean word could send her into a deep depression. She could dish it out but she couldn't take it. It was not in my nature to belittle her, even if maybe that's what she deserved.

At the same time, on her new diet, she was getting hotter every day. Skinnier, but with the same big ass. The new narrowness of her waist exaggerated her wide hips and ass, even made her small breasts more noticeable. Those long skinny legs would drive me nuts and her long hair was down to her ass now. Even her face got a little skinnier, showing her cheek bones and making her lips and eyes look exaggeratedly large. She was ridiculously fine now, and as vicious to me as she was good looking. We would have crazy angry sex. She would scratch me more than she used to, sadistically now, so my back was always covered in bloody wounds and as soon as the sex was over, she would find something to argue about. I was starting to feel like she hated me. She definitely hated to see me happy. She was so hot that I would take any abuse just to have sex with her, and I would almost always get only one nut, so I would make it last as long as I could. I started hating myself and even feeling a little suicidal, just plain trapped. Every day she would destroy my confidence, the main thing that women are attracted to even in the ugliest of men, so I couldn't even find another girl to take her place. I think that's really why she was doing that. She must have sensed that I was searching for another girl and instinctively tried to cripple me any way she could.

I had been hiding from Paloma from the convenience store for a long time. I hadn't seen her once for the entirety of my relationship with Reina. I had several reasons. At first, it was because I was afraid that seeing her would put me on some kind of flashback of all that craziness when I had the delirium tremens. Earlier in my relationship it was also because I thought I loved Paloma more, and I felt that just to look upon her would be cheating on Reina. Also I didn't know how to act in front of Paloma now that I had a girlfriend. I couldn't possibly go in there with a false air of indifference toward her.

I started longing for Paloma again, and the purchasing of alcohol that I associated with her, as I always did when I was feeling low. I was covered in sweat and scratches, even had hickeys on my neck, after one long, drawn out session with Reina, and I decided to go show off to Paloma. I knew she would be there. I asked Reina if I could borrow her truck so I could go buy some beer. She gave me the keys and I went to the store.

Paloma was looking just as fine as ever, and when she saw me all sweaty and sexed up, (also physically much larger than she had ever seen me, since that Zyprexa made me gain a lot of weight and muscle; I was 200 pounds and in great shape) we looked at each other like we never had before. The look she gave me was kind of shy and startled at first; she gave a little gasp, and then a sly smile that seemed to say, "you dirty dog" and the casual smile I gave her said, "I am a dirty dog. Just imagine the things I'd do to you..." I went home. Reina slept with her head in my lap that night as I daydreamed about Paloma and drank King Cobras, just like I used to in the bad old days.

One day, I had a lot of fun at work and I was in a great mood. I always had a habit that when Reina would go out with her friends to the club, I would stay up all night and wait for her to call me when she was safe at her house before I could go to sleep. This wasn't really out of a fear that she would cheat on me, although it slightly was; it was more out of a lingering fear that something bad would happen to her like when the sheriff beat her up. Tonight was one of those nights, and I was eagerly awaiting a call from her and planning on sharing my good mood with her and having some nice conversation. But when she did call me, it was the worst, most brutally abusive call I had ever received. It blew my mind. The tone of her voice was like a snarling dog behind a fence. When I hung up with her I felt like I wanted to kill myself. We had planned for me to take her out to the country bar, Whiskey Dick's the next day, but after that call, I didn't think I had it in me.

I was depressed all day at work and unfocussed, dreading the idea of going out with my mean girlfriend or ever seeing her again. My mom picked me up from work that night and Reina called me while I was in the car. I told her I had to cancel our plans because she was too mean to me last night. I didn't want to go anywhere with her ever again.

"What, you can't take it?" she kept saying.

"I shouldn't have to take it. Why should I have to take shit from anyone? I'm not mean to you. Why you gotta be so mean to me?" Then she started snarling at me again and the sound of it even shocked my mom. I hung up on her. I went to a bar and got $100 drunk that night. I was completely shitfaced and I broke up with Reina by text message. I had tried to do it over the phone but it was impossible to talk to her. We had been together for nine months. I had double vision and couldn't even walk straight when I got out of that bar, and I felt relieved, free at last. My mom came to pick me up and she was glad too. I slept soundly that night, until I heard a knock at my door. It was Reina. She didn't say anything, walked quickly into my room, gathered her lingerie, slapped me in the face and left.

The next day, my day off, I went to that same bar and got $100 drunk again, this time depressed and crying because I didn't know how to live without her, ignoring all her calls and text messages, none of which were apologetic in any way, just more abuse, rubbing it in, those "you'll never find another girl as good as me" type messages. One waitress tried to get them to kick me out for crying and being depressing, but the bartender was like, "Nah, let him get it out of his system." I was probably the highest paying customer that day after all.

A few times my mom or sister would come and tell me that she was at the door and I would tell them to turn her away. I couldn't even stand to look at her. I didn't see her for three weeks, and then one day she was at my door looking so gorgeous that I had to let her in. She was skinnier and more exaggerated looking than ever in a pink dress with little brown cowboy boots. We didn't even say a word. She had tears in her eyes and she hugged me like there was a tight vacuum between us. I took her to the bedroom, kissed her, pulled off the little white thong that barely concealed her vagina and came inside her five quick times without pulling out or saying a word. Then she told me that her mom had taken her to a party and tried to make her dance with her sancho, some disgusting little bald guy who wore a lot of flashy clothes. She hated him, and the whole thing had been so traumatic that it had driven her back to me. We got back together that day, but we didn't even make it through the night before I broke up with her again and went to the bar with another $100 bill in my pocket.

Three weeks later she showed up at my work. I

was stacking some stuff and when I saw her I jumped and knocked everything off the shelf. She was super horny and gravitational, and something was different about her. She hovered around me smiling a wicked smile, talking so sweet and batting the long lashes of her big eyes at me. I gave her some money and told her to buy two bottles of Beringer Pinot Noir for me and whatever she wanted to drink, and to go wait in her truck for me to get off.

"Pimp," she called me.

"You don't know what pimpin' is, baby," I told her. It was true. A pimp would never put money in her hands. She bought our stuff, my two bottles and a sparkling pink one for herself, and waited in her truck for about 20 minutes for me to get off. Then we drove to my house. In my bedroom, I asked her if she had been with anybody else and she said that she had been with a marine for two weeks but he went to Afghanistan.

"What?! That's how long it takes you to find a guy and fuck him?! Damn. Did you use a condom?"

"Yes." Knowing her, if she used a condom it was only because the guy wanted to, and either way it was most definitely a lie. Maybe it was the truth and she only used one and then convinced him to take it off.

"I haven't been with any chicks this whole time," I said.

"You know you're not getting laid tonight," she said.

"It's cool. I don't care as long as I got my wine," I said casually. She told me she was sunburnt from picking up trash at the zoo for community service.

"Would you put some lotion on my back?" she asked. And next thing I knew we were fucking. I made her cum twice, and then something I said pissed her off and she tried to get off me without letting me cum, selfish bitch, but I held her down and raped her quickly for like ten seconds so I could finish. She socked me right in the jaw.

"Get out of my house, you fucking whore!" I said. She put on her clothes and left, slamming the door, and that's the last time I ever saw her.

We would occasionally argue over text messages for the next three months. The usual argument was something like, I wanted her to come over to my house so I could fuck her again, and she wanted me to take her out and spend money. Neither of us would budge, and eventually we stopped communicating at all. Only a few months later, from spying on her through facebook, I found that she had married a tall white marine, almost as tall as her father. I hope they treat each other better than we did.

XLVI. I NEVER THOUGHT YOU'D LEAVE ME

I WENT OFF Zyprexa without telling my shrink. I had slowly been tapering off it since the day I started taking it. After breaking up with Reina I had gotten the shrink to double my dose of Klonopin to 2mg twice a day and I stayed on that. My violent temperament returned and I had a short fuse.

My sister had been hanging with this guy who I never liked, and she told me that he had gotten some text messages from someone who badly impersonated me and told her not to hang out with him. He had texted her the whole conversation and she showed it to me. As I read it, I became angry because this guy insulted my imposter and challenged him to a fight, believing it was me. For the next few weeks I became obsessed with beating up this guy for insulting my imposter and talked about it a lot, worrying my mom and sister.

As I was pushing shopping carts in the parking lot of Wal-Mart, next to Texas T's, I saw a guy coming out of the bar.

"Excuse me, sir. Would you mind if I bum a cigarette off you?" I asked him politely.

"Would you say please?" That was weird, kind of gay?

"Nah, I'm good." I turned away from him and went back to pushing my shopping carts.

"Why you rude little son of a bitch, I oughta kick your ass!" I heard him say behind me. I threw the shopping carts to the side.

"Alright then. You think you can kick my ass? Let's see what you got!" I started walking towards him. He ran around me and got to his truck as fast as he could, fumbling with his keys. "That's right, you fucking coward. You're a bitch, huh?" He nodded his head. "I call you a bitch and you nod your head?! What the fuck is wrong with you? Well get in your car then, bitch, and go home." I had half a mind to run up and kick the door of his truck and smash him as he was getting in. Some people!

The world is filled with bluffers and bullshitters who go through their days hoping they won't run into a guy like me who would love to call them out. All the guys on the patio of Texas T's had witnessed the whole thing and were laughing. He would probably never be able to show his face there again. I've been there plenty of times since then and never seen him.

My probation required that for six months, I was to attend drug abuse counselling classes twice a week, have a one on one meeting with a counsellor once every two weeks and do community service at a thrift store in Canutillo. I hated to have to quit my job; I had finally found one that I liked, and I could see promotion in my future, but there was no way I could make it to all those meetings and work full time at Wal-Mart without a vehicle, so I explained this to them and even gave two weeks notice for the first time in my life. I had about $700 saved up in my bank account. It was surprising how quickly I spent it on booze, cocaine, and opiates, the only drugs you can get away with while being drug tested on probation, since they all leave your system within about three days, maximum.

Every time I had to go downtown to those meetings, as soon as I was done, I'd go visit Granny in her nursing home nearby. I watched her rapidly deteriorate into senility, and it was unsettling. I knew she didn't have many days left, so I spent as much time with her as I could.

One night, after lifting weights and hitting the bag all day ferociously, as I did almost every day while my probation intensified, constantly preparing myself to go to jail in case I got caught violating, I sat on the couch eating two burgers and some fries that I had made.

Then the guy who had insulted my imposter came out of my sister's room. I stood up, got into a perfect stance right in front of the guy, who was very drunk, looked coldly into his eyes, and said, "Hey, I heard somebody was impersonating me, sending you text messages and telling you not to hang out with my sister."

"Yeah, what's up with that?" he said. I was still looking him in the eyes.

"I heard you insulted my imposter and challenged him to a fight, believing it was me. So that makes me feel like you insulted me and challenged me to a fight," I said. I hadn't blinked the whole time. He didn't know what to say when confronted with my suckerpunch stare, and his reaction to it was to go so far as to turn his head to look out the window. Wham! A mean overhand right to his soft cheek that knocked him onto the floor. He looked like he was searching for something on the ground and I realized that I had blinded him and he was unable to fight back. My sister helped him up and took him outside to his car. When she came back in she told me I better hope that guy makes it through the night because he was blind for like five minutes and I had definitely given him a serious concussion.

I made a mental note to hit guys on the cheek more often. It's a practical target. It's soft, so you can hit it as hard as you can without having to worry about breaking your hand, like you might if you hit a guy on a hard part of his skull. And it can cause blindness. Not everyone deserves the mercy I gave to that little dude by not continuing to beat him while he was blind.

Over the next few weeks this guy went around telling everyone that I went up to him holding a plate of food in one hand and knocked him blind with the other. Although it was untrue; I had no plate in my hand when I hit him; the plate was on the coffee table; I allowed this rumor circulate because it gave me a scarier and more ridiculous reputation.

This was also interesting because it indicated that a person's memory of the events right before a concussion can be altered by the concussion. So anything a person says about a fight where they got knocked out, like many of the things I've said (and will say...) about things that happened before I got a serious concussion, should be taken with a grain of salt. A man who got a concussion may very well believe that what he says is true, but nothing but a video camera, not even a bystander, whose perception is most likely skewed, especially if he was drunk, could tell you what really happened.

Later it turned out that my imposter was the guy's best friend, Dogoberto's cousin, just doing a little prank on him, and curiously, I had no desire to beat up that guy. I didn't know him personally, although everyone tells me I've met him before. I wouldn't even recognize him if I saw him. I thought his poor impersonation of me was funny, and I was glad that he had provided me with a reason to hit his best friend.

I went to Texas T's and there was this hot girl named Misty who worked there, but came in as a customer that night. I and almost every man in the bar were hitting on her and buying her drinks because she was dressed so scandalously. I had my arm around her for a minute and we were calling each other baby; then another guy bought her a drink and took her away from me. I had no problem with that. He took her away from me fair and square, and soon she would be back on my arm again anyway. I observed her body language and interactions with the other guys. A guy came up to my left and said, "Hey, that girl over there is my friend and she told me that you're making her uncomfortable by the way you stare at her."

I cocked back my right hand and turned to glare at him, ready to hit him in the face for trying to tell me what to do while I was drunk. He retreated quickly and said, "Hey, man I don't want any trouble. All I'm trying to say is, if you like her, go talk to her." I eased out of my violent stance but kept a mean eye on him.

"Alright, man. I'll take your advice. I'll go talk to her about this and see what she says." I went over to Misty and said, "See that guy over there?" I pointed at him, "He just told me that he's your friend and you told him I was making you uncomfortable by the way I stare at you. Is that true? Because I don't want to make you uncomfortable."

"No. You don't make me uncomfortable at all," she said, "and I don't even know that guy!" she laughed. I went back over to the guy and called him out, loud enough for everyone in the bar to hear and turn their heads to watch.

"You're full of shit, you bullshit motherfucker! She says she doesn't even know you. I feel like whooping your ass right now for telling lies and playing dirty.

Meet me on the patio if you ain't a scared little punk!"
I walked out onto the patio and stood facing the door,
smoking a cigarette, ready to flick it at him and attack
him while he was distracted by it, but he never came
out.

When I went back in, he was sitting in a far corner, defeated. I had punked him in front of everyone. I
continued to have fun with Misty, as she was passed
around by me and the rest of the players all night
until she left with no man. But who knows? She may
have met up with one afterwards. The whole time, the
dude had been mad dogging me from his little corner
and he still was. I decided to wait for him outside.
Last call came. I took three shots of Don Julio Añejo
in succession and went outside. People who were not
the guy kept passing by, until finally it was him.

"So you like mad dogging me? You ready to get
down?" I asked.

"No, man. I don't wanna fight you," he said. Why
the fuck would you mad dog someone if you don't
want to fight them? Bluffers were made to suffer.

"Too bad. You already fucked up," I said and bumrushed him. He leaned back and dodged the whole
thing, thought he was slick but I was one step ahead
and I kicked his front leg hard while he was leaned
back. He fell down and landed on his head. I thought
about stomping him, but I wanted to fight, so I told
him, "Get up, motherfucker. Let's see what you got."
He got up and ran for his life, with a limp from the
damage I had inflicted by bending his knee sideways,

to a truck that was driven by a girl. "What do you have between your legs? A fucking panocha? Come on! I'll even fight you from the corner!" I stepped back into the corner. He got to his ride and the girl came out, made some angry gestures and cursed at me. I laughed, walked out of the corner, whipped out my dick so she could see it, and took a territorial piss on the sidewalk of the bar. She looked away from my dick, disgusted, got in her truck and drove away.

Six probation violations: being in a bar, drinking, being out past curfew, assault, indecent exposure, public urination.

The next day I went back and drank all afternoon and night waiting for him to come back, intending to beat him mercilessly if he should dare show his face in my bar. He never showed. A song came on that reminded me of Reina. I tried not to cry but ended up putting my head down in my arms and sobbing. I missed her so bad. I didn't know how to live without her. When I looked up, my beer had been replaced with water and a telephone. A beautiful bartender was smiling at me, offering to call me a cab. I asked for her number and she said no; she had a boyfriend. I called my mom and she took me home.

XLVII. ONE FOR ONE

DOGOBERTO AND I took a lot of Klonopin and drank a
lot of beer one night. We got really fucked up. I was
used to the Klonopin; he wasn't. He got a call from
his girlfriend and they had a bad argument. He was
depressed when he got off the phone.

"I want you to punch me in the face and give me a
black eye so I can tell my girl I got in a fight and show
off to her," he said.

"Well, I can't do that unless you hit me back," I
said.

"Ok, we'll play one for one in the face."

"Alright." I walked around him to try to get a
good angle and give him a black eye. He leaned back
reflexively and dodged the first punch. Then he let me
try again. I missed his eye drunkenly. I hit him with
my right hand on his ear and some blood dripped out
of it. "Oh shit, man. My bad. I'm fucked up. I was
aiming for your eye but I missed."

"It's cool."

"Now it's your turn." He threw a twisting right
cross so that one knuckle hit the top of my eye socket
and another knuckle hit the bottom of my eye socket.

Accurate, but not a hard punch. He had held back.

"Hit me with your left hand this time," he said. I walked around and gave him a spring loaded overhand left that totally missed his eye and busted his upper lip wide open. Blood spurted out all over the floor of the garage. Just then his grandma called him, "Dogoberto! Come inside!" He went inside without hitting me again. I went home laughing.

The next day he called me on the phone sounding angry, "What the fuck happened last night?"

XLVIII. CONFESSION TO PALOMA

MY MOM AND I were talking about the circumstances of my birth. She had me when she was sixteen and a lot of people in my family looked down on her and treated her badly for it. She said, "How can you hate someone for having a child?" and it really struck me how messed up it was, the way I had hated Paloma for being pregnant during my insanity before I went to EPPC. I was disgusted with myself all over again.

I decided to go to Paloma and have a talk with her, the talk that I had always been too ashamed of myself to confess to her. As I walked to her convenience store I was so scared that my legs were shaking and I felt like I was going to shit my pants. When I got to the store I went to the bathroom, got some King Cobras from the fridge, paid for them, and then asked her, "Can I talk to you for a minute?"

"Sure," she said.

"Do you believe in supernatural stuff, like brujería?"

"No."

"That's good, because they say if you don't believe in it, it can't hurt you. Wanna hear a scary story?"

"Ok," she said uninterestedly. I told her the whole story with all its details of how a witch had put a hex on me and driven me to suicide, pausing occasionally as customers came and went, not wanting any of them to hear it. I told her how I came out of the mental institution, overly medicated and terrified and went to that church over there, crying and praying on my knees, begging God to send me a beautiful woman. She was starting to look uncomfortable. Where was this going?

"Then I ran out of matches and I came to this store to buy a lighter. You wouldn't have even recognized me then. I looked so crazy and I was all skinny with long hair and a long beard. When I saw you I thought, 'That's the most beautiful girl I've ever seen!' I'm sure you get that all the time."

"No, not really," she said, a bit sadly.

"Well, you're still the most beautiful girl I've ever seen and I fell in love with you at first sight! You were the answer to my prayers. After that, I would think about you all the time, and no matter how bad I felt or how scared I was, just thinking about you would make me feel better, like you put me on a high, and I would think to myself, 'I have to better myself if I ever want to be good enough for this girl' and I did get better. A lot of it is thanks to you," I said. Now she was beaming at me. I had never seen her smile so fully before. "So now I finally made you smile after all these years! You look so beautiful like that. I wish I could see you smile like that every day! By the way I never introduced myself to you." I told her my name. She repeated it questioningly, surprised that anyone should be named that and pleased at the unusual sound of it. She offered her hand to me with her wrist bent for me to kiss it. I grasped it instead.

We talked a little more on some other subjects. She told me that she lived with her boyfriend and her two sons.

"So that's why you were always so mature even though you're younger than me. I never knew you had a kid."

"I had my first son when I was seventeen," she said, a little nervously.

"There's no shame in that. My mom had me when she was sixteen," I said. "You're lucky to have two boys. I hope to someday have two sons of my own and one daughter." She closed up like those brightly colored sea creatures that vanish into their tubes when something passes by.

"I have to get back to work," she said.

"Ok, Paloma. It was real nice talking to you." I walked home that night with some weight off my shoulders.

The next day was Dia de Las Madres, the Mexican Mother's Day. I walked in, got some beers, and a single red rose. She looked a little nervous about the rose. Was I some kind of obsessed stalker? I paid for my stuff, gave her the rose respectfully and said, "Happy Mother's Day."

"Thank you," she said, with relief that it was not a

romantic gesture. We had an understanding. I walked out of there, certain that she would never be mine, and ok with it. I did not deserve her or wish to interfere with the stability of her life. My guilty conscience was relieved by giving her a Mother's Day rose as much as it could ever be. The guilt would probably be there for the rest of my life for having once thought so badly of a pregnant woman, but it was all I could do. It was nice to think of her as a special sort of beloved acquaintance. But I could never have her. Still, somehow she didn't have a ring on her finger yet, and I wished with all my heart that I was a different kind of man who could put one on there.

XLIX. BASTARDO

BY NOW YOU may have noticed the pattern that any story that starts with "I did a bunch of coke with Dogoberto" always has a fucked up ending. Dogoberto and I went around doing coke and barhopping all day. I was looking for a fight. I had woken up feeling violent, drank a half a bottle of 1800 for breakfast, and knew that I was going to find what I was looking for in one of these bars.

Later that night, Dogoberto's girlfriend called him, saying that she needed him to fix her car so we drove out to her. He tried his best but was unable repair the vehicle. She got in Dogoberto's grandma's van and he started driving us all back to our neighborhood. I still wanted to party though. I asked Dogoberto if I could borrow ten bucks from him. He owed me fifteen anyway. He gave me the ten, I did the last of my coke (we had done a little bit less than an 8 ball each and smoked a little crack with Lost in a hotel room) and he dropped me off at a bar.

I sat at a stool near the far end of the bar and flirted with the cute bartender girl innocently, not saying anything sexual to her, just joking around and giving her a little compliment every now and then. A guy from my drug abuse counselling class walked by me and we laughed when we recognized each other.

"Hey, we're not supposed to be here," I said.

"Yeah, we gotta keep this on the low. Hey, meet my cousin." He introduced me to some cholo guy. We shook hands.

"Come play pool with us," said the cholo.

"I'd like to, but I'm not wearing my glasses so I wouldn't be any good," I said. He looked offended for some reason and walked to the pool table. He passed by me again a little later.

"Bastardo!" he said.

"Bastardo? Do you got a problem with me?" I asked him.

"No, that's just what we call each other. Like, 'Hey! Bastardo!'" he said with a low five that I reciprocated. This guy was way too drunk and talking out of his ass.

"Ok then, 'bastardo!' you do your thing and let me do mine and we won't have any problems," I said.

"Come play pool with us."

"I told you already, I'm not wearing my glasses so I wouldn't be any good."

He waved his hand dismissively and walked back to the pool table without listening to my whole excuse, offended again. Then he came back one last time.

"Hey, you need to stop hitting on that bartender. That's my homie's girlfriend." I don't like anyone telling me what to do when I'm drunk. It didn't matter what it was, all this guy wanted was to tell me to do something and see me do it. Had it been his girlfriend, I would have been more understanding, and I'm sure it would have turned out differently if he had asked me politely instead of told me. It didn't matter. He had succeeded, because I did stop hitting on her.

I stood up, looked into Bastardo's eyes, saw him wobble slightly with drunkenness and lose his concentration momentarily. I blacked out. Then he was crumpled at the bottom of the barstools unconscious and a bouncer was dragging me out of the bar on my heels. I don't know what the fuck I did to him but I didn't have a scratch on me and he wasn't waking up. Then I saw a guy coming at me from my right in slow motion, running, throwing an overhand right. I turned my head to the left and rolled with it so that it didn't hit me but only slightly grazed my cheek painlessly. I smiled at him.

"You hit like a bitch, dog." I said.

In the parking lot, a bartender guy told me to get out of there, go home, and never come back to this bar again.

"I'd like to do that, but I wanna get down one on one with that guy who tried to suckerpunch me while I was restrained. Where is that fucking pussy?" I said.

"I'm right here," he said and took off his shirt. I took mine off too. I wanted to bite his ear off.

"He didn't hit you while you were restrained. You

were already out here in the parking lot," said the bartender.

"That's a fucking lie and you know it! Everyone saw!" I said.

"Hey, man, just go home. Don't you see, you can just walk away from all this," said a guy standing next to me.

"Shut the fuck up! This ain't none of your fucking business!" I said without taking my eyes off the guy who tried to hit me while I was restrained. Was it gonna be the left ear or the right?

"That's my son," said the bartender, "and you gotta understand, I have to protect my family. If you wanna fight him you have to go through me," and then he looked down and started counting on his fingers all the different blackbelts he had in various martial arts. I took a swing at him, but it wasn't right, something panicky about it in the moment when I switched my concentration from his son to him when I saw him look down, and I didn't really get my weight behind it. I hit him on the cheekbone mid-sentence.

I guess I underestimated this guy, or just didn't care to estimate him at all; to me he was just another opponent who had made the mistake of taking his eyes off me, but I guess he was pretty good after all, because it seemed like the instant my fist made contact with his face, I was on the ground. I don't know what he did, or how he put me there so fast, but I was there and he was stomping on my head, saying,

"Why would you try to fight me when you know I have superior training? Huh?! Huh?!" Because I'd rather die than back down from anybody, I thought, and considered the possibility of grabbing him by the balls and pulling him down, but before I could try that, two guys grabbed me by one leg each, stomped me in the nuts, and started dragging me around while a whole bunch of people, I don't even know how many, surrounded me and stomped and kicked my head and body.

All I could think of to do was try to cover my mouth and jaw so I wouldn't get hit in the teeth or a broken jaw. I don't know what possessed these faggots to take off my shoes and pants, but they did, and they dragged me around stomping and kicking me until I started to wonder if they were going to kill me. Then everybody suddenly dispersed and ran off. I got up quick. My boxers were torn and my dick was hanging out. The bartender I had been flirting with, who had also kicked me while I was down, said, "You have a small dick."

"I'm glad you got to see it," I said. She spat on the ground and walked away. I picked my shoes up and put them on, arranged my boxers to try to conceal my dick as best I could. "What about my pants?!" I yelled.

"Get the fuck out of here before we jump you again!" I heard someone say.

"Ok, but remember this! What's between me and you is between me and you! I ain't no fuckin snitch!" I yelled. Then I made a break for it. I needed to find a concealed route to my house so I wouldn't indecently expose myself to anyone along the way and be charged as a sex offender or something. But the cops were already rolling up. Fuck.

The cops didn't make fun of me or laugh. They didn't even seem like they had any laughter in them that they were holding back. They asked me what happened.

"I'm not trying to indecently expose myself to anybody or anything. I just got jumped by a bunch of people. I don't even know who they were. They didn't fuck me or anything but they jacked my pants for some reason, so I'm just trying to go home now."

A smiling guy from the bar came and brought my passport to the cops. Not my house keys or my pants though. The cops put me in the back of the car and took me to the detention center, gave me some county blues, and put me in a one man cell. There didn't seem to be any other criminals there that night. It was just me and the cops. I was cursing and yelling drunkenly at the people who had jumped me. "Why did you have to jump me, you fucking cowards! Why didn't you fight me one on one?! Am I that fucking scary to you, you fucking chickenshit motherfuckers?!..."

I went on and on until a cop told me to shut the fuck up, and then I punched the wall, which I immediately regretted because I fucked up my knuckles and I might have to go to jail and fight some more. I decided that my right hand could only be used now for eye gouging, palm heel strikes, and hammer-fists, grappling and so forth, and my mind began working rapidly on a new strategy for fighting like this against multiple opponents, who may very well want to fuck me this time.

I asked a passing cop, "So what's up? Am I going to be incarcerated?"

"You're not even under arrest right now. That's why you don't have handcuffs on. You're just being detained while we wait to see if anyone presses an assault charge on you. If someone does, we'll take you to jail. If not, we'll take you home." I stayed silent. They couldn't press charges on me. I had assaulted two people, but at least eight had assaulted me. What they had done was more illegal than what I had done. True to my word of not being a snitch, I stayed quiet until about four in the morning when I got dropped off at home.

My mom was horrified. I told her not to worry. I took a shower. I tried to go to sleep but I kept hallucinating weird shadows and random, wobbly, jiggling surfaces in the dark, so I took out the box cutter, cut a Zyprexa into four pieces, took one of those quarters and two Klonopin, waited for them to kick in and fell asleep when I saw the sun rising.

L. TAWDRY AUDREY

THE DAMAGE WAS not so bad. A swollen right eye, broken nose, road rash on my shoulder and butt cheeks. My nuts and pubic bone were sore. The vertebrae of my spine were swollen between my shoulder blades but there were no pinched nerves or slipped discs. Every part of my skull had been tenderized. Really, the worst part was the road rash on my shoulder because if I moved around too much it would open up and start to bleed, so I wasn't able to work out until it healed; also the damaged knuckles were something to worry about because they made me less dangerous. I had some bruises on my ribs and some abdominal pain. For about a week my shit would be black due to the presence of internal bleeding somewhere. I didn't feel like going to the hospital. I would find my painkillers elsewhere. I felt no loss of pride and walked with my head high everywhere I went. The guys who had jumped me were the real chickenshits. Had I backed down from them and walked home, who knows what kind of insanity might have haunted me after that.

I needed to get some pussy. I called up Audrey.

You may remember how I failed her once before. I wasn't worried about that now. If I had ever felt paranoid and violent, it was nothing compared to this. I put some brass knuckles in my pocket. I had never liked them, and always thought that in a fight I would be more dangerous without them, but now they were much better than the damaged knuckles of my right hand and I was glad I had bought them.

I stopped at Paloma's convenience store to buy a pack of cigarettes. She looked pissed off, not the type of woman to lick some knucklehead's wounds or feel sympathy for the loser of a fight. I almost told her, "You're a sight for sore eyes," but that was way too cheesy. I just got my cigarettes and left. That was the last time I ever saw her.

I took the bus to a convenience store by Audrey's house, bought two bottles of wine, and she ran up with her big bouncing boobs to meet me halfway. She looked better than the last time I had seen her. Her hair was longer, she had lost a little weight, and I could tell she had been working out because her ass and big legs were nicely shaped. She gave me a long hug and squeezed me tight.

"What the fuck happened to you?!" she asked when she saw how jacked up I was.

"I got into a little rough business at the bar last night," I said, and as we walked to her house I told her the whole story. She was impressed by my bravery, unwillingness to back down, and the general roughness of my style. Also she was just plain easy.

About halfway into a bottle of wine I was eating her out and fingering her. I hadn't eaten pussy in a long time. I made her squirt all over her couch. I had only ever seen that in pornos. I fucked her, stopping sometimes when she would ask me to put my dick in her mouth. She liked giving head and she was the best at it. For a little while I had my balls in her gentle mouth and was jacking off. I even tittyfucked her.

I fucked her hard, with all my pent up aggression and for a long time, and when I pulled out, she grabbed me by the dick, pulled me close, and aimed me so that every last drop of sperm went into her mouth. She swallowed it without taking her eyes off mine, said "Thank you," and then put my dick back in her mouth for a quick polishing so that it was perfectly clean. All I could say was "Fuck yeah!"

I fucked her a couple more times and left hickeys all over her breasts. Then we sat on her front porch finishing the wine. There was little romance between us and we both knew it. We were just cool fuck buddies. I would go back to her house every now and then. I stopped eating her out when she told me she had other guys she fucked, but continued boning her without a condom and she continued to drink my sperm.

One day she came to my house wearing a little black dress. I took her into my room and whipped out my dick to her.

"See that?" I showed her the weird sore that looked like some kind of hard, white boil on the outside of my foreskin. "I haven't fucked anybody but you and I got this. You might wanna get yourself checked." I wasn't mad at her. It was my own choice not to use a condom with her. We drank a bottle of Johnnie Walker Black that night, didn't fuck, and I never hung out with her again.

When I went to the urologist, she couldn't make head or tail of it. It wasn't a wart; it wasn't herpes; I didn't have any symptoms of chlamydia, gonorrhea or syphilis. She said it was probably an infected pimple and gave me some hardcore antibiotic pills. It went away and never came back. I went downtown, got a free HIV test and came out clean.

LI. WENT INTO MY HOUSE FOR A DRINK

CRACKAINE HAD JUST gotten out of jail. His sister was my front door neighbor. He, Arnufo, and I had two plastic bottles of cheap vodka and were drinking strong screwdrivers that had just little splashes of orange juice in them, sitting around being dumbasses. I had had maybe three of them when my sister came into the yard to get a drink off us. I went to take a piss on a tree. I heard Arnufo tell my sister, "You look really pretty tonight." Then, in my memory, it seems like I went to my house to get a drink, which makes no sense, and then Arnufo was backing away from me and I was asking him, "Why do you look all scared? I didn't come at you with violence. I just think it's disrespectful that you hit on my sister in front of me like that and I'm telling you."

"Sure, man, it won't happen again," he said, terrified for some reason. It looked like he had spilled some drink on his pants. We forgot about it and continued drinking peacefully all night until the sun came up. I went back to my house and fell asleep.

In the afternoon, my sister told me that when Arnufo had told her she looked pretty, I had said, as I

309

was taking a piss, "Shut the fuck up." Then Arnufo had come to me arguing that all he had done was give a polite compliment and so on, but was cut short when I took my left hand off my dick, grabbed him by the neck and lifted him about six inches off the ground, pissing on him while I held him there. All my veins on my neck and head were popping out and Crackaine had to come pry my grip off the guy.

I didn't believe her. I had absolutely no memory of doing anything like that, although I could admit to a small inexplicable gap in my memory. The story was later corroborated by Crackaine, though. I was now a little scared of myself. If I could black out and do that when I wasn't even very drunk, who knows what else I could do? I didn't even think I was strong enough to lift a 180 pound guy off the ground with one hand. What if I black out and murder somebody one of these days?

Everybody in the neighborhood was laughing about my special move: The Choke Piss.

LII. THE LAST DEVIL

WE MOVED INTO my Granny's house. She was living in a nursing home and it was wasteful for her house to be empty. It was a nice house in a much better neighborhood. No friends, no enemies, no nosy neighbors, just old people who minded their own business for the most part.

Soon, Granny started dying of natural causes. I went to visit her and she was there on the bed, choking and gasping for air. She looked like she was in a lot of pain. I don't know if she recognized me or not, but she seemed to be comforted by me holding her hand. I stayed there for a few hours like that, watching her die. I gave her a last kiss on the forehead and I knew that I would never see her again. On my way home, I was so angry that I had a strange desire to bite a man's face off. Every man I saw on my way home had a face that I wanted to bite off. I wanted to start with the nose. Granny died that night and left her entire estate to my mom.

In the morning I awoke to a big, muscular, winged, red devil on my ceiling, smiling down on me with white fangs, offering to lend me his strength, should we go together, biting people's faces off until we found our way to hell. I was sure it wouldn't take long to get there by that method. I popped two Zyprexa and went back to sleep. That was the last time I saw a devil. I've been on my meds ever since. What an amazing pill, Zyprexa. It actually keeps devils off you. I think I may be hopelessly violent without it, and chemically dependent for the rest of my life.

I got permission from my probation officer to go out of town to my Granny's funeral in Rochester. There, my mom, sister, and I met up with two of my uncles and my aunt at a hotel. I had Klonopin; my sister had Xanax bars; my aunt had Adderall tablets and some kind of big horse tranquilizer pills. We all had beer and we all passed the various drugs around to each other. My mom was not involved in this. She doesn't even drink and she stayed in her hotel room while the rest of us got fucked up. Everyone went to sleep but me. I stayed sitting at a little table drinking beer all night. I wondered if those animal tranquilizers even did anything. They didn't seem to have any effect until the sun came up and I got out of my chair. I fell down on my face and couldn't even walk! I was stupid retarded. I crawled to my sleeping aunt's purse, stole two Adderall, crushed them up on the table and snorted them. Then I was evened out enough for the funeral. They took a photo of us. You should see my face.

It was a small, peaceful funeral. We all took a turn

with the shovel throwing some dirt on the wooden box that contained Granny's ashes. Her grave was next to the grave of her second of three husbands, the one she loved the most and had no children by. We were all descendants of her mean, short tempered, womanizing first husband from the '50s. We would all miss her, but at least her death was not a tragedy. She was eighty eight and had lived a full life with a lot of love and happiness and many offspring.

LIII. A LETTER FROM MY GREAT GRANDPA TO MY GREAT GRANDMA

TAKE NOTICE: ELEANORE [Granny]

I have broken OFF with my girl friend & the both of us have decided to try AND make a go of what we have.

I, personally dont think it will work but, I will give it a <u>FAIR</u> <u>TRY</u>. It will take a considerable amount of indulgence on the part of both us.

I am going to expect the following from you and the kids:

1. THE HOUSE MUST BE KEPT CLEAN AT ALL TIMES.
2. THE TRASH MUST BE KEPT EMPTIED without a to-do about it.
3. The yard, both back & front MUST BE KEPT CLEAN ALL TIME.
4. WEEDS will have to be kept pulled & the grass trimmed AFTER each mowing
5. The grass will not be watered over 2 times

each week

6. The TREES & flowers will be WATERED both morning and late evening – until I give the word to STOP.

7. The grass will be mowed every 2 weeks without FAIL. MORE OFTEN IF NEEDED.

8. I AM NEVER TO HEAR FROM YOU OR ANYONE ELSE IN THE FAMILY ABOUT WHAT HAS HAPPENED IN THE PAST.

9. You will REFRAIN from making remarks about my working too much or too late.

10. YOU WILL ONLY CALL ME ON EMERGENCIES.

11. When I am ready to contact you, I will do so.

12. BREAKFAST WILL BE AT 7:00 A.M. & SUPPER AT 6:30 P.M. unless otherwise specified.

13. My clothes will be kept clean AND IRONED much better than they have been IN THE PAST. I have been ashamed to wear some of the shirts that YOU IRON.

14. DISHES WILL BE KEPT WASHED.

(OVER)

15. Richard [my grandpa] and Tom [his brother] WILL BE HELD RESPONSIBLE FOR THE YARD WORK & DISHES

16. You will BE held RESPONSIBLE FOR KEEPING the house and CLOTHES clean.

17. PADDLINGS WILL BE FREQUENT IF THE YARD WORK AND DISHES ARE NOT KEPT UP.

18. I will be out OF TOWN a good portion of the time. Dont expect me to WRITE.

19. ANY TIME I COME HOME & THINGS ARE NOT PROPERLY DONE UP – YOU WILL HEAR FROM ME. THE KIDS AS WELL.

20. I will controll all monies. You will be given $100.00 per month for GROCERIES. I will PAY ALL BILLS etc.

If ever a word is brought up about me going to the doctor or reference is made to what has happened in the past four or five months you can either pack up and leave or I will one.

The next time I leave, it will be for all time. I am trying to forget but if you cannot, and insist upon bring up things that have happened to and with me in the past with women. I shall get out and stay out. I dont need you that bad. I will miss the kids but, I will have to put up with it and get over it my own way and you will have to get used to me not being around and depending upon me for things.

We'll see how things work out.

I will not stand for people keeping tabs on me as if I were a baby I know what has been going on between... [The rest was cut off by the copy machine]

We found this photocopy of a letter in my Granny's house. Supposedly this was from during the time when she was divorcing my great grandpa. The reference he makes about "going to the doctor" is about when my Granny had him psychoanalyzed. The psychologist said that he was not crazy at all, just mean.

LIV. DRUNKEN HEARTED MAN

I CONTINUED TO violate my probation as I pleased, narrowly passing the urinalyses, and never getting a home visit from my probation officer, who would have found, if not some lingering evidence of my alcoholism, or my sister's weed to lock me up, a gun that I had acquired, an early '60s Smith and Wesson Model 10 .38 Special revolver that had been re-blued to look like new.

I drank and did coke and popped pain pills, went out on all the holidays, and never got caught. My probation was officially over on St. Patrick's Day 2014. I went out to a bar that day but found no pleasure in it now that it was no longer forbidden, and curiously, I slowly decreased my drinking naturally, out of lack of desire, until my alcoholism was under control for the first time in my life. Now I have a drink every once in a while, maybe once every two weeks at the most, and I don't even get drunk. Sometimes I even go months without wanting a drink. I think that's ok, better than not drinking at all like some extremist party pooper. One thing I absolutely never do, though, is drink and drive, or get in a car with a driver who has been drinking. I do drugs every now and then but not too much. I am even able to smoke a little weed occasionally when I'm in just the right mood for it. I think the ability to smoke weed without wigging out is a sign of good mental health.

One day I woke up at four in the morning, made myself a breakfast and drank a pot of coffee. Then I stayed around the house, really bored. I took the Smith & Wesson to the gun store, the same one I always go to, the same one that always rips me off, and sold it for $150. I bought it for $500 and I bet he'll try to sell it for $600. I hated to sell the gun because supposedly it had changed hands many times and would be difficult to trace to me, should I have used it to murder someone. I cashed my check at the bank at Wal-Mart.

I bought an all day pass on the bus and went back to one of my old neighborhoods.

I smoked a cigarette and did the sign of the cross. I went to the palm reading shop and looked through the door, tried to open it, but it was locked. The woman who gave me the evil eye opened the door. Her eyes were harmless now. As I had suspected for a long time, she was not the woman with the blue hood and shades; they were two different women, but this was definitely the one who had given me the evil eye. I apologized for not ringing the doorbell that I hadn't noticed. A palm reading from her would cost me $75 and I had to come back in two hours. It was 1:21.

I walked far to a liquor store and bought a bottle of Don Julio Añejo, my favorite drink, for when it was over. I stopped at Cincinnati Bar and drank two glasses of water. It was a hot summer day in late August, 2014. I walked back and sat in the shade of a building near the palm reading shop for about an hour and a half, terrified, glad that I had sold my gun and could not shoot myself, but still afraid that this woman might induce me to throw myself in front of a car or shoot me with her own gun and dispose of my body. The anticipation of facing your fears is the worst part. In my experience, when you finally do, it is always feels great, even if you lose.

At exactly 3:21 I rang her doorbell. The inside of the place seemed impossibly spacious compared to how small it looks from the outside. It appeared that many people worked there. I saw a huge bald man in another room. She led me to a tiny room with a curtain for a door. It had two chairs and a desk that was covered with little statues of Catholic imagery. I was relieved that I wasn't walking into some kind of openly diabolical work. I told her my whole story of why I had come to her, to face her, my worst fear, who was not so scary at all now. She read my scarred hands like an open book, not like a map of lines as most people tend to do, for about half an hour.

I can see how people can become addicted to her and come back and spend a lot of money on her, but I decided never to come back to this place. On my way out there were some more customers coming in who she was very familiar with. One was a beautiful girl. Was she a customer or some kind of initiate? If she was, I'm sure it was an expensive initiation.

The old huckster didn't give me a limpia. That only came with a tarot card reading and was more expensive. False advertising, it says clearly on the sign "FREE LIMPIAS WITH EVERY SESSION" but I was too scared of her to call her out on it, so I will never know what the procedure of a professional limpia is. I don't need a limpia from her anyway. I gave myself a good one a long time ago, remember?

THE END